A PATH IN THE DARKNESS

M. D. Cooper

ISBN-13: 978-1505701678
ISBN-10: 1505701678

DEDICATION

I dedicate this book to all of us.
May we find our path in the darkness.

ACKNOWLEDGEMENTS

Those who have read their fair share of science fiction will know that this book stands on the shoulders of giants. It is to those giants, whose ideas paved the way for books like this to be written, that I give my thanks and gratitude.

MARS

STELLAR DATE: 3227279 / 11.22.4123 (Adjusted Gregorian)
LOCATION: Mars 1 Ring (M1R)
REGION: Mars Protectorate, Sol Space Federation

Tanis walked into the elevator's main cabin, peering through the throngs of people for a seat near a window. She spotted one on the side that would have an eastern view and slipped through the crowd, managing to secure it before anyone else.

The captain's message instructed her to come wearing civilian clothing. She managed to find one complete outfit that didn't look military; a pair of tight, dark-blue jeans, a white blouse, and a burgundy jacket.

She pulled at the jacket as she sat, ensuring that the sidearm strapped to her side was out of sight.

The captain hadn't said anything about weapons.

Conversation buzzed around her as a thousand people all found seats and stowed whatever they were carrying. The sounds of vendors preparing food came from the balcony above the cabin.

Tanis took in the thousand sights, sounds, and smells, her senses on alert for any sign of danger.

<*Do you think you were followed?*> Angela, Tanis's internal AI, asked conspiratorially.

<*Who knows? You know I can't just turn it off.*>

Outside the elevator, on the surface of Mars1, the final few passengers were walking over lawns leading up to the entrance. To her left, Tanis saw a pair of cargo haulers drive away over the low hills surrounding the elevator, their beds empty.

The clock on the local net showed departure time in nine minutes. Tanis settled back, anticipating the view. She believed that no planet was more beautiful to drop onto than Mars. Perhaps it was because she had grown up there.

A young girl sat to Tanis's left, peering out the window with excitement.

"I can't wait to get there!" she said as she bounced in her seat.

"Easy now, dear," her father said from beside her. "We'll be dropping soon enough."

"I just can't wait to see Mommy." The girl smiled.

"I know." The father patted his daughter's head. "It's only been a few days but it feels like so long."

Tanis smiled at the girl, wondering what her life would have been like if kids had come into the picture. She hadn't been much older when she first rode the elevator down to Pavonis Mons.

She spent the rest of the time reviewing leads and lines of inquiry around the attacks on the *Intrepid*. She wasn't certain what the captain thought was more important, but he wasn't a man given to frivolities so it was likely important.

An alert came over the local net and audible systems giving the fifteen second warning for the elevator's departure. Tanis cleared the work from her mind and prepared for the moment.

A gentle shudder rippled through the deck and the elevator began to rise above the surface of Mars 1.

Tanis always found it somewhat incongruous that, due to centripetal force, space elevators had to climb toward the planet. Over the course of the trip, gravity from would decrease and the passengers would have a period of 0*g*. At that point the cabin would rotate and the passengers would re-orient with their feet facing down to the planet.

Even after decades traveling between space and planets, Tanis still found it took as long as an hour to shift her thinking about up and down.

Both rings and free-orbiting habitats always oriented so that their parent planet or moon was up. Almost all time in space was spent with a world hanging overhead. On the surface of a world space was what was hanging above.

The result was the feeling that you would fly off the surface of the planet into space.

With seventeen-thousand kilometers to travel, the trip would take over an hour. Tanis leaned back in her seat and gazed up through the angled windows as her home world grew larger above her.

The most distinctive feature of Mars was the Borealis Ocean, which covered the northern third of the planet. The southern two thirds consisted of a massive supercontinent broken up by small crater lakes and the larger Hellenic Sea.

Tanis recalled vacations she had taken with her family on the sea when she was younger. She found it odd that her father always insisted on leaving the shores of the Mariner Valley to go to another sea half way around the world.

After a few more minutes the Mariner Valley became visible and Tanis strained to make out the Melas Chasma where she had grown up.

She remembered the long, idyllic days of her youth swimming in its deep blue waters and spending time fishing and boating on the valley lakes.

Once, when humans first settled Mars, the Mariner Valleys were ideal sites for habitation. The mile-deep cracks in the Marsian surface offered protection from the sand storms and provided a safe haven for nurturing a heavier atmosphere. Today those initial habitations were curiosities that tourists could view in submarine tours.

To her left she could see Olympus Mons, the Sol system's largest mountain, a massive volcano which rose over twenty-two kilometers above the seas which lapped at its western shore.

Tanis had climbed the cliffs at Olympus's edge several times on training missions. At over nine kilometers high they were brutal, even in Mars's low gravity.

Once on the mountain it was almost impossible to tell it was a mountain at all. With a base nearly the size of the province of France on Earth it seemed more like a gently sloping hill.

Tanis enjoyed watching the clouds drift across the surface above her until the local net sounded the warning that full 0*g* was near and the cabin would flip.

Several minutes later the passengers found themselves staring up at the glistening latticework of Mars 1 and the MCEE with all their elevators, shafts and anchors reaching out into space.

It was quite the change from staring at the idyllic garden world.

Less than ten minutes later the elevator dropped within a shaft cut deep into Pavonis Mons. The shield volcano was amongst the smallest of the massive volcanos on Mars, but at over 8 kilometers above sea level it was still massive by any measure.

With its peak and most of its one-hundred thousand kilometers of slopes eternally sheathed in ice, the debarkation area for the elevator was deep underground with maglev train service out to the nearby city of Sheffield on the high, arid Tharsis steppe.

Tanis transferred to the train within minutes of the elevator settling within its cradle on the surface. The trip to Sheffield would take only several minutes and from there Tanis would transfer to a low orbit jump jet to the location the captain had provided on the island of Elysium.

It had been over a decade since she last set foot on Mars. She still remembered that fateful day when her family had sided with her ex-husband and all but ostracized her.

In retrospect, with a more measured eye cast toward her former spouse, she wasn't surprised he had cut ties with her. But she never expected her father to cut her off as well.

The urge to check in on him was strong, but she closed that train of thought off, that part of her life was over. Soon she would leave Sol and they would be a part of her past, nothing more.

<I'm sorry,> Angela said. *<I know we agreed not to talk about this, but you were thinking it so loud…I'm just…sorry.>*

Tanis sighed. *<It's OK, I should try not to think of it while I'm here. Seeing home, even if it was from thousands of miles, brought back a lot of memories.>*

<There are good memories there, don't forget them.>

Tanis nodded and turned her mind to work, sifting through reports to take her mind off thoughts of family.

Thirty minutes later the jump jet touched down in the city of Albor. Tanis hailed a groundcar and gave it the name of the restaurant the captain had provided.

When she arrived, Tanis saw that it was a small, street-side café with flowers overflowing its planters and the smells of good cooking coming from inside.

She entered and spotted the captain sitting at a table beside a window. He was wearing a plaid shirt and the image made her think of an old woodsman.

"Good morning, Jason," she said as she slipped into the booth.

The captain smiled and ran a hand through his hair. "A good morning indeed, Tanis. I'm glad you could make it on such short notice."

"Coffee, dear?" a slim woman wearing an apron with the café's logo on it asked Tanis.

"Yes, cream and sugar, please."

The woman poured a glass and, as Tanis reached out to take it, the captain put his hand on hers.

"Was the trip pleasant?" he asked.

Tanis had a moment to wonder if this was some elaborate ruse to get her alone and make a pass at her before she detected the nano he had slipped into her hand.

It contained a coded message and Tanis decrypted it as she replied, "It was nice enough, I took the scenic route down the Pavonis elevator, it was nice to see the valleys one last time."

The captain nodded as he sipped his coffee. "I remembered that you grew up there. I've sailed on them a few times, amazing views."

Tanis read the message as the captain spoke about his adventures on Mars's high seas.

<Enfield has a highly sensitive, secret package he needs brought aboard the Intrepid. It contains materials which will be needed for manufacturing on New Eden. We are to meet with a contact in a park near here. He will take us to the package.>

Tanis and the captain discussed pleasantries until the time drew near for them to meet their contact.

As they talked she wondered what the special cargo could be. There were dozens of things of incredible value already on the *Intrepid* and they had been successfully delivered by conventional means. She wondered if Terrance thought so little of her security on the ship—then again, he had sent her to pick it up.

The captain passed his token over the local net to the café and they walked out into the street toward the park. The walk was pleasant and only took several minutes. They kept up light banter about the weather and the things they saw around them—careful to not speak of anything more significant.

In the park they walked to a low wall overlooking a pond and leaned against it, admiring the view.

"Good morning," a man said with a smile as he walked past.

Tanis nodded in return and suddenly knew why she had been called in, the captain could never have picked up the message she had just been delivered.

<*It's coordinates and data for coded entry.*> Angela's assessment matched Tanis's.

<*Not often you get a message delivered by breath,*> Tanis replied.

She reached out and touched the captain's arm, sending him a coded message via the direct contact.

<*We're to proceed to an office tower a few blocks from here. There's a maintenance door we're to use around the back. From there I have pass tokens to get us into some sort of facility,*> Tanis said over the coded connection.

The captain merely nodded and said something about a swan in the pond.

The walk to the office tower was short and Tanis easily located the door they were to use. She placed her hand over the panel and passed the codes to unlock it.

They walked down a short flight of stairs and she unlocked another coded door.

Tanis had expected some sort of hidden laboratory or research facility teeming with scientists working on the next greatest breakthrough.

Instead, they found themselves in a small room facing a nondescript man sitting at a drab desk.

"Ah, you're on time, good," the man said. "If you'd please sit and give me your arm."

Tanis looked to the captain, who shrugged, and back at the man. "Why would I do that?" she asked.

The man frowned. "So that I can give you the package, it has to be injected into you. It's not something you can carry around."

Tanis weighed her options and decided to sit and offer her arm. If this was an attempt to kill her it was the oddest yet. She looked up the man whose breath held the message in the park in addition to this man and found connections to various Enfield holdings.

As far as she could tell, this was a legitimate hand-off.

"It's OK." The captain placed a hand on Tanis's shoulder. "It's required for the nature of the package."

Tanis looked into the captain's eyes. She saw only calm sincerity. He had never given her any reason to distrust him.

"Very well." She sat.

The man reached under the desk and placed a case on it. He opened it and withdrew a small needle.

"I won't hurt much."

Tanis wasn't worried about whatever pain a needle might cause, she was concerned about what it might deliver.

The man slid the needle into her vein and pressed the plunger. Tanis and Angela immediately began to analyze the contents.

<*It's some sort of nano cluster moving a container,*> Angela said.

<*I see that, too, but I don't see how to look inside.*>

<*It's making a beeline for your liver.*>

"Earnest said you'd try to open the package," the man said. "He asked that you refrain. It would be damaging to your health if you did so."

"Is that it?" the captain asked.

The man nodded and Tanis rose, again searching the captain's eyes for a clue.

Andrews shook his head no and gestured for them to leave. Tanis rolled her sleeve back down, even more determined to find out what strange nanoscopic cargo she was carrying.

Back on the street, she and the captain began to make their way to a maglev stop three blocks away. From there they would catch a jump-jet back to Mount Apollinaris and the elevator there.

Tanis noticed a man with long, dark hair cast an appraising eye at her as she walked past. She wasn't unfamiliar with receiving looks, but something about him struck her as strange.

She moved her nano cloud out, looking for any suspicious behavior. On crowded planet-side streets that was nearly an impossible task.

Stations and ships had rules about what could be done where and when. It kept things safe, predictable, and orderly. Planets were the embodiment of chaos. People lounged in entryways, groundcars sped past, and both humans and robots flitted through the air above.

A block from the maglev station something caught her eye. A man was leaning against a restaurant's doorframe appearing to be bored and disinterested with his surroundings, but his eyes flitted to her three times in ten seconds.

She watched him through her nano cloud and saw him glance at a woman across the street who also cast Tanis a furtive look.

<*We have company,*> Tanis said to the captain while passing him the faces and locations of her suspects.

The captain didn't respond, but increased his pace. Tanis slid a hand into her pants pocket, through a cut in the fabric, and drew her lightwand out of her leg.

<*By the way, don't die,*> the captain said.

<I don't really intend to.>

<Good, because the package you're carrying will self-destruct if you do.>

<You are going to tell me what this is when we get back to the Intrepid.> Tanis was not pleased with being kept in the dark.

<I promise.>

The man and the woman Tanis had identified before were moving toward them from the front, while another two women were approaching from behind. The street was too crowded with not enough cover.

Tanis stepped into a shop and the captain followed.

The store sold souvenirs for tourists and they pushed past people gawking over rocks from the bottom of the Borealis Ocean or meteor fragments from the Hellas Sea.

A man stood behind the counter wrapping trinkets and processing transactions. Tanis spotted a stockroom behind him and worked her way around the counter.

The man was too startled to speak as she pushed past him, finally gaining his voice and calling out as they slipped through the stockroom.

"Hey, what're you doing?"

Tanis ignored him and moments later they were pushing through a back door into a wide alley.

"Get to the train?" Andrews asked.

Tanis shook her head. "No. They'll be waiting for us. We'll double back and find a groundcar."

They broke into a run, moving away from the train station. Tanis had to resist breaking into a full sprint—there was no way the captain could match her augmented speed.

"Stop!" A call rang out behind them. It was a male, likely the man she first saw in front of the restaurant.

A shot rang out and Tanis felt a ballistic projectile whistle through the air near her right shoulder.

"I guess they don't know that they shouldn't kill me," she said.

"Could have been a warning," Andrews replied as they rounded the corner moments before two more projectiles whistled past.

Tanis cast a frantic eye up and down the street, looking for a way out of this mess. "There." She pointed two blocks over where taxis waited in front of a hotel.

The pair had to backtrack across the street they started on and Tanis knew it was likely that one of their assailants was doubling back. With no other option, she and the captain took off at a run.

Sure enough, as they approached the intersection, a woman stepped out in front of them.

The woman raised her gun and time seemed to slow for Tanis. She shoved the captain aside as the woman let out a cry and fired her weapon.

In a split second Tanis calculated the angle of the barrel and trajectory of the bullet. It would hit her. She jerked her prosthetic arm up and braced for impact while throwing her lightwand.

The lightwand entered the woman's face through her cheekbone, dropping her with a scream. Tanis raced toward the assailant, barely aware that four bullets had struck her.

The woman was writhing in pain as Tanis approached and tore the lightwand up and out through the top of her head, ending her pain.

The captain was beside her in a moment, scooping up the woman's weapon.

"Are you hit?" he asked.

Tanis grimaced and nodded as she picked up speed, pulling him across the street.

<She took three in her prosthetic arm—only superficial damage. One is lodged between two ribs, I'm working on pushing it out,> Angela supplied.

More shots rang out as they dashed across the intersection. One caught Tanis in the right shoulder and another grazed the captain's leg.

"Don't stop!" Tanis ordered while catching the lightwand as it fell from her numbed right hand. This was the last time she listened when someone told her to go anywhere unarmed.

People scattered as they ran down the sidewalk, shoving anyone too slow to move out of the way.

"Get down," Tanis called out to the people on the street, afraid that a bullet meant for her would end an innocent's life.

<Don't forget about your life,> Angela said.

<Believe me, it's very much at the forefront of my mind.>

Most of the pedestrians dropped to the ground, but enough took off running that Tanis and Andrews managed to disappear into the milling crowd long enough for them to make it to the taxi stand.

Angela had repaired enough of the nerve damage in Tanis's right shoulder that her hand functioned again. She swapped the lightwand again and grabbed the door of the first cab with her prosthetic arm, ripping it open and tossing out the driver.

The captain crashed into the seat beside her and Tanis hammered the accelerator while cranking the wheel. The groundcar spun around and took off away from the attackers. Several stray shots hit the back of the car causing Tanis and Andrews to duck instinctively.

"That was bracing," the captain said.

Tanis looked over to see that he was pale and shaking slightly.

"Are you hit anywhere other than the leg?" she asked.

Andrews looked himself over. "I don't think so, my internal checks all pass…I do seem to be having a blood pressure issue from the sheer terror," he said with a weak smile.

"I guess I'm more used to it than I should be," Tanis replied as she cranked the wheel, sliding around a corner, missing oncoming traffic by less than a meter.

The captain was gripping his chair and the dashboard. "I'm not augmented like you, you know. A bullet to the head—or a car for that matter—will kill me."

"Noted," Tanis replied. "I'm more worried about bullets, they're trying to hit us—the cars are trying not to."

The car's holo overlay showed two other taxis in close pursuit. Their attackers must have also commandeered transportation.

"Where is local law enforcement?" the captain asked, looking out his window into the air.

"It's inaccessible," Tanis replied. "I've been trying it for some time, but it keeps responding as busy. I'm guessing whoever is after us has some sort of a hack in place."

"What are our options?" the captain asked.

Tanis threw a cloud of nano into the air, sending it behind their car.

"Don't worry, we'll have these clowns off our tails in no time."

Angela directed the nano to the engines of the cars behind them. The electronics yielded to the military grade nano and the cars' engine stopped and the brakes engaged.

The nano sent back a final image of their attackers before the internal safety mechanisms engaged, saving the passengers from certain death as the cars went from one hundred kilometers per hour to zero in a matter of seconds.

Tanis saw the enraged face of the man she had passed on the street when they left the Enfield office tower. What was she carrying that he would go to these lengths to get it?

She slowed from her breakneck speed and programmed the car to take them to a nearby parking garage where they would switch vehicles before driving to the airport.

"Your nano is really quite effective," Andrews commented.

Tanis nodded. "Only the best for the TSF. But somehow I think that my nano is not worth a lick beside whatever is currently holed up in my liver."

Andrews placed his hand on hers, sending a direct message.

<I imagine you've heard of picotech…>

CALAMITY

STELLAR DATE: 3241790 / 08.15.4163 (Adjusted Gregorian)
LOCATION: *GSS Intrepid,* AI Primary Node
REGION: LHS 1565, 0.5 AU from stellar primary

Forty years later…

The *Intrepid* lost control of its drive system.

The ship's AI detected a fault in the neural nodes that managed the fusion engines. It failed over to the backup systems but those nodes crashed and went offline. Milliseconds later, power failures cascaded across the ship taking out key systems. In less time than a human took to blink the AI felt more than a fifty-percent reduction in its ability to think.

The AI, named Bob by its human avatars, ran through priorities. First on the list: take the fusion reactors and the antimatter annihilator offline while he still could. If they were cut off from him there would be no way to detect, let alone stop, a runaway reaction.

He initiated a controlled shutdown only moments before losing all access to the stern of the ship. The few sensors responding via wireless interface showed that the commands succeeded.

Bob gave the AI equivalent of a sigh of relief.

With the ship's reactors no longer producing power, the ship's systems began switching over to superconductor batteries. Several neural nodes powered back up for several seconds until an explosion amidships sent shock waves through the decks as one of the SC battery banks took on heavy load and overheated. Bob ran through the power distribution. It was well below even nominal draw, there was no reason the bank should have failed, let alone exploded.

More banks started failing—though less catastrophically than the first—until there were more batteries were offline than functioning. As a result, large sections of the ship were powered down and what neural nodes were left began switching over to internal backup energy.

Another explosion rocked the ship and reports streamed in from the bow. Visual inspection showed a large hole in the ES ramscoop emitter. Bob looked over the logs and could find no indicators pointing to any failures, anywhere. Everything *should* be working correctly.

With the ramscoop offline, the few small fusion generators running were now on stored fuel. Bob checked the reserves and found that, while deuterium and helium-3 were at acceptable levels, lithium was critically low. Yesterday's logs showed a million tons of lithium.

What was going on?

Bob dedicated what processing power was left in the remaining bow neural nodes to pouring through the ship's logs. He discovered subtle errors and inconsistencies. After a few minutes the realization dawned on him that his sensors were reporting false data. A minute later he confirmed even the positioning sensors had been reporting the starship's vector incorrectly.

They were not passing by the star named LHS 1565, they were falling into it.

The knowledge lent a sinister look to the star's dim red light. At a fraction of Sol's luminosity, and a mass of only 115*Mj*, it was on the smaller end of the stellar scale, not far beyond the threshold of being a brown dwarf—a fact that wouldn't stop it from vaporizing the *Intrepid* in its corona.

He took a fraction of a second to consider the notion of seeing starlight as sinister. Such an action was not something he had been capable of before his first mental merge with his human avatars, Amanda and Priscilla. Having his mind melded with theirs provided new insights and perspectives, the most prominent of which was currently suspicion.

It was also strange that in the two minutes since Bob had sounded the general alert, no humans had responded. Gollee was on duty at present, and he was never more than a thought away, but now the AI couldn't find him. What few internal scanners still functioned showed no sign of the on duty crew.

Before the ship had left Sol forty years ago there had been a few random failures that were chalked up to sabotage. The STR Corporation had gone to great lengths to stop the *Intrepid* from getting to the New Eden colony and many known sabotages did occur. Either some had gone undetected, or a second group had been involved.

Either way, whoever was shutting down the *Intrepid* was onboard now; but with the ship falling into a star, they wouldn't be for long.

Bob checked the status on the servitors he had dispatched to survey the damage across the ship and found he had lost their signal. He was losing all signal across the ship.

The wireless transmitters were going offline and his distributed network was dangerously fragmented. Bob shut down all but his primary node to prevent a schism and gained a small insight into what the fear of death was like.

Preservation protocols began writing data and algorithms to crystal in an attempt to store his latest state.

Those imperatives satisfied he reviewed the remaining options. Humans were needed to solve the riddle. His remaining transmitters received a response from only the closest stasis chamber. He looked over the list of humans within the pods and realized all may not be lost. Tanis Richards was in that chamber. If anyone could get to the bottom of what was going on it would be her.

Correction. It *had* to be her.

Bob initiated the protocols to retrieve the human and was about to provide her with a message on the general shipnet when all access beyond his node was cut off. He attempted to resend, but nothing worked. All physical connections were severed.

Bob spent several long minutes trying backup systems and alternative data paths. His desperation increased and, for the first time in his life, Bob wished for a body.

It would fall to Tanis.

ALONE IN THE DARK

STELLAR DATE: 3241790 / 08.15.4163 (Adjusted Gregorian)
LOCATION: *GSS Intrepid*, Officer Stasis Chamber B7
REGION: LHS 1565, 0.5 AU from stellar primary

Tanis stared at the holo alerts around her. The words didn't make sense. She checked the general shipnet and found the same information. This couldn't be right. She had been awakened too soon… or was it too late? Everything seemed to be offline or failing.

<*What the…*> Angela started. <*There's no wireless nets available other than the general shipnet, and I've only got local access to it.*>

<*I know… auths are timing out on every other net,*> Tanis said, feeling as though she was blind, unable to see data on the nets, limited to just her own eyesight and hearing.

<*This can't be right.*> Angela examined the ship's vector. <*We're falling into LHS 1565.*>

"I noticed that," Tanis said aloud, though her AI could hear her internal thoughts. Angela was a distinct entity, but also occupied a portion of Tanis's brain. Even if she didn't have access to auditory pickups, she could read many of her host's outermost thoughts.

<*Are we alone on the ship? Where's Bob?*> Angela asked.

Tanis didn't know. The ship AI's presence had always been close, like a looming mountain on the shipnets. One of the most advanced AI ever created, she couldn't imagine what would shut down or block it.

"First things first," Tanis said. "We need more intel. There's no data on the duty officers, but that doesn't mean they aren't around somewhere. Let's get to the bridge."

<*What about everyone here?*> Angela asked.

Tanis looked at the rows of stasis pods, her gaze lingering on Joseph Evans' in particular.

"They should be safe. Pods have their own backup power supplies. Besides, I'm going to recode the door and seal it."

Angela signaled her approval and within minutes they were moving through the ship to the bridge.

The corridors were empty, and only the occasional dim emergency light provided illumination. Tanis added IR and UV overlays to her vision, as well as a structural overlay to ensure she stayed on the right path. Angela released a cloud of nano to scout ahead and keep an eye out behind them as well.

<*There's nothing here,*> Angela said. <*Life support is offline engines are offline, energy interchanges are all dead. Everything is running on local power. When that dries up its going to get dark and cold in here really fast.*>

<*How long ago do you think this happened?*> Tanis asked.

<*Judging by the rate of cooling and the current temperature, not long ago. Maybe an hour. We've probably got a few days before things will start to get serious,*> the AI responded. Even though the cold didn't bother her, she was dependent upon Tanis for energy and connectivity. If Tanis died, she died.

Tanis gave a stoic smile. "Then we better get things fixed up. Plus, if we don't smash into a star we'll still freeze to death.

<*I don't think that's quite how it would work, you usually burn up before any smashing would occur,*> Angela said.

The empty corridors stretched on with no sign of life or recent use. She estimated the distance to the bridge to be just over a kilometer, provided there were no sealed hatches on the way, she would be there in a matter of minutes.

Tanis found herself wondering why she was awakened. No other stasis pods showed any signs of reviving their occupants and there was no data left for her on the net. It had to be Bob who brought her out of stasis, but why not leave her with some information?

They passed through the forward commissary, cutting behind the food stands and through Chef Earl's main kitchen, then into the executive dining room. It was a shortcut that would take them to a hall one level down from the bridge deck and only a few hundred meters aft.

The dining room was dark, chairs were stacked along the wall and the tables showed a thin layer of dust. It drove home that forty years had passed. By Tanis's reckoning, she had left this room only hours before.

It was odd that it lacked more recent signs of use; it was one of the closest dining rooms to the bridge. Surely the duty officers would have been eating here, unless they felt uncomfortable and were using the officers' mess only one level further down.

Tanis looked up who the duty officers should be and was surprised to learn she knew each of them personally. The first was GSS Lieutenant Collins, a man Tanis had not gotten along with particularly well before the *Intrepid* had left Mars. She had only spotted him once or twice afterward and was surprised that a supply officer had been added to the in-flight duty roster.

The next was Lieutenant Amy Lee. She had been stationed under Tanis in the Security Operations Center in the harrowing days before the *Intrepid* left Sol. Tanis knew Amy Lee reasonably well, but not as much more than an acquaintance beyond their working relationship.

The last of the three duty officers was Ensign Gollee. Tanis knew him from a few games of 4D chess they had played in the officer's mess, but had not worked with him professionally. She felt bad for Amy Lee and Gollee being stuck with Collins. If she had to spend three years with that man Tanis knew someone would be dead—him.

<*I hope Amy Lee and Usul are well. They were a very pleasant pairing,*> Angela said.

Usul was Amy Lee's AI. He wasn't a military pairing, like Angela, but had been with her family for several generations. When she made colony, he jumped at the opportunity to leave Sol and transferred to her.

Gollee, like most pilots, didn't have AI. Most of their extra processing space was needed for additional systems to handle plots and vectors. Collins was simply too low on the totem pole to be granted any military AI and he wasn't the sort who would normally attract an unchartered AI for a pairing.

<*Gah… I've glimpsed his mind,*> Angela said. <*You can get a feel for what a person would be like by looking at their data streams. Being in him would be like living in a prison.*>

Tanis reached the top of a service tube and stepped onto the bridge deck's maglev station. In all of her previous visits to the command deck Tanis was one of hundreds crowding the station and executive corridor. Now the emptiness was palpable; emergency lighting casting long shadows across the space as the echoes of her footfalls skittered up and down the hall.

Beyond lay the bridge's foyer; the place where Priscilla, or Amanda—the ship's two physical avatars—took turns providing the main interface between the humans and the *Intrepid.* The avatar's pedestal was empty and the holo emitters were offline. Even more than the main hall, this room had always been a riot of light and color—usually white, grey and light blue if Amanda was ensconced, or red, pink and violet if Priscilla was running the show. Tanis slipped through the darkness, a shiver ran down her spine and she couldn't help but feel like she was the only person on the ship.

There wasn't a single person who hadn't looked out into the cold, dark blackness of space and feared falling into it, lost and alone in the emptiness for eternity. Out here, far from even the most rudimentary civilizations, Tanis couldn't help feeling those thoughts creep into her mind again and again.

She took a deep breath, pushed the tendrils of fear aside and strode down the corridor to the left, past the executive conference room toward the bridge.

Her nano arrived first and sent an image back showing it to be empty, a fact she confirmed moments later as she stepped into the heart of the ship.

She drew another deep breath through her nose. There were traces of human pheromones. Her augmented olfactory system informed her that people had been here a scant five or six hours earlier.

Tanis felt the solitude pressing around her ease back as she settled into a duty station. The holo interface sprang to life around her and she brought up the previous month's logs.

They were blank for the last month.

"Well that complicates things," Tanis muttered. <*You got anything?*>

<*Negative,*> Angela responded. <*There's nothing here and no helm control either. Engine systems seem to be physically disconnected and on top of that we're nearly out of fuel. The ramscoop is offline as well and it appears the emitter is damaged.*>

"Are the habitation cylinders still spinning?" Tanis asked.

<*Not certain. I can't get any data on them. They do have their own self-contained power systems, so we can only hope they are. That's going to be one serious mess if those dropped to 0g.*>

"Speaking of 0g," Tanis said. "We've still got grav here in the crew areas."

<*I would expect so. The GE MBHs are fully self-contained. They generate their own power and are pretty hard to tamper with.*>

"So you're thinking sabotage as well." Tanis said.

<*No way could it be anything else. To knock out that many systems at once before Bob could get servitors or the crew after you would have to require subversion.*>

"It's gotta be Collins," Tanis said. "I can't imagine either Gollee or Amy Lee being involved."

<It could be anyone. We don't know if they were the only ones out of stasis when this all happened.>

"So we've got two things we need to do. We need to get to Bob, and get him control of the engines or we'll be having a really bad day."

<I project that we have either our initial pass, or our first orbit to break away from the star. Any further and we won't have enough v *to escape its gravity.>*

"What's the time on that?" Tanis asked.

<About three days.>

"We better get moving then."

Tanis left the bridge and worked her way back to Bob's primary node. Hopefully, it was intact and he had run the preservation procedures. With luck he would be fully activated and they could begin repairing whatever damage had severed him from the ship.

On their way she stopped at the officer's mess to see if it showed signs of use and to check for any clues. This room wasn't quite as Tanis remembered it. In the intervening forty years, someone had decorated it.

The previously white walls were done in several vibrant, yet tasteful colors and several new couches were also arranged throughout the room.

The serving area in the rear was stocked with fresh food and Tanis helped herself to a glass of water and a cold sandwich—she suspected it would be a while before she got to eat again.

Peeking into the walk-in refrigerator she stopped and deployed a series of nano probes. Around one of the racks, she saw a pair of feet. The probes took stock and fed the view to her HUD. It was Gollee; judging by the pallor of his skin, he had been dead for some time.

<More than twelve hours,> Angela said. *<With the moisture in here I don't think he'll be recoverable. Too much decay.>*

Tanis disagreed. There was always a chance they could bring him back. It was not too far above freezing down where he lay; it was possible to bring people back even after a day if the conditions were right. She crouched down beside the ensign and saw what the probes missed. There was a large hole in the back of his head. No, they wouldn't be bringing Gollee back.

<*Looks like it was done post mortem,*> Angela said. <*Someone didn't want whatever info he had to be extracted.*>

"So it would seem. I'll move him to the freezer and then we can continue."

Tanis hauled the ensign's inert form to the freezer and set him down gently. He'd been a good chess player. She was sorry they hadn't had the opportunity to know one another better. Closing the freezer door, Tanis took a deep breath and determined to pay back whoever had done this in like kind.

<*We need to keep moving. There isn't a lot of time.*>

<*I know.*>

Less than ten minutes later they were at the entrance to the ship AI's primary node. The entrance was a narrow corridor that was normally alive with scanners and holo readouts. Beyond that was a large, cube shaped space where the node resided. Tanis attempted to deploy probes, but found she lost contact with them the moment they entered the corridor.

<*Dampening field,*> Angela reported. <*Probably what's keeping Bob from controlling his nano or servitors outside the node.*>

"I'd wondered about that," Tanis said. "Well, here goes nothing."

She stepped into the corridor and immediately regained communications with her nano. They had stayed on course and were surveying the AI node. Tanis emerged from the tunnel and into the space the AI occupied. It was similar to the communications nodes she had visited on Callisto not long ago, albeit somewhat smaller.

The room was perhaps twenty meters per side. A catwalk ran around its center and while most of the power fed via conduit, communications between nodes and the ship were largely wireless, sent down ES waveguides that transferred comm through the ship. The node appeared to be offline at first, but the nanocloud reported that it was actually active, just running on backup power.

"You're here." The words were audible. Though she had never heard it aloud, it was the same timbre Bob's voice always had in her mind.

"You're alive!" Tanis said. "Angela and I were quite worried."

"If you can call this alive, then I suppose I am," the AI replied. "I'm crippled and trapped within this node. I have no external net access and a dampening field is blocking my control of nano beyond the node."

"We noticed that." Tanis nodded. "I think we can find the emitters and remove the field, but we need to know what happened. Where is everyone, how did all of this happen?"

There was a pause...just a second or two, but an eternity for an AI.

"I'm not entirely certain. Since the event I've been running through my logs and have found that there have been some gaps for some time. Almost as though parts of my sensory input had been altered to not pick up certain events, or certain people's movements."

"So you were blinded," Tanis said.

"In some respects, yes. I don't know if the sabotage was set up during those times, or if some of it had been in place since we left Sol. What I do know is that the timing was perfect. At first I thought it was a viral attack, but it quickly became apparent that it was physical. Only someone who knew my systems with fair intimacy could have done this. Earnest and

Abby built in many redundancies and they were all circumvented."

<*Have the attackers tried to breach this node?*> Angela asked.

"There was an attack made by servitors, but I managed to repel them with nano once they entered the node. I also have some limited feeds throughout the ship, comm paths that, while damaged, still have some bandwidth. I believe whoever has done this is trying to flee the ship via one of the stellar pinnaces. If they depart after our first orbit of the local star they'll have enough velocity to reach Sol in roughly one hundred years. I believe that is their plan."

"We need more people," Tanis said. "I can't go to the shuttle bays… which one is it?"

"Starboard A3."

"And deal with whoever is there and leave you unguarded. They could mount a physical attack here.

"I'll be safe," the AI said. Laser cannons lowered from the ceiling, and several armed servitors appeared on the catwalk, most likely the ones that had tried to attack the node. "I'm conserving power in case I need to use these systems."

<*Just be careful,*> Angela said with concern in her tone. <*You don't want to do any damage to your primary node.*>

An audible chuckle filled the room. "I'll be certain not to shoot myself in the foot. Go, find whoever this is, and stop them. We need to know if they have anything else planted on the ship before we begin to repair—and there isn't much time for that either."

<*She's right, though. We are going to need more people awake to handle this,*> Angela said. <*Can you access any of the stasis rooms to wake anyone?*>

"Unfortunately no, I barely managed to wake you. I'm also uncertain who I would wake if I could. I don't know who to trust. Amanda or Priscilla would normally make that choice."

Tanis nodded. "Well, for starters we could wake one of those two, but I think the best bet is to wake Joe."

There were others in the stasis chamber who could perform the required, but she had her own reasons for wanting Joe.

"You go to the shuttle bay. I'll send a preprogrammed servitor with a message for him." The servitor would lose contact with Bob once it was beyond the node, but the task was a simple one, which it could perform autonomously.

Tanis passed the new access codes to the stasis chamber. She left the node and began the trek to the starboard A1 shuttle bays.

The *Intrepid* was a colony ship, with all the supplies and equipment to establish humankind on a distant world. As such, the ship was equipped with a fleet of smaller vessels intended to gather resources within the destination star system and establish an economy. Amongst the complement were several pinnaces capable of the trip back to Sol.

Tanis's quarters were only a small detour and she decided to stop there and gather weapons and armor. There was no telling how many people she would be up against and the stasis suit she was still wearing afforded virtually no protection.

The personal seal over the door to her quarters showed no signs of tampering and Tanis removed it before forcing the panel aside. Even with the best filtration systems a fine layer of dust covered everything in the room, a tangible sign of the four decades she had been in stasis. To her it had been only an hour or two since making the bed and straightening her things; for some reason, seeing the passage of time here again brought the feeling of solitude to the fore.

Focusing on the task at hand, Tanis pulled off the stasis suit and slid into the base layer of her flexi-armor. It fit like a second skin, a second skin that could stop kinetic rounds. She retrieved a fresh canister of reactive material and held it to her chest; waiting for the base layer to finish initializing. A ready symbol flashed on her HUD and Tanis pressed the cylinder into a now glowing circle on her chest.

The clear liquid flowed out across her body, even covering her face in an all but invisible layer. The armor could absorb weapons fire from particle beams to ballistic firearms. Once the armor completed its startup routine she pulled out her shimmersuit. This top layer would render her invisible, even her scent and the sound of her movements would be masked.

Once the shimmersuit was in place, Tanis wore over five millimeters of armor and camouflage. She opened her personal weapons locker and retrieved the two slim blades hanging on the inside of the door. Each slid into sheaths on her forearms that would hide them from view. Next was a pulse rifle and pistol that she snapped together and slung over a shoulder. A final check of the armor and comm control systems and Tanis stepped into the hall, her body fading from view.

Anyone seeing her move through the silent and dark ship would have only witnessed a pistol and rifle floating through the air. However, even that wouldn't occur as Angela had the nanocloud roving far and wide. They would get plenty of advanced notice if anyone were nearby.

The A3 dock was on the lower half of the command and crew areas of the *Intrepid*. From her current position it was a kilometer aft, two kilometers starboard, and half a kilometer down. With the maglev trains and tubelifts offline it was going to be a long haul.

Releasing a stimulating combination of chemicals into her bloodstream, Tanis launched into a smooth lope, topping out at just over sixty kilometers per hour.

<*You're going to wind yourself,*> Angela warned.

<*I feel pretty good. I think I can keep this up for a kilometer or two.*>

<*I predict a seventy percent chance you'll cramp. You didn't purge your digestive tract before putting your armor on.*>

<*Would have taken too long. Which is why I'm running like this. We've gotta catch whoever broke the ship.*>

Tanis halted at an intersection she didn't recognize. Neither she nor Angela had the ship's entire layout stored in local memory. There was no reason to because no one expected the ship to ever be entirely offline. Aside from being uncertain about the route, there was another problem: the ship was designed to be traversed via maglev train. It was entirely possible that there would be no way to get to the dock from here.

<*I can't imagine that is the case.* They *got there.*> Angela added her two cents to Tanis's thoughts.

<*Good point.*>

Tanis considered the options and took a right. Several turns later she arrived at a large environmental transfer station. Conduits ran into massive induction pumps and then to their ultimate destinations.

<*What do you think? Down?*>

<*It'll save you a few decks. I'd do it.*>

Tanis walked to a railing that surrounded a series of large pipes which ran down through the decks. Switching her vision to IR she could see that they were still cooling and cast enough light to make out a catwalk twenty meters below.

She took a moment to gauge the distance and leapt over the railing into empty space. The catwalk rattled when she struck it and the lower half of her armor locked up, absorbing the impact.

"Handy stuff," Tanis commented.

Below was another catwalk, and she repeated the process until she was on the same level as the A3 docks. The catwalk at that level led through an environmental administration area and then into a general ship corridor. Angela supplied a possible map of their location, though it was extrapolated and could be inaccurate.

<Can't believe we didn't think to get one from Bob.>

<Heat of the moment and all that.>

Tanis worked her way through the corridors using her sense of direction—and a cloud of nano scouting ahead—to ferret out the path to the docks. It was slow going and the isolation was starting to make her see things.

Her thoughts returned to the endless blackness outside the ship, the knowledge that there were no habitats or worlds for light years, no repair yard to call, or tug to pull them away from the red dwarf she knew was outside the ship, ready to swallow it.

The closest humans beyond the *Intrepid* were seven light years away in the Epsilon Eridani system, they might as well have been on the other side of the galaxy.

Tanis wondered if that is where the saboteurs were intending to travel. Some of the larger ships in dock A3 were equipped with stasis pods; with a good pilot at the helm they could make the trip to EE in under thirty years.

She couldn't imagine anyone wanted to travel there. It was all dust cloud miners, not a single terraformed world in the system.

After another twenty minutes the first set of probes radioed back images of cargo storage areas. They had to be nearing the dock and Tanis picked up the pace, turning her focus to what she would do to whoever was behind this.

Before long her nano located the dock, they confirmed Tanis's suspicions: a Triton Class Pinnace was on the launching rails, powered up and ready to launch. Though there was no visible activity on the dock, Tanis approached cautiously all the same.

She wished for some backup, and her thoughts flashed to Joe; she imagined he must be revived by now, most likely with Bob, getting updated on the situation.

<*Too bad we didn't have some formation material; we could have left a comm string behind.*>

<*If wishes were fishes…*> Angela replied.

<*What?*>

<*Never mind.*>

The corridor terminated at the dock with both airlock doors wide open. Normally that wouldn't be possible, but with the entire ship essentially offline there was nothing to stop it.

<*If that ship launches we'll be sucking vacuum,*> Angela said.

<*Armor will keep me under compression, but air could be a problem.*>

<*Not really that funny.*>

Tanis didn't think so either, she was just thinking aloud… though it wasn't a thought Angela should have been able to overhear.

Tanis pushed the implications of that from her mind and crouched low, holding the pistol and assault rifle near the deck. It wouldn't do to have whoever was out there see two guns floating in the air.

Out on the dock there were several pallets of refined ore, ready for the space station that was to be constructed once the ship reached New Eden. They would make good places to hide her weapons while she surveyed the area.

Creeping slowly along the deck she reached the pallets and tucked the weapons under a strap. Tanis then pulled herself onto the ore and surveyed the dock. There still weren't any signs of people, but the pinnace's passenger ramp was lowered. Tanis decided to enter the ship. She could send a nano probe, but it was possible that the vessel's sensors would pick up its signal. She pulled her nanocloud in tight and jumped off the pallet.

The ship's ramp was only twenty meters away; Tanis kept her approach slow and steady when she heard a noise to her left. She resisted the urge to duck behind something, relying on her shimmersuit's ability to render her entirely undetectable.

It was Collins and another man she didn't recognize; they were carrying a bundle between them. Tanis realized how often she relied on the Link for data about the ship.

They rounded a pallet and Tanis got a better look at the bundle they carried.

It was Amy Lee.

"God dammit, why couldn't we just leave her back there?" the unidentified man asked.

"Because I don't know if she managed to get a signal off and I need to find out. It will affect where we can go," Collins replied between grunts.

Tanis knew that Amy Lee had a number of strength modifying mods. While she looked like a slim woman, just under 180 centimeters, she likely weighed over 120 kilograms.

"You told me we were going to Tau Ceti," the man said.

"Well, if she got a signal off, then we're going to Epsilon Eridani."

"What a shit hole."

"It's a shit hole with transports to Sol." Collins gave the man an aggravated look.

"I guess that's true," the man agreed. "I can't believe I signed on for this…two hundred years just to take out one ship."

"It doesn't matter. We were hoping the STR would succeed, but, since they failed, it was up to us."

The man nodded. "I understand. They have to be stopped. I just wish it wasn't taking so much time."

"There was no way they could be allowed to do that research at New Eden," Collins said.

"No way we could allow this ship's abomination of an AI to live either."

Collins nodded. "Leave her here for a minute; I saw some restraints in the security locker back in the dock ops center. You start the ship's launch process."

Tanis watched the unidentified man walk up the pinnace's ramp while Collins walked down a corridor toward the dock ops center. Stopping the ship from leaving was the top priority and she followed the unknown man up into the pinnace.

There wasn't a lot of room on the ship—a cockpit, common room, two cabins with two bunks each and a small cargo hold. Off the common room were stasis pods for four people, enough to get them to the closest system, and slip into regular insystem traffic without undue attention.

Tanis crept down the corridor to the cockpit. The man settled into the pilot's chair and she moved into position behind him.

<*Able to log onto the pinnace's net?*>

<*Working on it,*> Angela replied. <*Don't want to alert him.*>

Tanis waited; the intel that Angela could gather while the man was on the net could be invaluable.

<*Got it! He's Henry Freeman, a GSS pilot contracted to assist with the space station setup at New Eden before the* Intrepid *returns to Earth.*>

<*So not colony… I suppose that's reassuring.*>

<*I really can't imagine how. It doesn't change our situation,*> Angela said.

<*I just would be more surprised if a colonist was involved.*>

Tanis knew enough, no reason to let him prep the ship for launch. She pulled back her arm and swung at the man's head.

Right through empty air.

<*Holo!*> Angela said.

<*A damn good one too.*>

Tanis only had a moment's warning before her body was peppered with particle beam fire. She spun to see Collins in the pinnace's central corridor, rifle in hand.

The shimmersuit was torn to shreds, but the armor underneath saved Tanis from a grisly death. It dissipated the beams, though it grew uncomfortably warm against her skin. A few more shots and it would be searing. She dove behind the pilot's seat, the remains of her shimmersuit melting off and lighting her the chair on fire.

<*Damn…that was the best shimmersuit I've ever had,*> Tanis said.

<*I'm still trying to figure out how that holo fooled us.*>

<*Easy, neither of us really checked.*>

Collins had stopped firing during the exchange and Tanis peered around the smoking ruin of the seat. There was no one there. She crept cautiously through the corridor to the exit ramp. Her fleet of nano probes scouted outside the ship and showed Collins holding a gun to Amy Lee's head.

"Lieutenant Colonel Richards!" he yelled in her direction. "I've reversed the trigger on this weapon and I have it pulled. If I let go, it will fire and kill her. Come out where I can see you."

Tanis edged out onto the ramp. Amy Lee was conscious and there was fear in her eyes.

"Please, Colonel, do what he asks."

"Yes, do what I ask. Walk down the ramp."

Tanis did as she was instructed. "Clever bit with the holo. I can't believe I fell for it."

"Honestly—" Collins gave a throaty chuckle "—neither can I. I had no idea you'd get taken in so well. It worked pretty good at flushing you out. Now you walk toward those crates and Miss Amy Lee and I are going to get on the ship."

"How did you know to expect me? You weren't just waiting around on the off-chance someone came by, were you?" Tanis asked, stalling for time.

"Of course not, you forget that I subverted half the sensors on this ship, I knew you were coming an hour ago."

Tanis ground her teeth; it was stupid of her not to expect something like that. Just because she couldn't use the shipnet didn't mean the saboteur didn't have some sort of access to it.

She slowly edged back toward the crate as instructed; her only solace was the knowledge that she was moving toward her weapons.

Collins backed up the ramp and stood at the top, Amy Lee in front of him.

"Send her down," Tanis said. "There's nothing we can do now to stop you."

"I don't think so, you've proven to be very resourceful," Collins said.

Tanis backed up another step, her left hand within reach of her pistol.

"There's nothing to gain from this—" Tanis began to say as she reached for her pistol. Her fingers wrapped around the grip and in a single motion she raised it, pivoted and fired three shots at Collins's head.

He dove back into the ship, pushing Amy Lee as he did. She lost her balance and toppled off the edge of the ramp, the thud of her impact lost in the shots Tanis fired into the pinnace's entrance and hull.

The ramp began to retract and Tanis swore as she raced to recover Amy's body.

<*Hurry!*> Angela shouted in her mind. <*He's going to blow his way out of here, the dock's shields won't snap into place, it'll decompress.*>

<*I know! I can't leave her though!*> Tanis dropped her weapons and pulled Amy Lee into her arms as the pinnace rotated in its cradle. She was unconscious and Tanis slung her over a shoulder and turned toward the dock's entrance, breaking into a full sprint.

<*You have less than ten seconds,*> Angela said, her mental voice strained. <*The entrance to the dock has a pressure sensitive breach door. It should close even without power.*>

Behind Tanis there was a clang and a hum as the launch rails came to life, lifting the pinnace into the air. She cringed as the snap of lasers filled the air—heralding the end of the dock's bay doors.

The sound of atmosphere whistling out the door filled the air, followed by the sound of rending steel. Tanis found the energy within herself to close the last twenty meters to the dock entrance in record time while behind her the pinnace's engines roared to life, thrusting the ship out into space.

She raced past the entrance, narrowly missing the closing pressure doors.

<*You cut that too close.*>

<*You know I had to do everything I could to save her,*> Tanis said as she set Amy Lee's unconscious form on the deck.

Tanis could all but taste Angela's worry. <*We're still falling into a star. All you can do is still to come.*>

"Tanis! Are you alright?"

She looked up to see Joe running toward her. Seeing him caused a feeling in her chest she had forgotten about years ago. The look of concern and love on his face made her stomach do a pirouette.

Shame dampened the feeling of relief. She had always felt something was off with Collins. Now her lack of follow-through had cost Gollee his life and could be the end of the *Intrepid.*

"Yeah. I'm OK. He got away though." She gestured to the sealed door.

Joe skidded to a halt and wrapped his arms around her. Some part of her realized this was her first hug in over a decade; another part told the first part to shut up and enjoy it. She wrapped her arms around Joe and returned the embrace.

Joe looked down at Amy Lee. "Is she OK?"

"Yes, Angela just had some nano take a peek, she'll likely come-to in just a few minutes."

Joe looked Tanis up and down slowly with a quizzical expression. "Why are you naked?"

Tanis looked down at herself and her cheeks reddened.

"My shimmersuit burned off…I have my flow-armor on, but it's transparent," she smiled sheepishly.

"Looks good on you," he grinned.

<*I can change that,*> Angela said; a second later the armor changed to a matte grey from the neck down. <*If you had bothered to RTFM you'd know that too.*>

"Thanks Angela, what would I do without you?"

<*Be naked apparently.*>

"What are you doing here? Shouldn't you be with Bob?" Tanis asked Joe.

"I got Priscilla out of stasis. She's seeing to him and the ship, trying to figure out what the heck happened."

"And how to save our collective asses, I hope."

"Yeah, that too."

"We should get back up there. Nothing more we can do down here."

They woke a very appreciative Amy Lee and worked their way back to the upper decks by a more circuitous route than Tanis took on the way down.

"I can't believe I missed Collins being such an ass," Amy Lee sighed. "I mean…I knew he was an ass, just not this much of an ass."

Tanis grimaced. "Yeah, he was such an ass it practically functioned as cover."

"Did you find Gollee?" Amy Lee asked.

"I did, but he didn't make it," Tanis replied. "I'm sorry, Amy Lee."

Tanis turned her head to look at her lieutenant and noticed a strange look in her eye—one she hadn't seen before. If she didn't know any better she'd have thought it was satisfaction.

"Colonel, you know you can just call me Amy," she said.

The statement caught Tans off-guard. Amy Lee had always insisted on using her proper full name. Perhaps the four-year shift on the *Intrepid* as it crossed between the stars had finally loosened her up.

"Very well, Amy," Tanis smiled.

The lifts up to the command deck were offline and conversation ceased as the group climbed up a half kilometer of maintenance shafts.

At the top Joe waved for Tanis to stop.

"You may be all jacked on your super-soldier endorphins, but the rest of us mortals need a breather," he said with a wheeze.

"And how are you not covered in sweat?" Amy asked as she wiped her brow between gaps for air.

"This armor does an amazing job of dissipating heat; I'm not even warm," Tanis replied.

"Where can I get some of that stuff?" Amy asked.

"Uh...Callisto?" Tanis replied.

"Oh yeah, not likely I'm going to find any in the armory then."

Tanis dismissed an unspoken response. "Rest break over, let's get moving again."

The group started off at an easy run and Tanis replayed the confrontation on the docks in her mind, looking for clues in the details.

"Amy, Collins said you may have gotten off a signal to Sol about our situation. Did you?"

Amy shook her head. "No I didn't manage it, Collins shut down power to the area I was in before I could get it out."

"Good," Tanis replied.

"Good?" Joe asked.

"Yeah, the last thing we need right now is Sol knowing we're in trouble out here."

"I don't follow." Amy furrowed her brow. "I shouldn't have called for help?"

"No help will get here in time and if we failed to get a message back saying we're OK, they'll give the colony to someone else. It's best if Sol doesn't know about what's happening at all."

"Did you learn anything else about what Collins was up to, if he had any help?" Joe asked.

"I didn't, I was on the bridge reviewing logs when I stumbled across some irregularities. I attempted to ask Bob about them but he didn't answer, I tried to get a signal out when the bridge lost power. Collins showed up a moment later. All I know is that he somehow subverted a lot of systems." Amy shook her head. "I wish I knew more."

The group arrived at Bob's node several minutes later to find Priscilla standing in the midst of holo interfaces, trying to track the source of the ship's mass failure.

"What's the word?" Joe asked the ship's avatar.

Priscilla's eyes looked up from the display, while her hands continued to race across the interface.

"As best I can tell, we're looking at physical failures. We think that faulty parts were installed from the get-go. The sensors were also altered to ensure that they would miss the sabotage." Her mouth twisted with concern as she spoke. "I wish Amanda was here, but I can't get in contact with the stasis chamber she's in."

Tanis wrapped an arm around her shoulder. "I know how you feel, a lot of people I care about are out there on the ship, but we don't know if they're OK."

Priscilla nodded, her eyes showing thanks while she worked her holo interfaces.

"Amy Lee! You're OK," Amanda said with a smile. "With what happened to Gollee we were worried."

"I don't worry," Bob said.

"Thanks for the concern, Bob," Amy said sourly.

"I assume from your presence that Collins escaped alone?" Bob spoke audibly.

"That's correct," Tanis replied. "He was behind this—though I don't know for sure if he was alone. He strikes me as the sort who would have no problem leaving co-conspirators behind."

"So, when Collins wanted to disable the ship, he sent a signal through the system that triggered the faults and essentially fractured everything." Amanda continued with her report.

"Protocol indicates that we must wake the captain," Bob said. "We need his input on our next actions."

"You haven't done that yet?" Tanis asked.

"You are the ranking officer on the ship," Priscilla said. "Execution of command structure orders are your domain."

Tanis was startled for a moment. On the *Intrepid,* the pro-tem command structure was Captain Andrews, First Mate Mick Edward, Admiral Sanderson, and then her. With none of the others out of stasis, she was top of the list.

<Focus.>

Tanis drew a deep breath. "Yes, I should go wake the captain. Joe, you're with me; Amy, there's a security locker around the far side of the node. Arm up and keep Bob and Priscilla safe."

She turned to Priscilla. "I believe the ship to be clear of hostiles. I think your next step should be to get the servitors to set up a hard line out of the node and to take out whatever is damping this node. Then start physically analyzing the destroyed components. We'll want to give the captain as much information as possible."

Priscilla glanced at Bob's node and sighed. "We would *never* have thought of that!"

Tanis couldn't help but smile as she walked out of the node, followed by Joe.

"Good to see she still has their sense of humor," he commented.

"I think she has to. *We* could leave on a pinnace or one of the larger cruisers, but, no matter what, they would have to go down with the ship."

"I honestly don't think we could go either," Joe said. "There are two and half million people in stasis on the *Intrepid*. What cowards would leave?"

Tanis clenched her jaw. "I can think of one."

ESTRELLA DE LA MUERTE

STELLAR DATE: 3241790 / 08.15.4163 (Adjusted Gregorian)
LOCATION: *GSS Intrepid*, Executive Stasis Chamber A1
REGION: LHS 1565, 0.5 AU from stellar primary

Andrews rose from his pod. He rubbed his eyes for a moment, then gave Tanis and Joe a long, searching look.

"You're not on rotation before me."

"Yes, sir. There's been an event," Tanis said.

Andrews cocked an eyebrow and she brought him up to speed.

He gave a long sigh. "Lieutenant Colonel, I can see it in your eyes that you blame yourself. You can stop that right now. No one suspected that Collins was with the enemy. Though, being in supply and acquisitions he was well placed to get the sabotaged components aboard."

"Be that as it may, sir, I was head of the SOC. It was *my job* to suspect everyone."

"Save your recriminations for later. If we don't fall into this star and burn up I'll be sure to dress you down. In the meantime I need you…you both, at the top of your game."

Without realizing she had done it, Tanis found herself standing straighter and saw that Joe had done the same. The captain's calm surety was contagious.

<*That's why he's the captain,*> Angela's mental avatar gave a shake of its head.

"Take me to Bob." Andrews eased up from the edge of his pod.

Bob, Priscilla, and Amy had cleared the dampening field surrounding his node and the AI had access to the general shipnet once more. None of his other nodes were online, which was good; it avoided any issues of a fractured personality needing a merge—something never before attempted with an AI even close to his complexity.

"What's our situation regarding LHS 1565?" Captain Andrews asked the moment he stepped into the node.

"Well, for starters, we named it Estrella de la Muerte," Priscilla said with a smile.

"That's uhh…really encouraging," Andrews said. "But not that pertinent."

<*I have control of the dorsal array of sensors and have updated my calculations. We have thirty-eight hours before we reach the star,*> Bob supplied.

"If we could regain helm control, what are our chances of firing the engines to break free?" Captain Andrews initialized a holo display of the stellar system, examining the ship's vector and performing some of his own computations.

<*We could break free, but the action would use the last of our fuel and leave us adrift.*>

"I see we're lower on isotopes than we expected," Andrews said as he looked over their fuel situation.

"We think that the ramscoop was not performing correctly for some time, but the readings were being reported as though it were. The edges of this system have a lot of lithium, but we ended up missing it all," Priscilla supplied as she brought up the variances on a holo display.

Tanis leaned against the railing that overlooked the ten-meter drop to the bottom of the node. There had to be a way out of this situation, but she couldn't see it.

"Bob, can you show your best option for our breakaway burn on the holo?" Joe asked.

Bob complied and highlighted the point where the burn would take place. <*If we do a max burn here with optimal timing, and vectors line up better than optimally, then we will achieve breakaway velocities on this vector.*>

The captain expanded the holo to forty light-years. The vector didn't even come close to intersecting any other stars. The *Intrepid* would be adrift forever.

"Is there any chance we can correct that vector after the burn?" the captain asked.

"We'll have plenty of D2, but no lithium. Our fusion engines aren't designed to run without lithium and with the primary scoop emitter damaged we're not going to have much on the way out," Priscilla supplied.

"What a miserable little star." Andrews rubbed his jaw.

"I may have a way out of this, sir," Joe said as he walked around the holo and zoomed it back in close to the star.

Tanis gave him a smile, which he glanced at and returned.

<*I knew you'd figure something out—god knows I have no idea what to do,*> Tanis said.

<*Don't get too excited just yet,*> Joe replied.

"How accurate is this in regards to how the star will look when we pass it?" he asked Bob.

A slider appeared displaying a timeline and the ship's position.

<*Very accurate,*> the AI replied. <*Use the slider to set the position in the timeline.*>

Joe nodded and adjusted forward to where the ship was closest to the star. He altered the display to shift the *Intrepid* several lines of latitude north as it passed by Estrella de la Muerte.

"I see what you're suggesting," Priscilla said.

<*As do I.*> Bob didn't sound entirely convinced.

"Explain it for the rest of us, then," Tanis said.

"First—" Joe glanced at the node core "—maximize whichever is the opposing magnetic polarity to the star on our port shields at this position." His finger pointed to the representation of the ship on the holo.

<*Done.*>

The ship's outsystem trajectory shifted ever so little, with the breakaway velocity significantly higher than before.

"I get it now. You're going to push us off of that sun spot's magnetic field and use it to… well, I don't know what to." Tanis stepped away from the railing and walked around the display, trying to see if changing her view would reveal Joe's plan.

Joe zoomed the holo out again to a ten light-year radius around the star. It had them lined up with New Eden again.

"With the bounce off the sun-spot we'll be able to save the extra fuel to course correct and get to New Eden," she said appreciatively.

"Right and right," Joe nodded.

"Clever thinking." Captain Andrews was smiling; it was the first time Tanis saw him do so since they pulled him from stasis.

<*You've got a calculation error.*> Bob adjusted Joe's trajectory to show them once more missing New Eden and passing out of the human sphere without intersecting any other system.

"You're right," Joe said. "We need more fuel, specifically more lithium, but we don't need it until after we pass the star." He adjusted the display back to his original projection and then added a second path.

"We've been over this," Priscilla said. "The scoop isn't working well enough to pick up the lithium we need, and even if it were, there's not enough on that vector to fuel the burn you propose."

"Yes, but we have more than one ship," Joe said in agreement. "I'll take one of the heavy lifters and do a hard burn out to this asteroid ring at 30 AU. Signatures indicate that there is a high likelihood for lithium in some of these rocks. I find a big one, or net some smaller ones and boost like all-get-out to meet the ship on our outsystem vector."

"That's a risky proposition," Andrews said. "If you don't make it back in time Estrella de la Muerte will be your grave."

"I'm aware of that, sir, but if I don't try it, then things are a lot worse. Without this we drift forever." Joe's somber words reminded everyone of how dire the situation was.

Tanis felt a tightness in her chest, worry making it hard to breathe. If Joe didn't make it back, she would be left on the *Intrepid* without him… forever. She knew now, had known for some time, that she loved him. Loved him and hadn't even said the words to him yet.

"I'll go with you," she said to Joe.

"You're not built for it, you couldn't handle the acceleration." His voice was sure, but his eyes were sad.

"It's what, a max of seventy g's?

"Initial peak, yeah. Average closer to four or five."

"First"—Andrews gave both of them an unreadable look—"we have to decide if this is the plan we'll be pursuing. We need Ernest and Abby for this."

THE LONG SHOT

STELLAR DATE: 3241791 / 08.16.4163 (Adjusted Gregorian)
LOCATION: ***GSS Intrepid*****, Bridge Conference Room**
REGION: LHS 1565, 0.5 AU from stellar primary

Over the next hour, a frantic wave of organized chaos swept over the *Intrepid* as hundreds of crew were brought out of stasis. Repairs began immediately; the first to the upper command area's dedicated fusion plants. Abby delegated decision making to Earnest and organized a team of specialists—both human and AI—to re-initialize more of Bob's nodes and set to work with a vengeance.

Any plan other than burning up in the star required Bob to have control of the engines. Getting his nodes back online was the first step in that process. Only he could effect the precise burns needed.

A servitor poured coffee for the command crew sitting around the bridge's conference table. Joe and Tanis sat next to Mick Edward, the first mate. He stroked his beard as he examined the holo of the local system while muttering to himself. Captain Andrews was discussing Joe's plan in low tones with Terrance while Ernest appeared engrossed in the three holos and two hyfilms in front of him. At the end of the table, Hilda Orion, the ship's chief navigator, stared at the table's main holo projection of the LHS 1565 system like it had some secret it was hiding from her.

After everyone prepared their drink to their own satisfaction, Andrews called the meeting to order.

"We have just over twenty hours until we need to make the first burn. However, if Joe is to leave on his mission to pick up some rocks his window for departure is in seven hours."

The captain's words were serious and an additional weight settled over the room. Tanis reached under the table and found Joe's hand. He squeezed it in response.

<We're going to be OK. I know I can do this.>

"You've all had some time to mull over the events of the last few hours, as well as examine Lieutenant Colonel Richard's report. Bob has put together a precise timeline necessary to pull off Commander Evans's plan and it's up to us to decide if it is the best option, and if it is even feasible."

"Oh it's feasible, all right," Earnest said. "Totally insane, but quite feasible."

"There's also the extreme risk to you." Hilda looked at Joe and Tanis. "You will have to do an extremely hard burn to break free of the star's gravity well and then reach nearly 0.20*c*, decelerate *hard* at the far end, then capture a rock or two and boost *very hard* to meet up with us. One mistake and you're permanent residents of this system."

"We know the risk." Joe's expression was resolute, though he had expressed private concerns to Tanis about the danger to her.

Hilda snorted. "There's a far safer option. We rotate the ship and fire the engines to slow our approach to the star and break free. We coast to the system's scattered disk, collect what we need, repair, and then start a standard outsystem slingshot back on course." She projected her alternate plan on the table's holo system.

Earnest shook his head. "That requires a level of certainty that there will be the materials we need to properly fix the ramscoop. Without those, we'll have to dip into colony supplies to repair it. Even so we may not have what we need without creating industry and I really don't think there is enough material in this system to do that."

"But if Joe doesn't make his rendezvous then we won't be able to course correct and make it to New Eden," Terrance said.

There were somber looks all around and Earnest enlarged the holo. "If we don't get the lithium, we'll have to convert the engines to D2-only fusion. It'll take a few years with what we have on hand, but we'll be able to correct and make it to Epsilon Eridani."

Hilda pulled up data on the system. "A colony is setting up there, but the system is too young and hot for terraforming. It'll probably take us three hundred-forty five years to drift there."

The statement drew a whistle from Joe and an incredulous look from Terrance. "How long will it take to get to New Eden if Joe's plan works and we get the lithium?" he asked.

Joe adjusted the display. "Just under one hundred seventy-two years."

Terrance shook his head. "This is going to mess things up. Our timetable will be drastically altered."

"Our total journey will take roughly ninety-two years longer than expected." Earnest nodded his head in agreement. "It's unfortunate."

"Is it a large concern?" Tanis asked. "Most everyone will be in stasis for the duration. For all intents and purposes they won't care that it took an extra hundred years to get to New Eden."

"There's the *Dakota,* or whatever the next GSS ship is," Captain Andrews said. "If we take that long to get there, they'll take it from us."

"So we don't let anyone know, not until it's too late for them to beat us to the system. We can even send a probe from here along our original path and speed sending updates as though nothing went wrong." The solution seemed obvious to Tanis.

"There are other concerns," Terrance said.

Andrews cast an appraising look at Terrance; Tanis spotted the tells they both gave when having a protracted Link discussion. The captain nodded and Terrance slowly looked into the eye of each person sitting around the table.

"What I'm about to tell you does not leave this room. I want it classified at the highest security level in your internal systems."

Everyone nodded, though Tanis knew that only Joe, Hilda and Mick were unaware of the *Intrepid's* secret cargo—and the colony's secret purpose on New Eden.

"This ship is carrying the technology to manufacture picotech—pico bots, to be precise." Terrance let the bomb drop without any further preamble.

Nanotech robots were part of everyday life. The tiny machines were everywhere, and in everything. Picotech bots would be a thousand times smaller than nanotech. In the previous millennium they had been the holy grail of a million research projects.

Much of the research had been done on Juno, but the picotech broke containment and a pico-swarm devoured half the asteroid before fail-safes destroyed it and the swarm.

It wasn't the first pico disaster and afterward every government in the system placed a ban on all picotech research. Many corporations still carried out secret research at the edges of the Sol system, but with all of the data from Juno lost, most had started from scratch, and no breakthroughs had been made—at least none that were publicized.

"When you say carrying the technology, you mean functional tech?" Joe asked.

Earnest nodded. "Indeed. I worked it out over a decade before we left Mars. But it was impossible to do any manufacturing in the Sol system."

Mick sat back and ran a hand through his hair. "I can't believe you didn't tell me this." He looked at the captain. "I think I had a right to know. Hell, the colonists have a right to know."

"It's not like we're going to make pico on New Eden, we'll use one of the other planets for it. However, the tech is quite safe," Terrance said.

"Yeah, I bet that's what the guys on Juno thought before their bodies were consumed as raw resources, before half the world was eaten by the things."

Earnest scowled at Mick. "Those researchers had no idea what they were doing. My pico is rock solid. In fact, I'm certain I can use it to create femtotech."

Terrance shot Earnest a quelling glance. "That's just conjecture at this point. We have a lot of work to do with expanding on the picotech."

Hilda whistled. "Now I get why we're running such a massive mission, and why this ship is reusable. It makes so much more sense now." She smiled as she looked around the table. "Don't you realize? New Eden will become the economic center of the human sphere!"

Terrance smiled. "That's the plan at least."

"This is nuts!" Mick stood up, his eyes flashing with rage. "I can't believe you lied to everyone. This colony is a one way trip to death."

"If we don't die here first," Joe muttered.

<*I can't believe you didn't tell me,*> he said privately to Tanis.

<*I was under orders not to, same with Angela. I'm sorry,*> she replied.

"Mick," Captain Andrew's voice boomed. "Sit. Down. Now."

For a moment it looked like the first mate would comply, then he took a step backward. "No, hell no. There's no way. I have to stop you."

He turned and ran toward the conference room door. He was two steps away when the stun shot from Tanis's pistol hit him. His body fell to the floor and Joe rose to check on the man.

"He seems to be OK. Nothing a painkiller won't fix when he wakes."

Hilda looked pale; her voice trembled. "Why did he do that?"

"There's no record of mental instability in his record," Tanis said, after looking it up on the bridge net.

"I don't know." Andrews shook his head as he looked at the mate. "I've worked with him for over three hundred years, seen him do some death defying things, I didn't think he'd react like this."

Two servitors entered and lifted the first mate. Tanis sent them instructions to put the man into stasis for the time being. It was a mystery which would have to wait. It wasn't lost on her that she was now third from the top of the *Intrepid*'s command structure as a result.

"This doesn't change the fact that time is wasting," Earnest said, apparently unfazed by the first mate's mental breakdown. "It's only a matter of time before someone else works out what I've discovered. We need the fastest route to New Eden."

"Then it's Joe's plan." Captain Andrews fixed the commander with his unflappable gaze. "You're sure you're up to this, son?"

Tanis looked between Joe and the captain. Joe appeared convinced, but Tanis saw the slightest bit of tension around his eyes. He didn't want her to come. Not like he would have a choice.

"I am, sir. However—" he glanced at Tanis "—I think I should do this alone."

"I find myself in agreement," the captain nodded. "With Mick out of the picture, I need you here, Tanis."

Tanis knew that anything she said would sound petulant and selfish. The captain was right; she should stay behind. Even so, she wracked her mind for a reason she should go with Joe.

<*She should go.*> Bob entered the conversation.

"I find myself in agreement with Bob." Earnest cast a puzzled look at his holo displays. "For some reason, with Major…err…Lieutenant Colonel Richards on the mission, I project a significantly higher chance of success. Perhaps due to Angela's abilities."

"Glad to know I'm wanted." Tanis tried to cut the tension.

<Glad to know someone appreciates what I add to our partnership.>

"She's not enhanced to handle the high *g* burns." Joe shook his head.

<Please, just go along with it, I'll explain why later,> Tanis said to Joe.

He cast her a searching look, found her hand again and nodded.

"Ok, we'll go together."

"I'm not sure about this." The captain shook his head. "We're having trouble regaining control of parts of the ship and there are still rogue servitors and bots all over. I may need you here."

"You have Ouri and Amy, and don't forget that I organized a Marine division under Major Brandt. They're more than capable of regaining control of the ship."

<They will be sufficient,> Bob said, his tone more forceful that usual. *<Send Tanis.>*

The captain cast a quizzical look at the ceiling; Tanis suspected he was inquiring about the AI's strong insistence that she go. She also wondered why.

<Don't ask me, He usually doesn't weigh in on things like this,> Angela said.

Captain Andrews eventually nodded. "You'll go. I'll have Ouri get the Marine company out of stasis and we'll take care of things here."

"It's settled, then." Earnest shuffled his hyfilm together. "Tanis and Joe will take the *Excelsior*; it's our fastest heavy tug, which can boost a billion tons to 0.20*c*. You'll need to begin your initial burn in six hours and thirty nine minutes."

THE LONG DARK

STELLAR DATE: 3241791 / 08.16.4163 (Adjusted Gregorian)
LOCATION: *GSS Intrepid*, Bridge Conference Room
REGION: LHS 1565, 0.45 AU from stellar primary

????? ???r? t? Intrepid e???pe ??rn
???? ???r? t? end ?????e??r ? i???n ???n?? ? ind??

Abby and her team had been hard at work during the meeting. Thankfully, one of the first systems brought back online was the dorsal maglev. The train would shave at least an hour off their journey.

Joe and Tanis had visited an armory on the way to the train and both carried pulse rifles. Joe found light body armor while Tanis had opted not to add to her flow-armor, other than to strap two sidearms to her hips and throw a bandolier of power cells over her shoulder.

They sat beside each other as the train took off toward a station that would place them six kilometers from the A1 dock where the Excelsior waited.

With all the other maglev trains offline an easier route would have been to take a shuttle from the A3 dock, but when Collins left he had destroyed the other ships and much of the dock.

It was going to be a long hike to the *Excelsior*.

They hadn't spoken much since the decision to include Tanis and her discomfort at the silence was turning to annoyance. In the military, rank dictated decision-making. If you had a lower pay-grade, you shut up and did what you were told. The extra dynamic of a relationship added exhausting nuance to every conflict.

"Why am I getting the silent treatment?" she finally asked. "I thought you were OK with my coming."

"I've been waiting for you to explain why you are so insistent on coming," Joe replied. His tone was level, giving little away, but Tanis knew that meant he was upset.

"It feels silly; I know that logically going with you is not the right choice."

"You're right, it's not." Joe's voice was harsh and his expression softened. "Sorry, that came out stronger than I meant..."

"I seem to remember doing that myself from time to time."

"Who you?" Joe grinned and Tanis gave him a light punch on the arm. "I'm still worried, though. A seventy-*g* burn will make you weigh over six-thousand kilograms. Even in stasis that's a lot."

"I know," Tanis agreed. "It's not going to be comfortable, but I just found you—figuratively speaking—I'm not going to lose you."

Joe locked eyes with her. "I spent a long time chasing after you too. I don't want to lose you either."

<I may have a way to make this work out,> Angela interrupted. *<I think I can enhance Tanis's body to withstand the strain. You'll still want to be in stasis for the heavy burns, but the risks will go down drastically.>*

"Do tell," Tanis said.

<I can use your flow-armor to boost the structural integrity of your bones and organ walls. It's essentially what Joe's alterations allow his body to do under high g's.>

"That sounds a…bit risky," Tanis said, looking down at the matte grey armor tightly adhered to her skin. "Do I really need something like that? I already have a lot of structural enhancements. It's not like this is all flesh and blood in here," she said as she patted her stomach.

<I think it will help a lot. I'm in here too and that amount of pressure worries me as well. However your armor is designed to

withstand kinetic strikes much larger than these burns and will make the difference between a fun trip and lung collapse.>

"See, my concerns are not completely unfounded," Joe said. "I think you should do it."

<I don't need to do it now; we can do it on the ship. I have a suspicion that you'll need that armor on the outside before we get there.>

Tanis clasped Joe's hand. "Just the way we like it."

Neither said another word as the train continued to their stop; their hands didn't unclasp.

When the maglev stopped the doors opened into a pitch-black station. Even the emergency lighting was offline.

<So much for hoping another line would be online. You guys better get to it, it's a five kilometer hike to the forward docking bays,> Angela supplied.

<Pretty dark down here.> Tanis addressed Priscilla over the general shipnet. *<Any chance we could get some glow?>*

<Not very likely.> Priscilla's answer was short and her mental tone clipped. *<When we brought node eleven back online, a nasty virus leaked out; it's wreaking havoc with systems everywhere. We're doing our best to get it cleaned up, but until we do ship systems are going to be sporadic. That, combined with the battery bank that blew, has knocked whole sections of the ship completely off the grid.>*

<Is the virus human spreadable?> Tanis asked. It wasn't uncommon for system viruses to target a human's internal computers or AI. Because of human system viruses, nearly half of the average person's internal processing power and codebase was dedicated to intrusion detection and protection.

<Quite likely. I'd suggest you sever wireless connections, or at the least drop to low bandwidth with extra buffers.>

<Will can do,> Tanis said.

Joe had been listening in. He caught her eye and nodded.

<Keep us updated. We're on the second leg of our journey.>

<You got it.>

"They must have had a contingency plan in case any of us got out of stasis," Joe said.

Tanis nodded as they walked across the platform into the station's central plaza. She cycled her vision to a combination of IR and UV. The setting picked up enough ambient heat and background radiation to generate a picture of the room. Her navigation overlay filled in the rest, providing a false color representation of what the station looked like.

Joe's vision didn't have the UV pickup, so she sent him a point to point feed to help improve his sight.

"Thanks, there are some looooong drops on this ship."

"You're telling me. When they built it they really didn't give a lot of consideration to how hard it is to get between places on foot."

<*Tanis.*> Priscilla's voice came over the general shipnet. <*We've got some instances of rogue servitors in your area. It looks like there's an AI controlling that bad node and it's taking control of portions of the ship.*>

<*Are you going to be able to fend it off?*>

Priscilla gave the mental equivalent of a snort. <*Absolutely, the biggest concern is time, if it slows down regaining control of the engines then this party is for nothing.*>

Tanis signaled her agreement and nodded to Joe. They both unslung their pulse rifles and set them to an EM burst. It was a dangerous thing to use on a ship, but with everything offline there was little chance of secondary explosions.

"Servitors should show up pretty clearly on the IR," Joe said as they moved cautiously across the plaza. The station had several balconies and some large spaces with no cover. Tanis would feel a lot better once they were through it.

"Don't count on it, this room has a lot of reflective surfaces. Make sure you filter out your own image or you'll be shooting at ghosts."

"Not my first time using IR," Joe said with a smile.

Despite every hair on Tanis's neck tingling, nothing happened. They exited the station and began their journey down a long series of pitch-black corridors.

Unlike her mad race after Collins and Amy Lee, Tanis was acutely aware of her surroundings. The darkened halls took on a sinister cast and she found herself imagining twisted shapes lurching out from the shadows.

She shook her head to clear the images from her mind.

"You OK?" Joe asked.

"Yeah, just too many bad memories from darkened ship corridors."

Her augmented vision showed Joe nodding and he put a hand on her shoulder. She was glad he didn't ask for details. She didn't want to think any further on those past events.

Crew quarters and duty stations slid by on either side; after the first kilometer those were left behind as they moved into a region of supply depots and workshops.

"Well that's not handy," Tanis said as they came to a bank of lifts at the end of a corridor. "There's supposed to be a way to get down to deck 114B from here."

"What I'd give for a flashlight right now," Joe said while looking for an access hatch to a ladder shaft.

"Give it a second, I have my nanocloud doing pings, they'll find the opening."

Seconds later the nano spotted it and the hatch lit up on their HUDs. Tanis pried it open and slid down the ladder to the next deck; she put her back to the wall, scanning the cross corridors while Joe leapt through the opening and landed beside her.

"Such a show-off," Tanis said, worrying for a moment that it was the wrong thing to say.

Joe grinned. "Gotta keep limber."

<He fell for you even with all your snark, I suspect he knows what he's in for,> Angela commented on Tanis's internal worry.

They landed in an intersection and the corridor they needed was lit up on their HUDs. The path took them between entrances to massive workshops where machines lay dormant, prepared to fashion whatever ship's components were needed. Many of them would also assist in building the New Eden 1 space station on which the habitation cylinders would mount.

Joe stopped and put a hand on Tanis's shoulder. "Did you hear that?"

"Over my own breathing? No. It's weird to have the ship this silent."

"I could have sworn I heard something come from that opening ahead to the left." Joe gestured at the gaping doorway with his rifle.

"Then let's go nice and slow-like."

The pair crept through the corridor. Tanis never thought she would be in the dark, creeping down a hall in the *Intrepid,* worrying about being attacked by the machines that were supposed to build her future home.

A clang echoed out of the shop ahead.

"I heard it that time," Tanis whispered.

Another metallic sound sliced through the silence behind them.

"Fuck stealth," Tanis said. "Run!"

The corridor was featureless and indefensible; if they were going to be attacked from both ends they would be cut to ribbons. Ahead, the maps showed the corridor terminated in a sorting warehouse filled with various semi-autonomous robots, but at least it offered some cover.

The screech of metal on metal came from all around and Tanis spread her nanocloud further ahead. Not a moment too soon, a molecular welder moved into view from an angle they would have missed in their mad dash.

"Duck!" Tanis hit the deck a moment before Joe as a plasma beam shot over their heads. She rolled onto her shoulder and sent an EM pulse at the machine. Sparks flew and the plasma arm swung wildly, slicing through a part of the deck before finally going dead.

She swung her head to see Joe firing bursts at a series of light hauler mechs coming out of an adjacent shop. They crashed to the ground, but more of their brethren were assembling in the shadows.

Without another word they both got back to their feet and picked up the pace. The sorting depot was only a hundred meters away. Tanis checked on her AI to see that Angela was launching exploratory probes to attempt a signal intercept on whatever was controlling the robots.

<*Looks like it's our unfriendly neighborhood virus slinging AI.*>

<*It sure seems to know what it's doing,*> Tanis replied.

<*It may on a grand scale, but this sort of thing is my specialty.*>

Battling rogue AI was one of the reasons she and Angela had been paired to begin with, their skills suited one another quite well.

Several of the robots moved into the corridor ahead of them but then turned back once under Angela's control. As they dashed by, Tanis could see Angela's bots doing battle with those under control of the rogue AI.

<*Nice save.*> Tanis thanked her friend.

<*Say it, you'd be lost without me.*>

<*It goes without saying, are you jealous of Joe or something?*> Tanis smiled in her mind.

Moments later, Tanis and Joe burst into the sorting depot. They skidded to a halt as Tanis let her nano probes fly high to get a good view of their surroundings.

"Looks like it's powered down." Joe looked around, the tone in his voice indicating he wasn't too certain of his words.

"Just like those machine shops, eh?" Tanis said.

"Let's hope it's not *just* like them."

Tanis led the way while Joe kept an eye on the depot entrance, his rifle ready to send an EM pulse into the first non-sentient creature to appear.

<I've got them bottled up,> Angela said over the private net between the three of them. *<But the general shipnet is down here and I'm losing signal fidelity with all these machines around. In two minutes or so they'll be free again.>*

"Then let's not be here in two minutes," Joe said.

"Seems logical to me."

Their HUD overlays updated with a new route when they entered the depot. It led them past silent machines, and autonomous haulers, all the while praying Angela would be able to suppress activation of these robots.

<I've got better plans than that.>

As they passed, a few of the haulers stirred to life. The motion startled the pair at first, but Angela showed her plan on their virtual space. She would leave the haulers on pre-programmed paths and mission sets, and then fry their wireless receivers. It would effectively make them unhackable as well as provide a barrier to pursuers.

"Someone is going to hate us later when they have to clear up the mess that'll make," Joe chuckled.

"I'd pay to see the expression on their faces." Tanis smiled.

She rounded a suspension field sorter and found herself face to face with a closed door.

"That doesn't look good," Joe said.

"No power, no entrance." Tanis prodded the access panel.

"Aren't these things supposed to have manual overrides for when the power's out?" Joe looked around for a manual pump.

<Not in here,> Angela said.

"Well that's an annoying oversight." Joe stepped back and looked around. "There's a catwalk up there, map shows exits off it."

"Then that's where we're going," Tanis said.

They started climbing a seven-meter tall crane that rose near to the catwalk. It made the skin on the back of Tanis's neck crawl as she imagined the clear shots anything at the shop's entrance would have of her and Joe.

As if she were prophetic, the sound of robotic battle down the corridor ceased and was replaced by the sound of equipment rumbling over the decking.

"Move it, Commander. We're gonna have visitors."

"You mind if I at least make sure I don't fall?" Joe asked. He was at the end of the crane, getting ready to jump.

Tanis bit back another admonishment for haste and Joe leapt across three meters of open air. It looked like he wasn't going to make it, but he managed to hook an arm around the lowest bar in the railing.

Letting out the breath she hadn't been aware she was holding, Tanis ran up the last two meters of the crane and leapt across the space, landing on the top railing.

"Now who's the show-off?" Joe said through gritted teeth as he hung on. "Mind lending me a hand, Miss Monkey?"

Tanis leaned down and clasped Joe's outstretched arm, pulling him up and over the railing.

"More with the showing off!" He smiled, while rubbing his forearm where it had caught the weight of his body.

"I have this amazing new prosthetic arm, I may as well use it." Tanis grinned and then pointed toward an open doorway. "There's our way out of this mess."

They sprinted down the catwalk as the machine shop robots rumbled into the depot. Angela's haulers moved forward to block them, but even with the interference, several of the plasma beams came far too close for comfort.

Tanis dove through the door, and Joe slammed it shut behind them, pulling his hands away as several parts of the panel glowed white-hot from plasma impacts. He gave Tanis a hand and pulled her up.

"So it looks like we just added a half a klick to our trip." Tanis sighed.

"Damn evil AI," Joe grunted. "They're always messing things up. We've only got five hours to get to the *Excelsior* and prep it and there are still three klicks of space's-got-it between us and there."

"Let's get a move on, then," Tanis said.

18:05 ▯▯▯r▯ t▯ *Intrepid* e▯▯▯pe ▯ ▯ne▯▯er
4:47 hours to end of Excelsior mission launch window

Captain Andrews surveyed the bridge. His primary crew sat at their duty stations and everyone was briefed on the status of the ship and the plan. Commander Ouri reported in that Commander Brandt and two platoons were out of stasis.

<We had some contacts with the enemy, but we're on the maglev, headed to node eleven,> Ouri said.

<Good to hear, Commander. Keep me appraised of your progress,> Andrews replied.

He cut the connection and checked on Amy Lee's status. She had a group of ship's security officers clearing out servitors surrounding the ramscoop. They were making good progress and engineers would be able to diagnose the damage first hand within the hour.

<Captain, I've lost contact with Tanis and Joe,> Terry reported from the bridge's conference room where her team had set up to manage net security.

Andrew's stomach fell. *<Do we know why? Were they under fire?>*

<They've been under fire almost constantly for the last twenty minutes, but I think they've entered an area where the wireless feeds are down.>

<*There are more places without net than with,*> the captain replied. <*Do what you can; we need to know if we have to send a second team soon.*>

He would give her another hour. Tanis had been through far worse and come out unscathed. However, she had also come out very scathed from time to time. He still remembered seeing her return from her encounter with Trent on Mars 1, her left arm and a fair bit of her upper torso missing. Later, when she had merged her mind with the ship and the fighters to stave off an attack, she had nearly died but somehow pulled through. She would make it through whatever was going on down below.

<*Abby, how are things progressing with the engine connection,*> he asked the chief engineer over the Link.

He could imagine her grunt of annoyance at the interruption. <*It's going slower now that you are bothering me. We're having trouble, but nothing we can't fix up. If that damned rogue AI in node eleven could be shut down we'd be doing a hell of a lot better.*>

<*Ouri is taking a team to deal with it,*> Captain Andrews replied.

<*What, with guns?*> Andrews could sense her panic.

<*We need to shut it down; chances are it will have defenses.*>

<*We can't have node eleven damaged, with the issues elsewhere we need it to regulate the particle accelerator.*> Abby sounded frustrated, like she was being pulled in a dozen directions. Andrews knew just how she felt.

<*What do you propose?*>

<*Send Earnest with her, you just make sure he doesn't get a scratch on him. How are Tanis and Joe doing? Have they finished prepping the* Excelsior *yet?*>

<*No, we lost contact with them a few minutes ago.*> Andrews ran a hand through his hair. If things kept up it would be white before long.

<*You're just full of great news.*>

<They're in a dead spot on the shipnet. I expect them to be through it soon, but they've been in pretty constant combat for the last hour.>

<She better not be busting up my ship!>

<Abby, it will take a little bit more than Tanis with an EM gun to bust up the Intrepid.>

This time she did give her grunt of annoyance over the connection. *<I don't know about that. The girl has a knack.>*

17:44 ???r? t? *Intrepid e???pe ? ?ne??er*
4:26 hours to end of Excelsior mission launch window

Commander Ouri rode the dorsal maglev with two platoons from the *Intrepid's* 1st Battalion's Bravo Company and a fireteam of FROD Marines from Charlie Company acting as Earnest's bodyguards.

"Node eleven is seven levels down in Engine," Commander Brandt, the CO of B Company said. "The maglev doesn't go that close to it, but I plan to get off here anyway." She pointed to a small station one level in.

<That seems sound,> Casey, the company's AI agreed.

"Agreed," Ouri said. "There's bound to be resistance and maglev tubes are no place for a fight."

Ouri couldn't help but wonder what Tanis would do. Tactics and training were well and good, but Tanis always seemed to do things her own way and get superior results.

At least the colonel had the foresight to form many of the colonists with military background into a division. The regular GSS ship security types were good at policing and manning guard points, but fighting rogue AI in a powerless starship was a different story.

Getting Bravo Company had been a challenge in and of itself. No military units had been in stasis chambers that were under Bob's control and she had ventured on her own into one of the dark areas to bring Commander Brandt's company out.

Ouri didn't think of herself as someone who was easily scared, but moving through those dark corridors with nothing but her meager IR and a hand-light tested her resolve more than she cared to admit.

She had only encountered one rogue servitor and taken it out on the way to the company's stasis chamber. Once she had brought the soldiers out of stasis, she felt relief—not for their protection, but against the quiet and dark.

The barracks had auxiliary power and the soldiers had suited up in light armor. Ouri and Brandt had conferred and sent platoon one to protect Abby and her engineers while platoons two and three had the task of securing node eleven and stopping the rogue AI.

"What about the plasma conduits through that path?" Lieutenant Arin asked as she studied the train's holo display. "If the RAI breaches them we'll have nowhere to hide."

"I doubt that's likely. Judging by where the impellers are they don't have power—the lines should be clear," Brandt said.

Commander Brandt was a slight woman with thin, almost pixie-like features. Ouri wasn't alone in this assessment, she had heard several soldiers refer to her as "the Pix," something Ouri was certain no one had ever called her to her face.

"Commander, I don't see how you can be sure—" Lieutenant Smith began to object but received a cold stare from the smaller woman.

"Face the possible threat of plasma on the ship, or the certainty of it on the surface of that star out there. Your pick."

Ouri wasn't certain if it was the best team-building response, but time was of the essence. "Casey. Send the route to the platoon sergeants; they're going to need to arrange their teams."

Commander Brandt cast Ouri an unreadable look. Though they both shared the same rank, Ouri was GSS and her oak leaf put her above the other woman's bars. However, the fact that TSF didn't regard the civilian GSS ranks as legitimate didn't help her credibility.

"Make it happen, Casey." Brandt's glower turned to an expression of concern as the train suddenly lost power and slowed to a halt.

"Damn, we're still a klick from Engine," Brandt said.

"Looks like we're not taking the AI by surprise," Earnest said, shaking his head.

Brandt gave her orders and several fireteams pried the doors open and secured positions outside the train.

<*It's a vomit comet out here,*> one of the sergeants reported. <*The rail's gravity only covers about 4 feet and then you're getting tiny amounts from the particle accelerator and that's in waves.*>

The information went out on the combat net and the soldiers and Marines prepared for 0*g* maneuvers.

Ouri stepped out from the train. As expected, the maglev tube was too narrow and provided no cover. A fireteam from platoon two was pulling open a hatch that would lead to the access tunnels that ran alongside the particle accelerator.

Because the twenty-five kilometer long particle accelerator brought whatever the ramscoop collected to relativistic speeds, gravitational waves were produced. When it was fully operational it provided gravity for much of the crew areas of the ship. At present, the minute gravity it offered was more problematic than helpful.

Ouri and Brandt worked up a plan with the platoon leaders and determined that platoon three would take access tunnels on the starboard side of the ship and platoon two would stay portside. Earnest and his Marines, as well as the company HQ elements, would proceed with platoon two.

Ouri checked her rifle's load-out and loosened her pistol in its holster. Even though she was not an active combat participant in the platoon, she expected to be using her weapons.

The drop through the hatch caused an unpleasant lurch in her stomach as her organs shifted in 0*g*. Ouri still remembered the first time when she realized that being without gravity created a constant 'drop' feeling, like being in a fast moving elevator or a roller coaster the entire time. It took a lot of the fun out of low gravity work.

Earnest and his guards took up position next to Ouri as the platoon worked its way down a darkened corridor.

"This certainly makes things a bit more interesting, doesn't it?"

Ouri looked at the engineer, surprised to see that he was grinning.

"That's a curse if I ever heard one," she replied.

"Yes, yes, but an interesting one," he winked. "I almost feel better. I was waiting for the other shoe to drop and now, at least, it has."

"Isn't the ship severely damaged? We must be facing a serious delay in reaching New Eden."

Earnest nodded. "However, I'll get the opportunity to fix it out here with limited resources. Now that's a challenge!"

One of the Marines was shaking his head ruefully and Ouri had to shrug and put it from her mind. The only thing that mattered right now was eliminating the rogue AI and regaining full control of the ship.

"Stay sharp," staff sergeant Turin said. "Scan shows motion ahead."

<*Platoon three is engaged with the enemy,*> Casey reported. <*Two casualties, but they are making progress.*>

As if to punctuate the AI's message, a particle beam lanced over Ouri's head and she hit the deck. The Marines forced Earnest down and took positions around him, weapons at the ready.

"Give me blanketing fields of fire on that location!" a sergeant yelled. "Squad three, fall back to that cross-corridor and see if you can flank."

"Contact rear!" one of the Marines called out.

Ouri looked back and saw the shapes of servitors behind them. They were trapped in a narrow corridor with only a few conduits for protection.

The platoon's engineers were rapidly setting up stasis shields that were able to stop the particle beams, though they reduced the Marines' firing options.

Ouri took a position assisting the Marines in holding the rear of the formation. Her ship's security pulse rifle wasn't as effective as the Marines' but she had brought some of her riot control gear and clipped to her belt were three EMP webs.

She signaled her intent to the leader of the fireteam and lobbed the ball at the servitors. It bounced once and then sprayed a web over the robots. They were not hardened for battle and the web knocked them offline.

The soldiers in squad three saw the opening and dashed back down the hall to a cross corridor. Ouri's ship map showed that they would be able to flank the servitors attacking the front of the formation in roughly four minutes.

As she was checking the maps, there was an explosion and a part of the ceiling fell near her.

<Casey, what on Earth are they firing? How do servitors pose this much of a risk?>

<It would appear that several of the units ahead of us have plasma cutters that have been adapted into plasma throwers.>

"Sweet gods..." she whispered while watching plasma splash across a stasis shield.

17:35 ⍰⍰⍰r⍰ t⍰ *Intrepid* e⍰⍰⍰pe ⍰ ⍰ne⍰⍰er
4:15 hours to end of Excelsior mission launch window

Security drones had Tanis and Joe pinned down. The hovering robots were proving to be a far more effective foe than the welders and haulers had been.

Joe was across the corridor from Tanis, both were crouched behind a series of shafts that rose vertically through the deck. The shafts offered scant cover from the focused laser beams the security drones fired. Tanis's armor could take a few hits, but there were over two dozen of the drones out there—more than enough to overload its diffusion abilities.

"I really don't get why some AI is giving Bob so much trouble," Joe said as he ducked behind his cover—their IR vision showing a string of heated air where his head had been a moment before.

"Probably because he's doing his damnedest to get control of the whole ship from just one node. I don't think he, or the ship, was designed to work like that."

Tanis crouched low and darted into the open and back again, drawing fire. Joe used the opportunity to take out the drone that fired on him previously. The EM pulse hit the hovering bot and it fell to the deck in a shower of sparks.

"One down, what? Twenty more to go?"

"Something like that," Tanis said. "I can't get a good read; they have ionized fields that are blocking the nano. Angela can't get a probe past it to take them over. Even if she did, these things have good internal defenses. It would take an army of nano to knock 'em down."

"Sure would be nice if we had some of that pico tech," Joe said.

"I'd rather not be the first to try it out in combat conditions."

Joe laughed and took his turn drawing fire while Tanis hit two bots in quick succession.

"They're wising up," Joe said. "Nearly got me again."

"We need a new tactic."

"We need to bring pulse grenades next time."

Tanis laughed. It felt good to be back in the thick of it with Joe. They made an effective team as they fell into their old, comfortable place. She really liked that place.

"Then we need to improvise," Tanis said. They were still out of contact with the shipnet and neither had schematics for this section of the *Intrepid*. There had to be something in one of these conduits that could help.

<*Any chance you could try to extrapolate with some general probes?*> Tanis asked Angela.

<*Couldn't hurt.*> Angela's response was nonchalant.

Tanis suspected that her AI couldn't even be bothered to get worked up about life and death situations anymore.

<*Well, all things considered, a few automaton drones aren't much of a match for the pair of us. We could take them out with you naked only holding a plastic spoon.*>

<*Was that actual humor?*> Tanis asked.

<*I can do humor. I can do it even better when it's at your expense.*>

Tanis decided not to extend the conversation and held back her reply. It was nearly impossible to win a battle of acerbic wit with Angela. It was likely the AI spent the hours Tanis slept just thinking of comebacks and comments.

"So what's the plan?" Joe asked as he sprayed EM pulses at random.

"Angela's got a possible conduit carrying particulate matter for nano assembly in the fourth vertical conduit down on your side."

"Particulate matter? Isn't that engineering speak for explosive?"

"Samples indicate it could be aluminum oxide."

Joe paled. "Maybe we shouldn't be shooting at those things."

Tanis knew what he meant; few things were as frightening as a burning cloud of metal in an enclosed space.

"Everything is offline, it's not pressurized."

Joe's glance indicated how that knowledge failed to encourage him.

"EM isn't going to do the trick. I'm going to fire a focused pulse blast and see if I can crack it. You be ready to fry one of those things the moment the spray comes out," Tanis said.

Joe nodded, they were committed to this course of action and the only real option was to make it work.

Tanis used nano probes to get a good view of the pipe she had to hit. She held her gun out around her cover, using remote sighting to line it up with the target. A nod to Joe and she let loose with several shots. On the third shaped pulse impact, the pipe fractured and a cloud of aluminum filled the air.

The security drones were surrounded by the cloud and Joe took his shot at the closest bot. It exploded and ignited the powder. Joe's light armor wouldn't provide enough protection, but Tanis was ready. She leapt across the corridor the moment his finger pulled the trigger and landed astride him, shielding his body with hers.

The explosion was deafening and the pressure wave forced her body against his. Her armor locked up, protecting her—and, by extension, him—from the brunt of it. In a moment it was gone, having blown itself out.

"Wow, you are really heavy," Joe grunted.

Tanis sat up on her knees. "Is that any way to speak to a lady?"

Joe delivered one of his patented grins. "I know my lady isn't vain, she can take it."

Tanis laughed and stood, offering him a hand.

"Maybe I'm vain and you don't know it."

Joe glanced at her matte grey flow-armor. "You could make that any color or pattern you want and you picked matte grey."

Tanis shrugged. "It blends in with the ship down here."

Joe laughed and gave her a light peck on the cheek. "Yes, incredibly vain."

They walked through the remains of the corridor. The bulkheads had buckled and most of the pipes were cracked.

"Effective," Joe said.

"Appears to have been. Abby is going to kill us."

Joe kicked the remains of one of the drones. "Good thing those weren't hardened units."

Tanis nodded. "We're down to four hours. Based on the last reported readiness, it's going to take three to get the *Excelsior* ready."

"We can do it in two if we have to, we may just miss something we really wish we had later," Joe said.

"Like I said, three hours."

Tanis moved past the destroyed security drones and sent her nano scouting ahead. She followed slowly, leery of another attack.

"You have no sense of adventure," Joe grinned at Tanis as he caught up.

<*Are you kidding?*> Angela asked.

Joe laughed. "Yeah, you're right. I forgot who I was talking to for a moment there."

Tanis gave him a sour look. "I have a sense of adventure, but it's not like I go seeking trouble out."

Joe's laughter turned into coughing and Angela sent a series of incredulous faces over the private net.

"I'm serious," Tanis said. "I just seem to be around when trouble shows up."

"What about on the *Steel Dawn III* when you ran toward the nuclear bomb and not away from it?" Joe asked.

Tanis shrugged. "Someone had to take it out."

<*And when those mercs tried to take the VIPs hostage at that first ball?*> Angela added her example.

"I was there in the hall when they attacked."

"I seem to recall you going up into a crawl space to cut a plasma line. Then you jumped down with nothing more than a pulse rifle and your dress above your hips not three meters from the mercs."

Tanis shrugged as they rounded a corner into a wider, but still dark and net-less corridor. Her nano ranged far ahead, confirming the coast was clear and she picked up the pace. "Seemed like the best course of action at the time."

<We can't forget the mad rush to flush out those other mercs in the freighters.>

"That was classic Tanis," Joe nodded. "Only surpassed by our 'let's be bait' mission on Mars 1."

"OK, so maybe I don't actively avoid trouble." Tanis shrugged.

<We were just getting warmed up.>

"If memory serves, we were talking about the timeline, and the prepwork for the ship." Tanis gave Joe a somewhat annoyed look and sent a quelling thought to Angela.

Joe assumed a serious look, but a smile still played at the corners of his mouth. "Yeah, so we will probably need to fuel the ship up. Bob was going to see if he was able to make a connection to the bay on a highband channel. Docking control systems require pretty secure connections and he can't pass the encryption commands on the lowband wireless."

"What if there's no power?" Tanis asked as they turned into another powerless corridor.

"Docks can generate their own local power. Need it in case of emergency."

"How thoughtful."

Joe laughed. "Yeah, I guess it is fortuitous. Fueling the *Excelsior* could take an hour, depending on the pump specs; we don't have access to which system is in that bay right now. Then there's some equipment checks we'll need to do, system initialization processes, supply loading, that sort of thing."

"It occurs to me," Tanis said, "that with all these other ships onboard, couldn't we use them to help alter our trajectory?"

Joe gave Tanis a quizzical look.

"What?"

"You didn't look at the proposal stream?" Joe asked.

Tanis had to admit normally she would have looked at every solution proposal that was postulated for a scenario. This time she had ignored them all, fixated on the one that would put her on a ship alone with Joe for several days.

"Uh, not all of them, no," she replied.

"Huh…that's unlike you."

<He doesn't know the half of it.>

Tanis shrugged and Joe continued. "It was determined that, with the local gravity fields, the amount of force we'd have to use would cause too much structural stress. Normally, with all systems online that sort of thing could be compensated for, but as things sit it would severely damage the ship."

"I guess that makes sense." Tanis agreed. "Be nice if we had one of those 'tractor beams' they have in the science fiction stories."

Joe grinned. "We may as well wish for 'warp drive' while we're at it."

Tanis laughed. "Or 'transporters'."

A minute later, the nano reported back that it had reached the docking bay with no further signs of aberrant technology. Even better, the bay had power and access to the general shipnet. Tanis used the Link through her string of nano and reported in to the bridge.

<We're about three hundred meters from the bay, sir. A bit behind, but we'll make it out on schedule.>

Captain Andrews' mental tone conveyed a momentary surprise and then deep relief. *<Lieutenant Colonel, you have no*

idea how glad we are to hear from you. You've been out of comm reach for over an hour.>

<You don't need to tell me, Sir. This ship is one big place when you're huffing it as well as fighting random construction equipment.>

<Are you and the commander alright?>

<Right as rain, sir.>

<Good to hear from you, though. Oh, thanks.> Tanis had sent her full report on the journey thus far, including a detailed accounting of the fights with damage estimations. *<Good job, thanks for not breaking anything too much.>*

<Just doing my best. How are things going with our uninvited guest and the engines?>

<Ok, though Ouri and Brandt haven't secured the RAI yet.>

<So, OK, relatively speaking.>

The captain laughed. *<Yes, relatively speaking.>*

<Squad three, where the fuck are you?> Commander Brandt swore over the combat net.

<Nearly there, we're taking positions now.>

Ouri surveyed the platoon. At least four soldiers were down and the stasis shields were showing signs of giving out. Judicial use of EMP grenades had evened the odds, but the platoon was still pinned down.

<DO IT!> Squad three's sergeant yelled and the sounds of withering slug fire tore through the hall. Squad one took the opportunity to rush the servitors and less than ten seconds later it was over.

"Good work, Three," Brandt said. "Squad two, I want you to send your runners for medical attention and stay here with the wounded."

The commander turned to the rest of the platoon. "What are you waiting for? Get moving!"

The platoon encountered a few more servitors, but was able to quickly dispatch them. Ten minutes later, they arrived at a broad cross corridor that created a square with a maglev station, a series of shops, and the entrance for the node where the rogue AI was holed up.

"Feels so wrong without any people," one of the soldiers whispered before his sergeant told him to shut up.

Ouri couldn't help but agree. She had been through this section of the ship a few times and had spent some time in the shops strung along this corridor. It had always been bustling, packed with people. The silence itself was almost a physical threat.

Brandt linked platoon two's command net with platoon three's and laid out a plan. Ouri saw that platoon three had encountered more servitors, but none lobbing plasma. They had only suffered two casualties.

<The entrance to the node the RIA is lodged in is between our positions, about two hundred meters from us, and one hundred from you.> Brandt addressed her lieutenants and platoon sergeants.

As the officer in charge, Ouri would have to approve the plan, but she doubted that she'd have anything to offer that Brandt hadn't thought of.

<I'm expecting some heavy resistance down this corridor. The node has some serious firepower protecting it and I'd be surprised if we don't encounter a fair number of unfriendlies out there as well. I want platoon three to go in first and push hard. There are a number of shops on your end that should provide good cover. Hole up in those about twenty meters from the node entrance, or as close as you can make it. Once you have them distracted we'll advance down the corridor and attack any positions that are exposed to us.

Keep in mind that the node turrets and security drones will be hardened, so your EMP weaponry will have no effect on them. Your only route with them is kinetic force, but we can't damage the entrance to the node, or the systems inside. Surgical shots only.>

The lieutenants and platoon sergeants proposed some specific tactics which Brandt accepted before glancing at Ouri. <*Do you approve, Commander?*>

<*Approved,*> Ouri replied.

<*Command approval noted.*> Casey logged the event in the company's logs.

Platoon three began its advance and Ouri watched the action on the command net, impressed that the soldiers worked so well together considering that they had only trained as a unit for a few weeks before the *Intrepid* left Sol.

The platoon made it within 30 meters of the entrance to the RAI's node and reported that they could advance no further without suffering casualties. Brandt gave the command and squad one moved out into the corridor where they took positions behind several curved bulkheads.

Squad one was made up of sniper teams who took low positions in the corridor behind portable ES shields and searched for targets in the firefight between platoon three and the node's security forces.

<*Engage.*> Brandt gave the order over the command net and the sharpshooters let fly with thirteen-millimeter rounds from ballistic rifles.

"Abby would have kittens," Earnest whispered near Ouri.

"Not a lot of choice," she replied. "Kinetics are the only thing we can hit them with, short of explosives."

"Oh, I understand," Earnest smiled. "She would, too, but she'd still have kittens."

The snipers were changing positions—it would not take more than one or two shots for the security drones to locate them. However, there were six fewer security drones than there were mere seconds earlier.

Platoon three held its position while squads three and four advanced down the corridor under the cover of the sharpshooters' fire. Once they had taken cover, squad one moved past their positions. The process repeated until platoon two was within fifty meters of the RAI's node.

<I have movement to port of our position,> Casey reported over the command net.

Moments later, a particle beam shot from the hall behind them into one of the sharpshooters.

Brandt had used the sergeants and lieutenant in the company HQ to augment the fallen Marines from the previous engagement. Ouri, Earnest, and the four Marines were all who remained in the command position. Ouri looked at the Marines and nodded. "On me."

Trying not to think about what she was doing, Ouri unslung her kinetic rifle and activated her targeting computer. In one quick motion, she darted across the corridor while one of the Marines provided cover. She slid into the darkened entrance to a shop and searched for heat signatures in the corridor.

Another particle beam lanced out from the darkness and hit the deck where a sharpshooter had been just a moment before. Ouri tracked the shot and let fire with a series of rounds from her rifle.

Two Marines slid into the entryway behind her and in seconds added their fire to hers. An explosion and a shower of sparks provided confirmation that their bullets had found a target.

Brandt sent orders to the sharpshooters instructing them to advance down the corridor—putting more distance between them and unknowns behind their position. Ouri sent a remote probe down the corridor searching for more adversaries, wishing that she had the ability to generate nano on demand like Tanis did.

The probe scanned the corridor as it went, eventually coming across the remains of a security drone that had been pulverized by Ouri and the Marines. It proceeded another ten meters and sent an alert as it flagged two more security drones advancing down the corridor.

Ouri sent the data stream to the Marines and once the security drones were in range they opened fire. A few particle beams lanced out in their direction, but none hit and a minute later the drones were down.

"Not sure why they bother making things like that," one of the Marines grunted. "They're not good for much more than target practice."

"We didn't expect a war on the ship," Earnest said as he, Brandt and the final Marine crossed the corridor to Ouri's position.

Ouri laughed, "I'm not sure why not. I think there have been wars that were safer than being on the *Intrepid*."

"This?" one of the Marine's asked. "This is a walk in the park. Though you have a steady shot there, Commander, even if you are GSS."

"Shut up and cover our backs," Brandt barked back at the soldiers. "Ouri, they've cleared the entrance, let's get in that node and shut it down."

Ouri couldn't help but notice that there was a touch more respect in Brandt's tone. Not much, but a touch.

Earnest ran a hand through his hair as they walked down the corridor and muttered a stream of concerns under his breath. At the entrance two Marine techs were breaching the doors.

"Allow me," Earnest said and passed his hand over the physical override panel. The access panel glowed green and the door slid open. The techs stood aside and a squad of Marines pushed past Earnest into the node.

"No need," he said, "my physical command code will have overridden the node's internal securi—" His statement was cut short by the sharp crack of several ballistic rifles.

Ouri pulled him back from the entrance, covering his body with hers.

"Report!" Brandt called in.

"All clear," one of the Marines called back.

"Oh shit…" another gasped.

"Commanders, you better get in here."

Ouri stepped in, Earnest and Brandt behind her. The Marines were standing on the right side of the node staring up at something hanging from a data conduit. As Ouri rounded the corner she realized it was Amanda, her wrists chained to the conduit and several data cables jacked into the base of her skull.

Her mouth was twisted in a rictus of pain as she gasped, "About time. Please, get me down from here…"

Ouri signaled the Marines who stood on the railing and cut the chains with small plasma torches. They caught Amanda as she fell and Earnest bent over her, examining the cables plugged into her.

"So this is how the rogue AI was able to get control of so many systems," he said. "He used her access to the entire ship. Really quite clever."

"I'm so sorry," Amanda whispered. "I tried to stop it, but it just pulled what it needed from my mind. I could see it attacking you and trying to keep the ship falling into the star. It's insane!"

Ouri had heard of insane AI, but only as rumor. How Collins had managed to corral an insane AI and get it on the ship boggled the mind.

Earnest brushed the sweat-soaked synthetic hair back from Amanda's forehead. "Don't worry; I'll have you freed from this thing in a moment.

<You can't have her! She's mine! She promised I could keep her!> the AI screamed across the local net.

Earnest looked at Amanda with a puzzled expression. "You promised it could keep you?"

“I did no such thing, I don’t know what it is talking about,” Amanda rasped, concern filling her features.

Ouri saw Earnest pull out several small tools from a pouch and detected a nano-swarm releasing from him.

“Just another moment,” he muttered and then popped the connectors from the back of Amanda’s head.

“Oh, thank my blessed mother!” she gasped and then passed out.

<*Bob, you should be able to control this node again,*> Earnest sent over the shipnet.

In an instant, Bob’s presence swelled into the local net and, with a snap, the node shut off.

<*It is done,*> Bob said. <*Begin the reinitialization process for this node and bring Amanda to me.*>

17:31 ⍰⍰⍰r⍰ t⍰ *Intrepid* *e⍰⍰⍰pe ⍰ ⍰ne⍰⍰er*
4:11 hours to end of Excelsior mission launch window

Dock A1 was huge, even by the *Intrepid*’s standards.

It held a large assortment of ships, from a pair of thousand meter cruisers, to the heavy lifters (of which the *Excelsior* was the largest), down to smaller tugs and shuttles. Overall, there were more than thirty ships in the bay, all brand new and ready to build a colony.

“Look at that thing,” Tanis said as they approached the lifter in its bay. “It’s all engine.”

“It is designed to move up to B2-12 planetary objects.”

Tanis whistled. “That’s what, nearly the size of Mercury, isn’t it?”

“Yeah, though mind you it will move those rather slowly. For what we need it will do perfectly. We’ll be able to boost a couple billion tons up to 0.10*c*." Joe paused and looked at Tanis. "Last chance to opt out, it's going to be dangerous"

"I know that, Joe. I'm pretty used to dangerous. Remember your little bit with Angela back there?"

"This is a different kind of dangerous. You're used to scenarios where you have control. Here you'll have no control. If things go bad, there will be nothing you can do."

"You know"—Tanis smiled at Joe—"you'd be surprised how often you can manage to affect the outcome of a bad situation if you put your mind to it."

Tanis paused, but Joe didn't say anything, just giving her one of his introspective stares. She resolved to say what was on her mind, to simply be straightforward about her feelings.

"Like today…it hit me…I love you. Not that I just love you, but that I really *love* you. I know, it's crazy. Me, in love with a vac jockey, but it's true." The words spilled out, she knew it sounded lame; wished it could have sounded as good as the feeling that was inside of her.

It took a moment for Joe to react. He looked stunned, then surprised, then a slow smile spread across his face. He pulled her close and crushed her in his arms before loosening his hold, gently pressing his body against hers.

"It was earlier, after Collins got away," she said quietly. "When you came down the corridor and I realized that I didn't care what happened, as long as you—"

Her words cut off as his lips covered hers. It was soft at first, just a brushing that froze her for a moment before she responded. Tanis breathed deeply and felt herself melt into him. The intensity increased and moments later their tongues were exploring each other's mouths and hands were stroking each other's bodies.

<Uh…normally I go elsewhere when this sort of thing happens, but we do have to get the Excelsior *ready to fly. There'll be plenty of time for hanky panky once we're underway,>* Angela interrupted.

Tanis stopped and moved her head back so she could see Joe's light brown eyes. "She does have a point. We do have work to do."

14:41 ⍰⍰⍰r⍰ t⍰ *Intrepid* e⍰⍰⍰pe ⍰ ⍰ne⍰⍰er
1:22 hours to end of Excelsior mission launch window

Joe handled the fueling of the ship, as well as making certain it was equipped with all the detection and grappling systems they needed to catch their prey in the darkness on the edge of the system. Tanis worked through the checklists, ensuring that supplies were stocked, life support had the appropriate raw materials, and that there would be some items to use for extracurricular activities.

<*On schedule, sir,*> she reported to Captain Andrews at T-60 minutes.

<*Things are looking up on our end as well. The rogue AI has been shut down. Your Commander Ouri performed admirably at that task.*>

<*Good on Ouri.*> Tanis was glad Ouri had the chance to prove herself. She had always suspected the botanist turned GSS officer had what it took in combat.

<*She did and performed quite well, as did your makeshift Marine company,*> Captain Andrews replied.

<*Sir, they* are *Marines.*>

Andrews chuckled before replying. <*I'll let you get back to it, Lieutenant Colonel. I see you've sync'd your countdown with the bridge. Contact me at T-10.*>

<*Aye, sir.*>

Tanis reclined in one of the three acceleration couches in the cockpit. They were also capable of functioning as stasis pods and she had double checked each one's function in that respect.

Things that tested just fine at 1*g* could break quite easily at seventy.

The space was small, but somehow cozy. A holo display rose up over the main bank of controls, which were both holographic as well as physical. Ships like the *Excelsior* were often used and abused. As a result, they had more backup systems than a Cruithne hooker.

Luckily, that was not the case with this ship. It was brand new, also constructed at the Mars Outer Shipyards, just like the *Intrepid*. System logs indicated its only journeys had been a few short shakedown hauls. It had never actually moved any mass other than its own, but all simulations showed that it would have no problems with the task set ahead of it.

A faint murmur in the back of her mind informed Tanis that Angela was conversing with the ship's AI, a somewhat surly individual named Troy. He had been shut down during the trip and hadn't expected to be pulled out of the AI version of stasis for another eighty years. Tanis had been surprised to find an AI on the *Excelsior*, but Joe had informed her that it was common to have high-grade engineering AI on heavy lifters. They were often moving things that could destroy worlds if mistakes were made.

<He's not that bad, you know. He'd just planned out exactly what he'd be doing when he was brought back out of stasis and now he has to re-prioritize,> Angela said.

<You'd think he could be a bit nicer about it, though.>

<Troy's never been integrated with a human. I don't think he really gets stuff like that very well.>

<That's odd… Aren't all ships' AI required to spend at least a year integrated … that whole, to have humans in you, you must first be in a human thing?> That was one of the reasons Angela had originally been placed with her. There were simply some things AI were not rated to do unless they first spent time in a human.

<Transport ships, yes, but lifters like this, no. They just want the ones who are best at the moving-big-things math. Troy is top of his class when it comes to that.>

<Well, he's going to get a chance to prove that real soon.>

<Are you ready?> Angela asked.

<As I'll ever be. Do you think it'll hurt much?>

Angela's mental tone took on a soft cooing. *<Yes, dear, it will.>*

Tanis nodded and watched as her flow-armor slowly absorbed into her skin. At first it was merely uncomfortable, like the increased pressure on the outside of the skin when entering a lighter atmosphere. Then the pressure began to build and all of Tanis's bones began to ache.

<I've turned off your pain receptors as much as I can without knocking you out,> Angela said.

It got worse and Tanis ground her teeth, determined not to scream as she felt the flow-armor crawling under her skin, felt it along the outside of her skull.

"I think this hurts more than high-g…" Tanis gasped.

<Almost done,> Angela replied.

A minute later the pain lessened, replaced by an overall throbbing throughout her body.

<It should ease up shortly.>

Tanis lay back in the acceleration couch and wiped the sheen of sweat from her brow. She heard boots in the hall and Joe entered the cockpit.

"Uh… Why are you naked again?"

13:34 ⍰⍰⍰r⍰ t⍰ *Intrepid* e⍰⍰⍰pe ⍰ ⍰ne⍰⍰er
0:25 hours to end of Excelsior mission launch window

<*T-10, sir.*> Tanis reported in to the bridge. Joe had completed the fueling and ensured all of the grapples and webs were in place. Supplies were stocked, and all of the other hundreds of things on the checklists had been examined by both human and AI.

They were ready.

<*Very good, Lieutenant Colonel,*> the captain's voice was as smooth and calm as ever. Tanis had never seen the man lose control once. Even now, falling into a star, he sounded perfectly composed. <*Ensign Teer.*>

Captain Andrews had Linked the *Excelsior* with the bridge net.

<*Aye, sir. Opening outer bay doors.*>

Tanis switched the holo display to show the rear view. The *Excelsior* was facing into the *Intrepid* and would be backed out on magnetic rails. From there, maneuvering thrusters would rotate the ship and ease them away from the *Intrepid.* Once they had reached a safe distance, the antimatter engines would ignite and the *Excelsior* would begin its journey.

<*Confirming outer bay doors opening. ES shield showing green,*> Joe reported from his station.

<*Aye, ES Shield reports green.*>

Tanis thought she could detect the slightest strain in Ensign Teer's mental tones. She couldn't blame the woman. Now that the doors were open, the view was filled with the angry red glow of Estrella de la Muerte. Suddenly the name that was so funny before didn't seem quite as amusing. The possibility that she would die under the light of this dim red star was not lost on Tanis.

"You know, we look at stars all the time, but this is only the second one I've seen up close. Hopefully it's not the last." Joe echoed Tanis's thoughts.

She looked over at him, his face betraying none of the uncertainty of his voice as his eyes flicked over the displays and then came to rest on her. They stared at one another for a moment, then Joe stretched out his hand and Tanis took it in hers.

"I love you."

"I love you too."

They got lost in one another's eyes as the ship slid to the edge of the ES shield on the magnetic rails, the red glow of the star filling the cabin.

"I know I've seen vids of them, but I never really expected a red dwarf to be so…red," Tanis said.

<*What were you expecting?*> Angela asked over the *Excelsior*'s general shipnet.

"I guess that's what Jupiter will look like after they light it up the rest of the way," Joe said.

<*Dimmer, I'd imagine.*> Troy joined the conversation.

"I'd hope so," Tanis said. "It would make everything on the terraformed worlds look like it was covered in blood."

<*They'd have to re-bio the plants too. Photosynthesis is brown under a red star's light,*> Angela added.

<*T-60 seconds.*> Ensign Teer's voice came over the Link.

<*Abby just reported in. Bob has full control of the engines and they even have the backup LF scoop emitter online. By repulsing off that sunspot we'll be able to match plan A1 and achieve breakaway as projected. We should be able to maintain the planned vector and meet you at point B2.*> Captain Andrews sounded just a little pleased—enough to confirm Tanis's suspicion about his previous stoicism.

<*Good to hear,*> Tanis said.

<*Good luck,*> Priscilla said privately to Tanis. <*I hope you take this time alone to do what you should have some time ago.*>

Tanis laughed to herself. <*I think this enforced celibacy is going to your head. But, yes, I have every intention of satisfying that little need.*>

<*Good.*>

The *Excelsior* maneuvered away from the *Intrepid* by thruster until the colony ship was no longer in line with the heavy lifter's engine wash. During the process Angela shut down and Tanis set her couch to fully recline before turning to Joe.

"I'm ready, good night."

A cover slid over the pod and the stasis field snapped into place.

"Good luck," Joe whispered as he prepared the *Excelsior* for its first burn. The engines began their initialization process; hydrogen and anti-hydrogen readied to mix and annihilate one another. He kept one eye on the status indicators while getting comfortable in his couch and beginning his physiological alterations in preparation for extreme *g*.

As a pilot, Joe was physically altered in several ways to protect him from the extremes of spaceflight. Structural supports interlaced his brain with nano netting to hold it in place during rapid course alterations. His bones were also reinforced with carbon nanotubes, this lessened the risk of fractures being caused by normal movements under high *g*.

Within his skin—indeed, most of the soft tissue in his body—lay a latticework of liquid crystal which began to harden, creating a rigid structure that would keep his body from simply flattening when the *Excelsior* boosted at 70*g*. Even the walls of his body's cells hardened, preparing for the impending pressure.

Joe's brain turned off pain receptors, it was going to hurt, there were no two ways about it. However, he needed to be able to function; there was no point in his body telling his brain that 70*g*s were excruciating, he already knew that.

<*Engine status is green,*> Troy said.

<*Commence ignition,*> Joe responded.

He looked down at Tanis in her pod and wished that she could experience what he did when flying. She was not bad at all behind the flight controls, Tanis wasn't a pilot in the sense that she lived for it. Joe lived for it. There was nothing like feeling the thrust of a ship thrum through his body, threading obstacles and arcing around worlds. Gravity and radiation were his wind and rain, forces he floated on and soared through.

Tanis probably felt the same way about him when it came to a pitched firefight. She normally acted cool and reserved, but he had seen that primal grin on her face when engaged in battle. He'd seen it on her face when she killed—something which was hard to reconcile with her serene look beside him in the stasis pod.

The *Excelsior's* engines thrummed to life, bringing him back to the task at hand as they slowly built up the antimatter reaction. The first thrust would ramp up to 10*g* and then calibration checks would run for thirty minutes. After that, there would be a few course corrections and then the 70*g* burn would commence.

Based on current projections, that burn would last for six hours. Joe checked that the ports on his shipsuit would line up for the fluid transfers. Before the 70*g* burn, his heart would shut down and an external pump would take over circulating his blood—or rather, what would be taking place of his blood at the time. The extreme pressure would force the oxygen right out of regular blood cells. Specialized nano cells would be taking over for the burn, each equipped with microscopic stasis fields for carrying the necessary chemicals to keep him alive.

<I could have done this on my own, you know,> Troy interrupted his shipsuit check. *<No need for you delicate organics to risk your hides.>*

Joe laughed, no mean feat with his body weighing over a ton.

<You may have been top of your class, but you're young.> Joe glanced at the various readouts, making certain everything was within nominal ranges. The ship may have had burn-in runs, but by and large this was its maiden voyage.

<You do know that AI age faster than humans, mentally speaking. Just because I'm only ten years old doesn't mean your sixty years have anything on me.>

<Experience is the best teacher. You know that is true for all sentient beings, biological or otherwise.> It was true enough. When scientists first began to experiment with AI they carefully taught the machine intelligences how the world worked, what was right and what was wrong. They treated their creations like children and raised them, often even loved them, as such.

The sentimentality was mistaken as a quirk of the creators and when the process was commercialized, a nurturing environment was not a part of the young AI's upbringing. While the alterations allowed the AI to grow into their full potential quickly, they lacked compassion, something that was difficult for them to understand or relate to.

The dichotomy led to a series of terrific conflicts between humans and their creations. Sides were chosen and the Sentience Wars erupted in the Sol System. The lines did not divide evenly and AI and humans drew up on both sides of the battle. While any one conflict was short, the overall upheaval lasted from the early twenty-third century to the late twenty-fourth.

In the end it was a third faction of AI who convinced both sides to cease hostilities and created the Phobos Accords, a set of rules and guidelines for the raising and upgrading of AI. The non-compassionate AI and the humans who sided with them—a group not far removed from machines themselves—were offered the option of re-education or expulsion from the Sol System.

Interestingly, most chose re-education. It would seem that seeing many of their fellows die had actually taught them compassion and understanding a different way.

With the Phobos Accords not anyone could create an AI, just as not anyone was fit, or suited, to create and raise children—though human creation was far less regulated than that of AI.

In the current age nearly all AI were created from a merging of directives and imperatives from groups of parent AI. The process was analogous to the merging of DNA to form a human child, yet, as intelligent as the modern AI were, still no one could determine precisely what the temperament or potential of a young AI would be.

Because the brain of an AI—like the neural enhancements in a human's brain—was not digital, but analog, they grew and strengthened based on experiences and stimulus. Digital systems were used for computers and Non-Sentient AI, but to place a Sentient AI in a digital environment would be akin to a lobotomy on a human—and, of course, very illegal.

The *Intrepid* had no NSAI nodes. All the AI onboard were sentient, though there were far fewer than normal, what with Bob running nearly all systems and not really needing assistance.

<*Maybe we wouldn't be in this position if there were more traditional AI structure on the* Intrepid,> Troy mused, having been half-listening to the thoughts Joe let spill onto the public net.

<*I couldn't speak to that,*> Joe replied trying to avoid the conversation. <*I'm not an AI Structure & Systems Specialist.*>

Joe's mental tone told Troy to let it go and the AI complied. The pair returned to the business of reviewing engine stats and ensuring the ship was holding up.

<*Ready for final course corrections,*> Troy reported.

<*Calculations are confirmed by my nav processes.*>

<*Onboard nodes agree.*>

Joe established a connection to the *Intrepid* and was connected to the bridgnet.

<Captain Andrews. We have triple agreement on our plotted course.>

<Very good, Commander. Please send the data to our net.>

Joe uploaded the navigational data to the *Intrepid* and waited for the response.

<We have triple agreement on your data as well, in addition to a third party match from what our sensors can see. You may proceed with your burn at your designated A marker.>

<Affirmative.>

<Commander.> Captain Andrews waited for Joe's response.

<Yes, sir?>

<Good luck.>

<Good luck to you, sir.>

EXCELSIOR

STELLAR DATE: 3241791 / 08.16.4163 (Adjusted Gregorian)
LOCATION: *GSS ???e??i?r*
REGION: LHS 1565, 26.8 AU from stellar primary

????? ???r? t? ??ter?id ?r??p
???? ???r? t? Intrepid e???pe ? ?ne??er

Tanis opened her eyes a moment after the stasis field snapped off. She could feel Angela re-initializing and ran a check on her body to ensure there was no structural damage.

A face loomed over hers.

"You seem to be all in one piece."

She grinned. "I don't think I would have broken into multiple pieces no matter what."

"Well, not unless the ship did." Joe laughed. "Everything seem OK?"

Tanis held up a hand and moved all of her fingers. "Right as starlight. How did our burn go?"

"Hurt like hell." Joe rotated his shoulder and grimaced. "Well, didn't hurt at the time, but it always aches like crazy when my cells de-crystalize."

As he rolled his shoulders Tanis couldn't help but imagine running her hands over them, feel the muscle rippling below the skin. Everything certainly looked like it was alright from where she sat.

"Well then, we have more than enough time for a good rub-down." She held a hand in the air and let it fall. "We've got what, 0.3*g*?"

"Good guess, just a little over. I worked it out so that we could have some thrust for this part of the trip."

"That'll be just enough to have a bath if we don't get too energetic."

"There's a bath on this thing?" Joe asked.

"I finished all my preflight work an hour before you were done yours, so I had a build-out bot swap the second cabin for a hot-tub," Tanis said with a mischievous smile.

"Most dangerous flight of our lives and you make sure it has a hot-tub." Joe shook his head as he gave her a hand to pull her out of the stasis pod.

"Seemed like the right move at the time. Besides, nice warm water feels good on the muscles after a hard burn."

"Where did you get it from anyway?" Joe asked.

"It was set aside to be put in the gym facilities on one of the cruisers," Tanis shrugged.

"Someone's gonna be upset about that."

"What, before or after we're the heroes of the day for getting the ship the fuel they need?"

"Good point."

"So, what's to eat? I'm starved," Tanis asked aloud as she welcomed Angela back into her mind.

"I, ah…hadn't gotten anything ready."

Tanis gave Joe a peck on the cheek, something that felt weird to do, but nice nonetheless. "You just couldn't wait to talk to me."

"Well, more specifically to see if you were dead or alive."

Tanis laughed. "Well, I won't last long without some food. I only had the one BLT while we were getting ready."

"So several more BLTs all around, I imagine then?"

"It's like you can read my mind."

"Not yet."

<You're not missing out on much.>

"Woe unto anyone who stands between me and a BLT." Tanis grinned and loped out of the room in the low gravity with Joe close behind.

In the wardroom she opened the refrigeration unit and snapped the stasis field off. After extracting the lettuce, tomatoes, and strips of bacon, along with butter made from the *Intrepid*'s own cattle, she closed it and snapped the field back on. Joe was setting the baking unit to make a loaf of Tanis's favorite rich brown bread.

"You do pay attention."

"Well, that and I seem to recall being sent to the commissary more than once to get you a BLT made just so."

"Don't pull that on me." Tanis turned her head sharply, causing her hair to rise up and wrap around her face in the low gravity.

"Mfphh."

Joe let out a burst of laughter. "Classic."

Tanis unraveled her hair and stuck her tongue out at him.

"I do, and I remember you always stopping by to ask me if I wanted anything from the commissary. And don't let that bread rise too fast in the low-g."

"Yes, sir." Joe grinned and double-checked the pressure he had set in the baking unit.

The cooking plate was warmed up and Tanis placed the bacon on it, breathing in the aroma of sizzling fat.

"I tell you, this enhanced olfactory system I got really has its benefits."

"I can imagine. It smells damn good to me, I can't imagine what it must be like for you."

"Pure heaven." Tanis flipped the bacon over. She glanced over her shoulder at him again, this time slower. "You, on the other hand, are going to need that bath pretty soon."

"I'll distract you." He opened the baking unit and pulled the fresh bread out.

"Oh god... That smells absolutely delicious."

Together they sat at the small table and began preparing their meals. Afterward, Joe rose to prepare two cups of coffee, heaps of sugar for him and cream and sugar for Tanis.

"So how long on this *v*?" Tanis could have checked the shipnet, but she really just wanted to hear Joe talk.

Now that she had allowed herself to acknowledge her love for him, she realized how deep his affection for her must run. Perhaps he had been holding back and was now behaving differently around her.

<*No, he's been like this toward you for some time; you were somehow totally blind to it. Even the captain noticed how he felt about you,*> Angela said.

<*Everyone knew we were in love but me?*>

<*Pretty much.*>

<*That's a little embarrassing.*>

"Another thirty hours, then we rotate and begin braking. We won't need to do a hard break, though. The relative velocity of the asteroid group we're closing on is near to our relative speed. About twelve hours at 5*g* should do it, depending on the local medium and what we home in on."

"Good, then I can stay up for it."

"I did plan it that way." Joe smiled.

Tanis leaned an elbow on the table and locked eyes with him. "You know just how to use that smile of yours, don't you?"

A look of innocence crossed his face. "I have no idea what you are talking about. There is no pre-meditation in any of my actions. I'm a natural, go-with-the-flow sort of guy."

Tanis cocked an eyebrow. He was serious; it was one of the things that drew her to him. There was nothing faked about Joe; his behavior wasn't artificial, no looking in the mirror to examine smiles and expressions. Every action, every look from him was totally natural and in the moment.

Tanis envied that. Nearly everything she did was crafted—all of her actions, responses, everything. Well, except for her repartee with Angela. That was the one place she got to be herself. Maybe she could learn something of that from Joe.

Of course, she wasn't always like that, not before Toro. Tanis stopped that train of thought, Toro was the last thing she wanted to think about right now.

"So what do you have planned for the next thirty hours?"

"Well, that bath sounds good. Is it a double?"

"Do you really think I would go to all the trouble of putting a bath unit on this ship if it wasn't big enough for two?"

"Good point." He chewed thoughtfully for a moment. "Then I suppose we should give it a test-run. Once we reach our target set of possibilities, it'll be all work."

"Hurry up and wait, eh?"

Joe nodded. "Pretty much."

"Sounds a lot like everything in the service."

"Oh, sweet stars above, this feels great," Tanis said as she slipped into the water. She hadn't realized until they were done eating how weary she was. It had been over twenty-four hours since coming out of stasis on the *Intrepid*; plus a full day's work back in the Sol system—which was mind-boggling—before that. Stasis provided no rest and she felt it.

Joe was at the edge of the tub, stepping out of his ship suit, his back to her. She watched the muscles on his shoulders ripple beneath his skin. A slight sheen of sweat made the light brown flesh look delicious.

Tanis stretched out, arms above her head and toes pointed—just barely touching the far side of the bath. She draped her arms over the edge of the tub above her head, waiting patiently. Joe hadn't watched her undress, he'd faced away the entire time, she wondered if he wanted to see the whole package at once.

"Hurry up, slowpoke." She flicked some water at his back with a foot.

Joe chuckled, his shoulders rising and falling gently. "Just give me a second, getting all these ports disconnected from the suit and closed up. They don't really help the mood."

"Pfft. You saw me with my arm blown off and my lung flapping on the ground. I can handle a few fluid transfer ports."

"All set." He stepped out of his ship suit's legs and turned, his bemused smile shifted somewhat as he took in the sight before him. Tanis arched her back and took a deep breath.

"What are you waiting for?"

"No idea." Joe grinned and bent over the tub, planting a long kiss on her lips.

Tanis returned it, her arms draping over his neck. A tremor raced through her body, a thrill that started in her loins and radiated outward, her breath caught at the wonder of it. She opened her eyes to look into his, her nose wrinkling with a smile.

"Get in here, mister." She reached up and pulled him sideways into the tub; gently, so as not to send all the wonderful hot water into the air—a serious problem in low gravity.

Joe's shoulders bunched up as he lifted his body on the edge of the tub and swung his legs over the side.

She moved toward him and ran her arms down his chest. He released a long, trembling breath, not removing his eyes from hers. Wordlessly, Tanis slid around his body and wrapped her legs around his torso from behind. With deft fingers, she began to massage his shoulders, his arms, his back.

"You have the most amazing fingers." Joe stroked her calves with his fingernails.

"I'm not objecting to that, either."

He moved forward in the tub and then spun around; fast enough that she didn't move and they were now facing one another.

"You've finally lowered your shield, Miss Richards."

"It's at least on low power."

His hands slid down her torso and held her waist gently. "Who knew such a fragile thing was under those crisp uniforms and battle armor?"

"I'm no one's fragile thing."

Joe's eyes drew up, worried at first, and then smiling as he realized she was joking.

"But I'll make an exception for you," Tanis whispered.

Their lips met again; it was gentle at first, but passion took over and, before long, they were pushing and pulling at one another, as though they wanted to become one being. Then Joe's hands were in her hair, pulling her head up, and he ran his lips under her chin, tracing the outline of her jaw. Without warning, his hands dropped to her breasts, first cupping and then tracing outlines around her swollen nipples.

Tanis was in heaven, she had always secretly worried that Joe was attracted to her only because she was a firm, commanding woman—worried that he wouldn't take charge in lovemaking. She was wrong, happily, joyfully wrong.

He wanted to possess her as much as she wanted to be possessed.

She could see it in his eyes, feel it in the way he held her body, know it in the way he dug his fingers into her back.

When they joined it was beautiful. He opened his mind to her and she to him. Their thoughts and emotions co-mingled in a way Tanis had never experienced before. For a short time they became one being.

Afterward, they lay in the tub not moving, basking in each other's presence.

"You're absolutely amazing," Tanis said as warm thoughts of love and satisfaction suffused her.

"You're not so bad yourself." Joe's patented grin filled her vision. "I think I'll keep you."

Their lips were nearly touching, Joe's weight was pressing down on her, skin sliding gently against skin, hands idly tracing patterns on one another.

Tanis's eyes locked with his, wide with entreaty. "Promise?" Her voice quivered with a vulnerability she didn't even remember having.

"Guaranteed."

They didn't part right away. He held her for some time, stroking her hair and randomly kissing her lips, cheeks and neck. Eventually, he slipped out and rose from the water, his skin glistening. He bent and lifted her out of the bath, aided by the fact that in the current gravity she weighed less than thirty kilograms.

She sighed contentedly and reached for a towel, handing one to Joe before wiping herself down.

"That was… unbelievable," Tanis sighed.

"Glad you think so, I've been waiting to do that with you for some time."

"If I had known you were that good, I don't know that my resolve would have held out so well back before we left."

Joe laughed. "Ready for round two?"

Tanis's eyes widened. "Already?"

As it turned out, they both fell asleep within moments of laying down in the double bunk. Angela set the temperature just a touch warmer in the room and dimmed the lights before striking up a conversation with Troy about the best way to net more than one of the asteroids.

25:04 hours to asteroid group
-0:42 hours to Intrepid escape maneuver

Tanis woke first and reached out to feel the slumbering form of her lover.

Her Lover.

How long had it been since she had last been in love? Eleven… Twelve years now? Well, *she* had been in love. As it turned out he hadn't felt exactly the same way. Not something Tanis was worried about with Joe. It was obvious he was completely committed to her, the fact he had pursued her for nearly a year was ample evidence.

Though it wasn't entirely true. She had found him damn attractive when they first met back in that sector chief's office on the MOS. The next day—had it really been only one day later?—when he saved her life in the VIP corridor, she knew she could love him.

Of course, there was no way they could have a relationship while in the TSF with her being his commanding officer; so she had stuffed those feelings down deep and pretended they didn't exist. But the longing slowly forced its way to the surface, and now those feelings were front and center, no chance of going away.

Thank the starlight.

Joe stirred beside her.

"Good morning, sleepyhead."

"It's morning?"

"I really have no idea; we didn't really establish a ship-time."

"Close enough, I guess." He rolled over and looked at her, his eyes warm and smiling, if a bit bleary and sleep-laden. "You have no idea how completely awesome it is to wake up next to you. It's unbelievable."

"I believe it." Tanis grinned. "I am completely awesome, after all."

Joe laughed and hugged her to him. It was the best wakeup Tanis had experienced in years. They had sex again, another slow, sensual episode, the kind that she loved to have in the morning; apparently so did he.

"I promise some acrobatic events in the future." Joe said afterward. "But this just feels like slow and relaxed time."

"I have absolutely no complaints, mister." Tanis smiled, pulling the covers off and stepping gingerly onto the cold deck. She began her morning stretches while Joe watched from bed, head propped up on one arm.

"You do this every morning?"

"Of course, don't you?" Tanis touched her toes, and then wrapped her arms tightly around her legs, folding double and looking at him with her head between her calves.

Joe whistled, admiring the view. "Not really, but I heartily endorse you continuing the practice."

Tanis laughed—something that looked and sounded odd in her current position. "Get up and get dressed you lazy man. There's breakfast to be had, I could eat a buffalo!"

"Did you stock buffalo?"

Joe dressed and left to get coffee brewing while Tanis finished her stretches. She slipped into a fresh ship suit and followed a few minutes later. The small wardroom was down a short hall and the smells of cooking oatmeal greeted her. She stood in the entrance watching Joe prepare two bowls, heaping brown sugar on them.

"Oh boy, oatmeal," Tanis said.

Two things that grew really well in hydroponics: sugarcane and oats, in space you had to like oatmeal.

"And coffee, the most important meal of the day," Joe said as he set the cups on the table.

"Thanks for the joe, Joe," Tanis grinned.

"You're welcome and you have no idea how much I love that joke." Joe's sardonic tone took a moment for Tanis to parse.

"Ah, not down with the Joe-jokes. Noted. So what's on the schedule for today?"

"Well, the AI let us sleep long, as I'm sure you noticed." Tanis nodded as she chewed and he continued. "So we're fifteen hours from the slowdown burn and then ten hours from there until we reach the A group."

Tanis nodded as she continued to spoon the oatmeal up. "So what else do we have to eat?"

Joe laughed. "I guess we are a bit behind on the meals."

"The extracurricular activities did help in the hunger department too."

"Well, we could do waffles, bacon—I think there's sausage."

"Bacon and waffles! I stocked some great syrup."

An hour later they were on the bridge, studying charts and updated scans, looking for the spectral lines that would indicate lithium. There were a few good candidates and Tanis was lancing laser beams out at the rocks, looking for the right type of reflection.

The *Intrepid* had passed the time of its escape burn nearly two hours ago, but at just over fifteen AU from the star, the *Excelsior* would not receive confirmation of its success for another twenty minutes. Tanis found herself worrying about it more than she expected. Normally she didn't stress about things she couldn't control, but there were a lot of people she had come to care for on the ship.

If all went well they would be back onboard the *Intrepid* in forty-five hours.

Joe reached out and touched Tanis's arm. "I've got a pretty good candidate here," he said and put the asteroid up on the bridge's holo display. "Looks to be in one piece and has some good amblygonite deposits, maybe even as much as forty percent by mass."

The rock was just over a kilometer in diameter and massed a hair under twenty-three trillion tons. Tanis calculated the rough amount of thrust it would take to bring the object up to the required velocities.

"It's kinda big."

"Yeah, but see here and here..." Joe pointed at the display. "That's all dust, we can knock that off and probably shave almost ten trillion tons."

"That's a lot more manageable. How do we knock it off?"

Joe brought up another display. "We use a thumper. We shoot it at the object right where the dust is. It breaks apart into smaller projectiles that slice through the dust, and then balloon right before they hit the solid part. They essentially shove it quickly and it gets it away from the dust. Once on each side, with some repositioning in between, and we'll have a much lighter load."

The plan looked good to Tanis. The one rock would give them all of the lithium they would need and would be much easier to haul in than several smaller asteroids.

"Sounds good. Doesn't look like we'll need to alter course much to reach it."

"Yup, easy peasy."

"Speaking of peas, I'm hungry!" Tanis gave Joe a quick kiss and dashed off to the galley. What she really wanted to do was take her mind off the *Intrepid* and its escape burn.

Twenty minutes later they were completing a dinner of grilled cheese and tomato soup when Angela interrupted their discussion about beam rifles.

<Something is wrong.>

"That's not terribly descriptive," Tanis said.

<The Intrepid *isn't there.>*

Tanis felt her heart jump and saw a look of panic cross Joe's face.

"What do you mean it's not there?" Her appetite fled and Tanis put the remains of her sandwich down.

<We should have been able to see them come out from behind the star five minutes ago.> Angela said. *<But there is no signal, nothing.>*

Angela's worry was palpable; Tanis could feel it bleeding into her, amplifying her own fear.

"There's something else, isn't there?"

<I'm picking up high levels of x-ray refraction from the far side of the star.>

Tanis looked at Joe. They both knew what that meant.

Estrella de la Muerte was a red dwarf, and, like most red dwarfs, it was prone to solar flares. The flares were no more violent than a flare from Sol, but because the *Intrepid* was passing much closer to the dim red star than it ever would to a hot yellow star like Sol, flares were a much larger concern. Even without the heat, red dwarfs had another danger when they flared: X-Rays.

Estrella de la Muerte had been recorded to emit x-ray bursts over 10,000 times greater than Sol during flares. If such a burst hit the *Intrepid,* the ship would be turned into a lifeless husk.

"Sweet fuck," Joe whispered.

"Do we have readings on the x-ray intensity?" Tanis asked.

<Not yet. I'm just picking up refraction. The light will take a bit to hit the outer halo of asteroids and then bounce back to us, about another four hours. We won't know until then how bad it was.>

<It may have just knocked out their comm capabilities,> Troy said.

Tanis was a bit surprised to hear him offering comfort. Maybe she had misjudged him, or maybe he didn't want to think about being lost in this system for eternity either.

"Finish up," Joe said. "We're going to be hard at it for some time."

They wolfed down the rest of their food and then ran to the bridge. The two humans and two AI deployed a relativistic probe to get a view of the far side of Estrella de la Muerte while carefully examining the entire spectrum of the star.

The red dwarf had a rapid rotation and, before long, an angry blotch came into view. The sunspot the *Intrepid* had been using for magnetic repulsion had erupted.

"It went up..." Joe said softly. "It didn't read as being that volatile, it should have held."

<*It was a full scale flare from the looks of it,*> Angela said. <*But we don't know when it went off. It could have been before or after.*>

"Or during," Joe said.

"We'll know more shortly." Tanis brought up the data on the probe's trajectory—the ETA was twenty minutes.

No one spoke in the intervening time. The probe was racing to where the *Intrepid* should be. It was traveling at 0.8*c* and would fly past before arcing around the star and back toward the *Excelsior*. An alert flashed on the holo display as the data came streaming in.

No sign of the *Intrepid.*

"It's my fault." Joe put his head in his hands and Tanis rose to sit beside him.

"It's not. Everyone had the same data you did. They knew what flares are like on red dwarfs. We don't have any evidence that the *Intrepid*'s magnetic repulsion caused the flare. Red dwarfs may be small, but that sunspot was still larger than Earth. It's unlikely that the ship caused it to go up." Tanis laid out a rapid-fire series of rationalizations.

<*I've got readings on the intensity.*> Troy interrupted and brought the information up on the display.

It was bad, not quite 10,000 times the x-ray level of Sol, but close. A major flare. Plasma detection from the probe indicated that the flare went two million miles out into space, well beyond where the *Intrepid* would have been.

No one spoke for several minutes. Tanis forced the thoughts of the colony ship's destruction down, refusing to consider them. She could tell that Joe was doing the same, while Angela was running math on possible alternate vectors the *Intrepid* could have possibly taken.

Everyone followed her example and helped in the search. Signals were sent out and the probe was set to orbit the star in ever-widening circles. Tanis prepared a meal after a few hours and brought it back to the bridge where she and Joe only picked at it.

So many people. There were two and a half million colonists on the *Intrepid* who went into stasis with the sure expectation that they would awaken to their new world, their new system, ready for them to shape and to create the future they always dreamed of.

An anomaly signaled on her interface and she focused the low-band radio antenna on a section of the search grid that seemed to have a bit more noise than expected. Then she heard it.

"*Static*...Say again...*static*...*Excelsior,* do you read? This is the...*static*...*trepid*. Do you read?"

Tanis's heart leapt into her throat and she waved at Joe, putting the feed on the bridge audio.

"*Intrepid*. This is the *Excelsior*. We read you, and boy are we glad to hear your transmission."

Joe let out a whoop as he brought up the trajectory that matched the *Intrepid* at the position the signal had revealed. The main display shifted to show the new outsystem path of the colony ship.

Tanis glanced at the distance and saw that the *Excelsior* was one hundred-thirty light minutes from the *Intrepid*. It would take over four hours to hear back. In the meantime variations on the initial message continued to come in.

"I suddenly have a bit more of an appetite," Joe said as he reached down and picked up his BLT. He polished it off in two bites and then took a long gulp of water.

Tanis set the probe to intercept the *Intrepid* before she devoured her food as well.

"That's the great thing about a BLT; they don't get any worse for sitting for an hour or so."

"Well, the tomatoes get a bit soggy."

"Adds to the texture," Tanis grinned.

The pair sat in silence for several minutes, the adrenaline surge wearing off, leaving them slightly heady and still just a bit anxious.

"I'd like to know more about you, Tanis," Joe said at last. "I mean, I know *you* pretty well, but I don't really know much about how you got to be you."

His timing seemed odd to Tanis, but maybe it was the relief in finding the *Intrepid* that caused him to ask—and she knew what he was asking about.

"Outside of work I don't have a lot to tell. I enlisted when I was twenty-two. When the *Intrepid* left Sol I had just passed fifty years in the TSF."

Joe nodded slowly. "It's your work I find myself wondering about. I've been through the shit with you more than once and you've had my back and I've had yours. The Tanis I know doesn't match the one I heard about back in Sol."

Tanis didn't respond immediately. This was one of the reasons she hadn't wanted to get back into a relationship, she knew she would have to explain Toro.

"You want to know about Toro." The leaden words dropped off her lips.

Joe nodded. "I know you don't want to talk about it, but I need to reconcile the two Tanises."

"You don't need to apologize," Tanis said after a long pause then took a deep breath. "It's about time I told the story."

THE BUTCHER OF TORO

STELLAR DATE: 3223427 / 05.05.4113 (Adjusted Gregorian)
LOCATION: ⍰*SS* ⍰*r*⍰*t*⍰*r*⍰⍰, stealth approach to asteroid 1685 Toro
REGION: InnerSol Stellar Space, Sol Space Federation

Lieutenant Colonel Tanis Richards reviewed the intel and the plan. She didn't really need to; both the plan and the intel were hers, but this mission felt like one of those—one of the ones where something would go sideways.

<*You have good reason to think that,*> Angela said in agreement.

<*Just because there's no way a sane person would get involved with the Cardid cult? Or is there another reason?*>

<*I think the cult is a good enough reason.*>

The TSF surveillance drones had made several passes near the asteroid, passively pulling readings that gave clues as to what was going on in the interior of the asteroid.

Toro was one of several bodies in the inner Sol system that orbited Sol in resonance with Earth and Venus. From each of those world's point of view it appeared that Toro was orbiting them. This meant at certain times cargo could be 'dropped' from stations near either of those worlds and Toro would appear to accelerate to pick it up. At other times Toro could 'drop' cargo and it would fall into the outer solar system.

The asteroids also had a well-placed elliptical orbit. Perihelion brought it almost to Venus, and at aphelion it went beyond the orbit of Mars. Because of this, Toro had extensive docking and cargo transfer systems built around its three kilometer length, but those facilities told just a part of the asteroid's history.

High concentrations of Olivine crystal had drawn prospectors to the asteroid in the twenty-third century and its interior was riddled with mines and processing facilities. At one point, when both the mines were at their peak and cargo flowed through the station, it had a population of over a hundred thousand.

Over time, the valuable minerals had all been extracted and less cargo came through as Ceres's massive spaceport had been constructed.

Eventually, only a few caretakers and robotic cargo handlers were left; that's when John Cardid came into the picture. Thirty years ago he rented space on the asteroid for an undisclosed purpose. The Terran Bureau of Investigations suspected that he was involved in illegal human trafficking in addition to paramilitary activity. Over the years he had built up his presence and it was now estimated that there were over ten-thousand people on Toro.

Five years before, he bought the entire asteroid and had halted its cargo-handling operations.

The fact that the asteroid passed near many InnerSol worlds was far more concerning than the loss of its meager cargo transfer facilities. The TBI stepped up its intelligence gathering in concert with the TSF's counter-insurgency division.

It was slow work because John Cardid was very secretive and Toro was difficult to scan due to high concentrations of ferric crystals and iron oxide. This only served to increase suspicion.

Tanis had been involved with the investigation into Toro for several years. The TSF knew that several shipments of military weapons had found their way to the asteroid, which was reason enough for her to go in, but until things escalated the TBI had maintained jurisdiction.

Now things had escalated.

Four months ago, a group of highly public figures had, apparently of their own will, taken a transport to Toro for a visit. They never returned and only a few transmissions indicating that they intended to stay had been sent out.

Amongst those now considered to be abducted were several actors, sports professionals as well as two former senators and one sitting senator.

Tanis knew it was going to be a mess.

The TSF strike force didn't have enough intel to make a clean, surgical strike, but the public and political pressure had forced the brass to make a move.

The TBI had ceded jurisdiction and Tanis, as the lead investigator on the TSF side, had been sent in.

She had done her share of tours and often took a very active role in the field operations that resulted from her investigations, so this was not new territory. Given more time and intel, she would have been more than happy to run the mission, but this rush-job was going to be trouble.

She reviewed the packet containing the orders for the TSF *Arcturus*. It granted her broad discretionary powers and, in matters regarding the mission, Captain Arsenal was under her command.

She prayed she wouldn't need to issue those types of orders.

Closing the packet, she flipped to the entry points the Marines would take, as well as the sectors each platoon would clear when the TBI agent assigned as liaison entered the ready room.

"Going over this shit show one last time?" Bremen asked.

Tanis nodded. "Looking for whatever it is that I missed; we just don't know enough about what we're getting into and there has to be some clue that can help."

"We just have to clear a few dozen square kilometers of station with one battalion of Marines, kill the bad guys, save the good guys and pray no one who isn't supposed to gets hurt," Bremen grimaced. "What could go wrong?"

<*You have such a way with words.*> Angela's tone was droll.

"I'd prefer more than just a battalion," Tanis said without looking up from her holo projections.

"I hear you. Three hundred and eighty Marines is nothing to sneeze at, but for all we know we're up against ten thousand humans and who knows how many bots? I wouldn't mind a different assignment right about now."

Tanis glanced up from her notes, casting a harsh look at the TBI agent. That wasn't the sort of attitude that got the job done. She was happy he'd be staying back on the *Arcturus*.

Several minutes before the briefing was to begin the battalion commanders were all present and talking quietly amongst themselves. She was pleased, a lot of Marines would not be happy to have a battalion commander who was not a Marine as well. Punctuality showed respect.

<You've earned a bit of respect over the years,> Angela commented.

<Usually Marines only respect experience gained while wearing a Marine uniform, let's hope these ones are a bit more forgiving.>

The battalion's 2IC, Major Ender, was sitting in the front and gave her a crisp nod. Tanis had talked with Major Ender a few times to get a feel for the battalion and how they would react to a new temporary commander. It was a relatively good arrangement, the 242 was well respected, and their former commander, a Colonel Chen, had recently been promoted to general. Since the TSF had unified all branches, it was possible for her, a lieutenant colonel in the intelligence branch, to be put in direct command of a Marine battalion.

The rest of the room was filled with the company and platoon commanders as well as their sergeants. Tanis looked them over slowly, they were all veterans of at least one significant engagement; they had all seen the dark underside of humanity.

If Tanis's intel was right they'd see that underbelly's underbelly today.

"Thank you for all reading the pre-briefing docs. This meeting is really just a formality. You've seen the vids and know that something is rotten on Toro. We're going in to clean it up.

"Try not to kill the good guys, cover your sectors and keep your eyes out for Cardid. Use non-lethal force if possible, as much as possible."

Tanis stood, arms akimbo. "Questions?"

A platoon sergeant named Williams raised a hand. "What's not in the packet? It's light on what is likely going on in there and I bet you have a hunch."

<*Forewarned is forearmed,*> Angela said privately to Tanis.

"I don't have solid intel, but I think they're doing illegal genetic hybridization research."

"That warrants a visit from Force Recon Marines?" Williams asked.

"That's not the whole of it... I think something darker is going on, but all I have are crazy whispers about it being 'true evil'."

"They're in for it, then," a Lieutenant named Anderson said. "Because we all know that Williams is God's own right hand."

The comment raised some chuckles, but Williams didn't look pleased.

Tanis nodded to the major who proceeded to run over each company and platoon's assignments. When it was done, the group broke up to brief their men.

Tanis took the ship's dorsal maglev to the bridge. The *Arcturus* was one of the TSF's newer destroyers. It measured just over three hundred meters long and seventy wide. What it lacked in size it made up for with speed and stealth. The ship's antimatter engines could boost it to over a quarter the speed of light and the output from the engines could be focused, making the ship difficult to detect.

Toro was speeding through space at this phase of its orbit and the *Arcturus* was running a 1.3*g* burn. As a result, the trip to the bridge felt more like an elevator ride with the maglev's seats rotating ninety degrees to put 'down' below Tanis.

The *Arcturus* could accelerate in any direction: forward, backward, or spinning on either axis. As a result, just about any surface on the ship could be down at any given time. Most of the time, however, it moved forward so the decks were all perpendicular to the length of the ship, making it feel more like a tower than a wet navy ship.

The bridge was in the center of the vessel and the trip was short. Tanis stepped onto the command deck, noting the navigation holo, which confirmed that the *Arcturus* was only two hours from reaching the asteroid. Toro was near perihelion, its closest approach to Sol, and the *Arcturus* was approaching in the asteroid's shadow, all but creeping up on it.

The holo showed Toro spinning on its long axis, several docking stations and cargo facilities forming a ring around its center. When humans first settled on Toro, it spun at a sedate speed of roughly eight centimeters per second. To provide more significant gravity, close to 0.5*g*, it was accelerated to fifty meters per second.

The complicated burns needed to match the rotation of the station would give away the *Arcturus* and ruin the element of surprise. Tanis and Captain Arsenal had agreed to a plan where the TSF cruiser would move to a position ten thousand miles behind the station and Marine assault transports would close the distance.

"Ready for action?" asked the captain.

"Everything seems to be in order," Tanis replied. "I don't know about ready. This will be some messy action, are you prepared to provide supporting fire?"

"The composition of the asteroid may cause a few issues with targeted laser strikes, but we think we have the solutions to work around those."

Tanis nodded. "Let's hope you don't need to test those solutions, there's still enough crystal in there that refractions could be messy."

"Finer beams and higher power should do the trick—we'll melt anything we come in contact with rather than letting the light bleed out. The *Arcturus* has enough reserve power to turn Toro into Swiss cheese if needs be."

"Well, if everything is good on your end, I'm going to head down to the hangars and gear up."

"Godspeed," the captain replied in parting.

Tanis took a short series of corridors and ladders down to the hangar level where the Marines were suiting up into their powered armor. She approached the 4th Platoon of Bravo Company. The lieutenant, an overly slender man—odd for an orbital drop Marine—named Tippin, rose from inspecting his weapon and saluted her.

"Glad to have you in the 'toon, Colonel Richards."

Tanis returned the salute. "I hear you're the best in the outfit."

"Damn straight we are, if you don't mind my saying it. The boys and girls of the 4th Bravo have seen more action than the—" Tippin said before stopping himself, uncertain of how casual he could be with a CO who was an MICI and not a Marine.

"I believe the current joke involves the president's mother?" Tanis asked.

Tippin coughed. "Yeah, I think it does."

Tanis chuckled. "Why don't you show me to my armor?"

"Williams, hook Colonel Richards up with her gear," Tippin called out to the sergeant who had asked several questions during the briefing.

The sergeant trotted up and looked Tanis over. "I warrant I've got some that will fit you without too much adjustment. Do you have any load-out or weapons prefs?" he asked.

"I prefer to take tactical shots, what do you have for rifles?"

"The 242 issues M948 concussive pulse rifles for station combat, but those aren't terribly accurate. A lot of the boys and girls use MIV particle rifles so long as the proton beam cartridges stay behind for on-station missions," Williams said, raising his voice and casting a hard glare at a Marine who was checking his gear.

"The MIV is a nice weapon," Tanis said while nodding agreement about the proton cartridges being left behind. "Do you have any of the MIV6 model? I can live with the electron beam."

"Sure do." Williams selected a weapon from the company's armory and handed it to Tanis who looked it over, approving of its maintenance.

"Do you have any ballistic weapons as well?" Tanis asked. I find that bullet fragments make for some of the best suppression."

Williams grinned. "I sure do, how's a S901 suit you? We have the recoil dampeners on them as well as the flechette or ballistic rounds."

"Excellent," Tanis said, slinging the MIV6 over her shoulder and taking the S901 from the sergeant.

"Do you need any close range weapons?"

Tanis patted the duffle she had slung over her shoulder. "I have that taken care of."

Armoring up took over thirty minutes to complete. Because there was the very real possibility that the Marines would be exposed to vacuum on station entry and possibly later if combat breached any pressure seals, full EVA armor was the order of the day.

The Marines armored up co-ed style right on the hangar deck. This meant stripping down to nothing and starting with the base thermal layer, which also provided compression against vacuum. Tanis had brought her own and had it on in a few minutes, fighting a grimace when the suit's plumbing attachments hooked up to her body.

The actual armor Williams had selected for her was a scout style that started with a second tight-fitting ballistic and thermally refractive mesh. From there the armor's plating was applied, hooking together to form a partially assisted exoskeleton. She pulled the helmet on, first attaching the back to her suit and then snapping the face-plate on.

Her internal HUD updated and pulled in the stats from the armor, providing air, power and integrity reports. While the software cycled through all the checks, Tanis tested her range of motion. Everything felt good and she pulled several packs of power and physical rounds from the armory, sliding them into various clips and slots on the armor.

"Everything check out, sir?" Major Ender approached and gave the abbreviated salute Marines used whilst in armor.

"A OK," Tanis replied. "Your crew takes care of their gear, tests are all green."

Major Ender and Tanis exchanged a few other pre-combat pleasantries before the major left to join his platoon. Tanis wasn't sure why he came over in person—perhaps it was to ensure that the new CO was in good hands.

<*Or he thinks you're attractive,*> Angela laughed.

<*No one is attractive in armor,*> Tanis scoffed at the idea.

<*Sometimes I think you don't exist in the same reality as the rest of us.*>

While Tanis had spoken with Williams and gotten into her armor the time had ticked away. It was now t-minus 15 until drop. She climbed into the 4th Bravo's transport and racked in. The rest of the platoon was already in place, Sergeant Williams prowling through the lot, inspecting armor and gear, slapping and swearing his pleasure or dismay.

Once Tanis racked in he gave her a final check.

"Everything looks good, sir, you know your stuff," it was high praise from a platoon sergeant.

"I wouldn't still be alive if I didn't," Tanis replied.

"Fair enough," came Williams's response. "Still, not often you see a non-Marine officer who knows her asshole from her elbow. Sir."

Tanis wasn't certain how to respond, Marines were often more familiar with their officers than the regular TSF, probably because all officers in the Marines rose up through the ranks. She didn't have to worry about a response as Williams had already moved on, checking the lieutenant's gear before racking himself in.

The next several minutes were filled with the sounds of Marines mentally preparing for combat. For some it was catcalls and curses, others prayed, others said nothing and simply looked forward stoically. No one was asleep, which was almost unusual.

Right on its mark the transport 'dropped'. In reality the transports boosted out of the hanger on acceleration rails, but these were Force Recon Orbital Drop Marines, and as far as they were concerned, they always dropped.

Once clear of the *Arcturus*, the transports fired their main engines—short run antimatter burners—and the ships went from 0*g* to over 6*g* in seconds. Tanis gritted her teeth and watched the clock. The burn would run for almost three minutes and then the transports would rotate and reverse the burn to break. Within five minutes they would be disembarking onto Toro.

"Love this shit," one of the Marines called out as the transport rotated and Tanis fought the feeling of weightlessness in the pit of her stomach.

Then the burn hit again, this time eyeballs out, and Tanis squeezed hers shut. She knew they wouldn't pop out, but she still hated the feeling of them pulling at her eye sockets.

Right on time there was a loud clang and the transport grappled onto an external pad on Toro's South Transport Station.

In the blink of an eye, Williams was at the hatch, opening it and yelling for the Marines to get on the pad and make it secure.

There was about two-thirds regular gravity on the pad, but it was exposed to vacuum.

The Marines disembarked from the two exits by squad, covering corners and moving into position, the two-thirds gravity allowing them to race across the space in long bounds.

Tanis and Lieutenant Tippin were last off the transport; the moment they were out it boosted off—better able to provide cover and assistance from space than on the pad.

The platoon secured the landing platform while squad one's first fireteam—one/one—worked on breaching the airlock. The immediate area clear, one/two set up shielding behind one/one and took up positions to provide covering fire when the lock was breached.

Tanis dispersed nano around the airlock and took cover to the side. Tippin joined her and they monitored the events over the combat net.

<*Lock breaching in three, two, one…*> Corporal Jansen provided the count over the combat net.

The airlock doors slid open and one/one moved in to disable the inner airlock. Behind them one/three set up an ES shield to seal the airlock against the vacuum once both doors were open. The electro static shield was calibrated to hold in atmosphere but allow humans to pass through.

<*Lock set to breach, pulling back, in three, two, one…*> Jansen said as one/one moved back through the ES shield and took

cover on either side of the lock. The inner doors slid open and one/two tensed, ready for incoming fire.

Tanis sent her nano through the lock and into the corridor beyond, feeding the data stream to the platoon's combat net. The Marines' HUDs updated, providing a real-time clear visual of the inside of the corridor provided by the nano.

Three/one signaled that they detected no movement and held their position while one/one moved back into the airlock and began advancing down the corridor.

Tanis checked the battalion-wide combat net. All transports had successfully dropped off their platoons and all platoons had completed their breach procedures. Everything was running like clockwork.

The battalion AI, Bruno, reported that no communication attempt had been made while the transports were boosting in and even after the breaches were complete no signal had come out of Toro, though he had been making the required communication attempts.

Angela had directed several nano to find the nearest communications hub and she was working on breaching the station's cryptography.

<*ETA?*> Tanis asked.

<*It's good, but not that good, I should be through in a minute or so.*>

Tanis posted the update on the battalion-net. Bruno was also working on breaches in four other locations where company captains were positioned with nano capable of managing the hacks.

Her attention was brought back to her physical location as shots rang out from within the station.

Based on the nano-scan, one/one had entered a large cargo holding area that, while not filled, had enough crates to hide several dozen of the enemy. The squad reported that they had shielding up to protect the corridor and called for re-enforcements.

Lieutenant Tippin signaled for the rest of squad one to move into the corridor. Squad two and three took up positions near the entrance, ready for the signal to rush in.

Tanis rose from the position of cover she and Tippin shared and took up a position near the entrance alongside two/three. Tippin followed suit, taking up position with another fireteam.

Down the corridor and in the warehouse, squad one signaled that they were in position. They were keeping the enemy suppressed with pulse rifle fire, but the enemy was bringing in more heavy weapons to eliminate the Marines' cover.

Williams led the next fireteam in and Tanis followed after with hers. Tippin instructed three/one to stay behind and cover the entrance while the rest of the fireteams moved down the corridor.

Tanis stepped out into the space and took a position behind several crates. Both sides were using pulse rifles—a sane precaution when neither really wanted to punch holes in the station.

Several of the other platoons had also run into resistance, though none had any details on the nature of the defenders yet. Tanis's nano had made it across the warehouse and she directed it to get in close for a better look at who they were up against.

She let out a verbal cry as the image of the enemy appeared in her mind. At first she thought what she was looking at was a mask or exo-armor, but it wasn't, it was what these men and women actually looked like.

The thing that stood out at first were the long, tapered spikes driven through their eyes and out the backs of their heads. Out of their mouths, more spikes jutted, some appearing to have been driven through the lower jaw. Below the head their bodies were cacophonies of plas and steel mixed with flesh. There seemed to be little consistency, other than the horror it induced.

In some places metal plates appeared to have been screwed into flesh, in others attached by having more of the spikes pounded through. Some limbs ended in weapons, others in claws of steel, bone or some mixture.

Tanis had seem her variety of mods, some more extreme than these, but the nature of these alterations were grotesque. No clean surgical cuts or mergers had been done. It was like a child with a sledge-hammer had mangled these people.

It was evidenced in the blood and puss that oozed from all over their bodies, from horrible things like smashed remains of eyeballs stuck to faces to genitalia half cut off, hanging between legs.

The weapons fire had masked something even worse: the once-human creatures were all hissing and screaming. Not in pain or fear, but in anger and rage. They seemed oblivious to the fact that they were monstrous horrors and were entirely focused on their brutal anger.

Tanis had been in the TSF for most of her life and had seen a lot of horrible things in the field; when she was younger there were things that had caused her to freeze up with fear or horror, but it had been some time since that had happened—until now.

"What is it?" Williams was beside her, giving her shoulder a slight shake.

Tanis shook her head, making eye contact. "Tell the Marines to be ready for what they're going to see. The enemy is not pretty," she told him at the same time as the battalion AI.

Williams gave her a quizzical look, but nodded. "We're working to flank them," he said. "They're really just focused on a frontal assault. Every now and then one of them runs out charging at us too. They're not too bright."

"You can say that again," Tanis muttered.

Tippin and Williams were good at their jobs. Within several minutes the Marines were flanking the enemy and Tanis was at the forefront. She wanted to see for herself what these things were. Maybe there would be some clue explaining what had happened to them and how they were able to function, let alone fight on the side that had done…whatever had been done to them.

"Sweet fucking…fuck," a PFC named Chang said. "What are these? Are they really humans or just some crazy bot used to scare off visitors?"

Tanis's nano had performed a detailed scan and she knew the answer. "They're fully human, many of them had this done to them in the past few weeks."

One of the fallen creatures moved, twisting so its sightless spike eyes faced Tanis. "You'll join us, join us or die!"

The words were almost unintelligible, the creature's tongue working around the spikes in its mouth, getting sliced further as it worked out the words.

"Fuck no!" one of the Marines yelled and put a ballistic round from a sidearm into the thing.

"Perez, stow your shit!" Williams yelled. "We're not assassins or executioners, no matter what these things are, we don't execute the wounded."

Williams didn't appear rattled by what he saw, but his lack of actual discipline for Perez showed that even the gunnery sergeant was having trouble with the nature of the enemy.

<Squad two, you're taking the lead; one needs a breather,> Williams instructed.

<Have you gotten into their network yet?> Tanis asked Angela.

<I have… But I can't seem to find anything.>

<What do you mean?>

Angela took a moment to respond. *<There's nothing here, they've totally wiped the net. Basic systems are in place for station*

keeping, but there is no data about personnel, arrivals, departures, anything.>

<*So they wiped it?*>

<*It would seem so.*>

Tanis let out an audible sigh. <*Keep hunting and let me know if anything turns up.*>

<*I'm not sure why you still give such obvious orders sometimes.*>

The platoon moved further into the station. On several more occasions they engaged the strange horrors in combat, each time defeating them with no losses other than small slices of sanity.

By now all of the other platoons had also encountered the enemy. There were a few variations, different types of materials, weapons and—in some cases—blades instead of spikes had been used.

One platoon encountered a creature that appeared to be three or four of the horrors assembled into one. It ultimately required incendiary grenades to bring the creature down.

<*Some of these people were altered in the last day or so,*> Angela reported. <*I can't find any traces of anesthesia in their systems, nor can I see any defensive wounds.*>

<*What are you saying?*> Tanis asked. <*That they did this to them while awake and these people just took it?*>

<*I don't know that,*> Angela replied. <*But that would fit the evidence I see. There's something else as well. They seem to have very high levels of endorphins in their bodies.*>

<*I hope that doesn't mean they were getting off on this.*>

<*Few possibilities are pleasant.*>

Tanis updated the company commanders with the data she had and advised additional caution as it appeared they were not facing forces that would fear pain or death.

The battalion combat net showed many of the platoons engaged with the enemy. One appeared to be vastly outnumbered and Tanis worked with Bruno and Ender to re-enforce it.

Once the warehouse was secured the platoon moved further into the station, working their way toward one of the elevators that ran down into the core of the asteroid. They encountered only light and sporadic resistance. Other platoons hit harder opposition, but the 242 was amongst the best and pushed through with only light casualties.

The 4th Bravo reached the entrance to the facility serving the elevator. This area of the station had been mainly used for cargo transfer and so there were only two small lifts that dropped down into the asteroid.

As the two/one moved into the small foyer, the lift on the right opened up and a grotesque figure shambled out. It was over nine feet tall and appeared to be made up of multiple humans. Heads and limbs protruded from a variety of locations. There were also robotic limbs and things that appeared to have come from either the animal kingdom, or pure imagination.

Most of the limbs ended in weapons that started firing immediately. A plasma bolt burned through one of the Marines in the lead fireteam before they could get behind cover. Williams was hollering for CFT and ES shields and the platoon shifted into offering as much support for the beleaguered two/one fireteam as they could through the narrow entrance to the lift foyer.

Tanis sent in a swarm of nano to attack the thing. It had good countermeasures, but Tanis and Angela collectively began to breach them.

<*What are these things?*> Tanis couldn't believe what the readouts from the nano probes were reporting.

<*There's no synthetic backbone to this thing, the human brains are directly interfaced.*> Angela's mental tone contained a rare tremble of horror.

Tanis felt a twinge of phantom pain in her mind at the thought of it. The humans that made up that monster were organically linked at the neurological level, something that was banned by the Phobos Accords because of the complete and utter insanity that always ensued.

Humans were not wired to organically share their mind with other beings. AI and synthetic interfaces erected careful boundaries that allowed humans to participate in direct data assimilation and virtual worlds while maintaining their sense of self.

As Tanis recovered from her shock, another plasma bolt melted off a Marine's right arm and brought her back to the physical world.

Pulse rifles were having no effect on the mass the dozen humans that constituted the horror presented. Several Marines fired electron rails which the creature's ES shield shrugged off. Most of the platoon fell back to small ballistic weapons; while those could penetrate the ES shield, once they did they were slowed and caused little damage.

The Marines were not panicking, but if they couldn't make a dent against this thing they would have to retreat. Something she doubted that they would do with wounded in the field.

<I bet you wish we brought proton magazines, sir,> Williams said over the combat net.

<Keep holding it at bay,> Tanis replied, *<I have a plan.>*

She unslung her S901 and loaded in a magazine of armor piercing 20mm rounds. Moving down the corridor she fired several rounds into the wall, opening up holes into the elevator foyer on the far side of the room from two/one.

She quickly flipped out the magazine and swapped in incendiary rounds.

<I don't think that will stop it,> Angela said at the same time as Williams.

<*I don't intend it to, but it will distract it from two/one while you do what you have to do, Angela.*>

<*What do I have to do?*> the AI asked.

<*Burn its minds,*> Tanis said as she started firing the incendiaries through the holes in the wall. It had the desired effect and the horror shifted its attention, sending plasma bursts in her direction. The molten star-stuff blasted through the wall and Tanis made sure she wasn't where the thing was aiming.

<*I won't be able to keep this up for long, Angela. Do it, that's an order!*>

The AI didn't respond but Tanis could tell that she was following the order. At least just one of them would face court martial for the action. The Phobos Accords, which were created at the end of the century long Ascendance War, governed not only human and AI interactions, but also the things you could do to a sentient being's mind.

Burning a mind was tantamount to a war crime.

Angela directed the nano that had entered into the horror's body into its brains and set them about their task, burning out all dendrites that facilitated higher functions. The act would turn each of the horrors' brains into something that could do no more than power the organs under its control.

Normally the process could be done in a dozen seconds, but with the number of brains in the creature it would take a few minutes.

Tippin directed several fireteams to follow Tanis's example and moments later they were rotating incendiary fire to keep the thing guessing where the next assault would come from.

The work became easier as the number of functioning limbs on the creature decreased. After what only turned out to be four minutes from the time the elevator door opened to when the thing dropped, the platoon stood down, every one of them knowing they could have easily died in this encounter, a thought made all the more sobering by the realization that two

Marines had died and three others were in no shape to continue on.

Tippin and Williams triaged and adjusted the affected squads, sending a total of eight Marines back to the position three/one held at the entrance.

One/one hauled the horror out of the lift and dropped it in a corner. One/two joined them in the lift and the eight Marines took the ride down into the asteroid to secure the landing below.

Tanis passed on what they had come across to the other platoons and what they had to do to take it down. The responses she received were heartening. No one condemned her for burning the minds—not after they saw the thing and the destruction it had wrought.

She gave the order that company commanders could use their nano for the same action if necessary and she would take the heat.

When the Phobos Accords had been written she couldn't imagine the intent had been to protect horrors like the one she had destroyed—at least not in the heat of battle when it was killing her Marines.

<*The TSF will understand the circumstances,*> Angela said. <*The AI courts wouldn't. Thank you for making it an order.*>

Tanis nodded, she wasn't quite ready to speak yet. Instead she monitored the nano she had sent racing ahead of the lift, anxious to see what awaited the Marines when they arrived at the bottom.

"Now I believe in a god," Tippin said as he stared down at the horror.

"Why is that?" Williams asked.

"Because I know there's a devil."

"Not for long." Tanis felt anger drag her out of perseveration over her actions. "We're going to go down there and kill him."

As luck, or perhaps a god, would have it, the Marines only faced light defenses at the bottom of the lift and several minutes later the platoon was working their way through the asteroid itself.

The gravity was lighter here and magnetics in the armor's boots helped keep them attached to the deck plating. Tanis always found it a bit awkward and ended up turning hers off. When the gravity was too light to hold her down at all she'd switch them back on.

Reports came over the battalion's combat net of more horrors and other things like them. Only one other platoon had encountered one in tight quarters like the 4th Bravo had. They managed to blow out a wall with explosive rounds and sucked the thing into vacuum. The other encounters all took place in more forgiving surroundings for the Marines and they were able to use flanking and explosives to take the creatures down.

The platoons were all in the asteroid itself at this point, facing an endless stream of new enemies, few as difficult to take down as the multi-human horror, but none easy. The Marines worked their way through the nightmare with stoic determination.

Tanis despaired, doubting they would find any humans to save in the place. Every person, using that term lightly, was a monster and attacked them on sight, never saying a word, though shrieks and moans were common.

By the count Bruno was keeping, they had killed over a thousand of the probable ten-thousand inhabitants of Toro. The 4th Bravo and several other platoons were closing in on what the net showed to be a large, open chamber near the center of the asteroid. Chances were that they would find the other nine-thousand occupants there.

If they had all been turned into monsters this would get very messy.

The platoon moved down a final corridor toward the central chamber, Tanis's remaining nano, scouting ahead, flew out into the expanse first and began sending back data.

The chamber matched what the net said and was five-hundred meters long and thee hundred wide. Being near the center of Toro there was no gravity here, save for a small pull backwards. It was roughly oval and was *full*.

They had found the rest of the occupants.

Creatures of all shapes and sizes floated in the space, more than the nine-thousand Tanis's intel had estimated, there had to be at least twenty-thousand or more. It was hard to be sure because so many creatures consisted of more than one human.

"Welcome," a voice boomed out, "it is so nice of you to come and join our union."

Tanis could make out a figure roughly a hundred meters into the chamber. It was drifting closer and the vague outline began to take shape.

It was John Cardid...plus a few other people. His head was present and appeared to be attached to a mass of human bodies with a variety of other heads sticking out his 'torso'. His arms consisted of additional people and his legs were each made up of two people.

"By order of the Inner Sol Government, I command you to surrender," Tanis called out.

"Right, because he's going to do that," one of the Marines said quietly.

"I have to say it... But I hope he doesn't. I'd very much like to see this...guy dead," Tanis replied.

John Cardid had started chuckling as he heard the statement. "I don't think so, even now my forces are flooding out through paths not on the station's plan to flank you. You'll join us or die. Chances are that you'll join us even if you do die."

Almost as one, all of the figures on the edges of the space began to push off and, like a slow wave, all of Cardid's followers moved toward the platoon.

"Platoon…retreat." Tanis sent the command over the combat net to the entire battalion as well. <*We can't overcome these odds, but we'll be back with some friends.*>

The 4th Bravo began to move back up the corridor, keeping an eye out for the flanking forces Cardid had spoken of. Tanis and one/one were moving backward, covering their escape, and one of the Marines planted a few high explosive charges on the walls as they went.

"Can't cause a 'cave-in' in zero-*g* but it can block them and their plasma bolts for a bit."

Tanis nodded her approval and when they were at a safe distance the Marine detonated the packs. The shockwave rippled past them and back down the corridor; the walls turned into high-speed gravel. Most of it ricocheted around the point of the explosions with a few working up and down the corridor. It wasn't a moment too soon as fire began to impact the debris cloud.

<*Double-time,*> Tanis called up. <*Not a lot of cover back here.*>

The platoon picked up the pace, but they were soon slowed down by the flanking forces.

They were able to move, but slowly, fighting for each meter. The Marines were beginning to crack. When a series of spider-looking things crawled out of a tunnel a few began to fire wildly in all directions, screaming.

Williams was there in an instant, shouting them back into control and then calming them. Tanis was impressed with his abilities, but knew they couldn't last.

The platoon was taking hits, running low on ammunition and close to losing it.

<*Arcturus, come in,*> Tanis called the cruiser, passing the current sit-rep. <*I need evac for all platoons, pick up the teams*

holding the egress points first, then have the birds hold positions in these locations.> She provided the data over the Link and Captain Arsenal acknowledged.

<*I have targets for your lasers as well,*> Tanis said as she passed up the data that Angela and Bruno had worked up, over a hundred coordinates that would clear paths ahead of the Marines and hopefully slow down their pursuers.

<*This will open up the interior of Toro to vacuum,*> the captain objected. <*You'll kill everyone in there!*>

<*I won't kill us,*> Tanis barked back. <*That's pretty much all I care about right now. Do it. That's an order!*>

Tanis suspected he was consulting his packet for a way around the order. There wasn't one and she knew he would comply.

Her expectations were confirmed as a section of the tunnel a hundred meters behind the platoon disappeared in a white-hot flash. The tunnel shook as the rock rapidly expanded and the Marines felt their magnetic boots turn on full as air whipped past them into the vacuum.

Several exceptionally grotesque enemies flew by as the air rushed past, eyes bulging, but still firing at the Marines. Tanis couldn't believe it and kept moving up the corridor to the platoon's evac point.

It opened up a few minutes later as another laser blast erupted ahead of the platoon, cutting away a wide opening that led to the surface of the asteroid. The Marines rushed into the space moments later and used their armor's thrusters to avoid the white-hot walls of the wide shaft. At the top their transport awaited, three/one hanging on the sides, firing at the monsters that seemed not to care that they were dying in the vacuum.

The battalion's combat net showed that all of the platoons were on their transports; the 4th Bravo, being the furthest in, was the last out.

Looking down, there were dozens of holes on the surface of Toro venting atmosphere, but there were also several small ships taking off from the asteroid itself and the stations surrounding it.

Even though they should be evacuating, all of the ships moved into attack vectors, aiming to take out the Marine transports.

<*Take them out,*> Tanis called into the *Arcturus*. This time there was no argument. Laser fire crossed the space between the cruiser and the attackers. It was invisible in the emptiness of space, but the results were instantaneous as dozens of the attacking ships exploded.

The Marines had all locked down in the transport and Tanis took her seat, watching the external monitors. Below them the holes from the Normandy had almost all stopped venting atmosphere. Suddenly a large crack appeared across the center of Toro, then another appeared laterally.

Because of the increase to Toro's rotation to create artificial gravity, carbon nano-struts were in place to re-enforce the asteroid. Cardid, however, had not added additional support to compensate for the new tunnels and chambers.

Those changes, in addition to the laser fire burning holes in the role proved to be too much and Toro began to tear itself apart.

In a slow motion dance of destruction, the asteroid tore itself apart, chunks breaking off and swinging out into space, while others smashed into the ring of stations. Explosions blossomed and, by the time the transports were docking on the *Arcturus*, Toro was no more.

The Marines were silent as the transports docked. They stripped out of their armor with no banter and carefully cleaned the blood and gore from their gear.

Tanis was working with them, cleaning the armor and weapons she had used. There were a thousand other things she should be doing, but she needed the time to collect her thoughts, to try to put together what had just happened into something that made sense.

"Colonel Richards!" a voice called out behind her. Tanis turned to see a squad of MPs standing behind her. One of them, a major named Indras, stepped forward.

"Yes, Major?" Tanis asked.

"I am here to relieve you of command of the 242nd Marine Battalion and place you under arrest."

Several of the Marines around her turned sharply and bristled, a few reached for their weapons. She may not be a Marine, but apparently going through Toro had made her enough of one for them.

"What is the charge?" Tanis felt like the ship had fallen out from beneath her, yet she didn't feel alarmed, she didn't know how to feel anything.

"Violation of the Phobos Accords, violation of the TSF code of conduct, use of weapons of mass destruction against civilians, and other crimes against humanity."

"There were no civilians and no humanity on Toro," Williams barked. "On whose orders are you doing this?"

Brennan was with the MPs and shook his head. "I forwarded the feeds, what you did was unconscionable."

The major's eyes were hard and unblinking. "On the orders of the president of InnerSol and the joint chiefs. Come with us, Colonel Richards, we are to confine you to quarters."

Tanis set down the weapon she had been cleaning and followed the major; the other MPs forming a box around her as the Marines hollered and swore at their backs.

CRACKING A FEW EGGS

STELLAR DATE: 3241792 / 08.17.4163 (Adjusted Gregorian)
LOCATION: *GSS ⍰⍰⍰e⍰⍰i⍰r*
REGION: LHS 1565, 27.0 AU from stellar primary

⍰⍰⍰⍰⍰ ⍰⍰⍰r⍰ t⍰ ⍰⍰ter⍰id ⍰r⍰⍰p

Tanis ended the story with a small choke as she remembered the Marines calling after the MPs, their commanders just barely stopping a mutiny on the *Arcturus*. She looked up at Joe to see tears in his eyes; he reached out and wiped one from hers.

They didn't speak as they embraced for several minutes, Tanis found herself sobbing as emotion she had bottled up for so long came crashing out.

After she had regained control of herself, Joe spoke. "But it wasn't that bad, they didn't discharge you or imprison you."

Tanis nodded. "Once they watched the full sensory vids and the investigators sifted through the ruins they realized that I had made the right call. Cardid was planning an all-out assault on several habitats and would have killed millions. It was only because we caught him by surprise that we were able to stop them. He had more powerful defenses, but they weren't online because he didn't want Toro to be targeted before he launched his assaults.

"So I didn't lose my commission in the end, I got a slap on the wrist for violating Phobos and knocked down to an LCO."

"And you got the media lambasting you."

Tanis nodded, the tears welling up in her eyes again. "That was the hardest part. Pretty much everyone I knew shut me out, including my husband."

"You were married?" Joe was a little shocked.

"Yeah, his name was Peter, I married him when I was fifty-five, I know, a little early for marriage, but I thought we were in love."

"I guess he didn't take Toro too well," Joe said.

Tanis shook her head ruefully. "He didn't care about what I did on Toro. He always got off on me being the tough girl who kicked ass and took names. He divorced me because he didn't want the career damage that being married to me would—" Tanis's voice broke and she took a moment to regain her composure "—that being married to me would cause," she managed to finish.

Joe wrapped his arms around her and held her for several minutes as she cried softly.

"Thanks… I haven't spoken of him since the day he left me, I didn't expect it to turn me into more of a mess than talking about Toro did."

"So I guess he's not the type of ex we have to say nice things about. We can call him super-douche."

Tanis snorted a laugh. "Total ass-hat. The guy left me with nothing, I was unhirable and had to stay in the TSF, which I pretty much hated at that time for betraying me. I put in for colony the day after he filed for divorce." A fire was back in Tanis's eyes as thought about the day.

Joe shook his head slowly. "I'm sorry it went down like it did, you certainly didn't deserve the raw deal you got. I have to admit, though, I didn't learn about Toro until you joined the *Intrepid's* crew. There was all sorts of scuttlebutt about how you got on the roster."

"Really?" Tanis asked. "How did you not hear about Toro? I blew up an entire station. It was practically the only thing in the news cycle for weeks."

"I was on a mission when it went down. I had heard people talk about the Toro disaster a bit, but even after you came onboard I didn't look into it—I wanted to form my own opinions of you, not be poisoned by someone else's."

"I'm glad you didn't, '*Killed twenty-thousand people*' is a hard first-impression to lose. The redacted mission report isn't much better. Thank starlight that the captain and Anderson had access to the classified version or they would never have let me aboard." Tanis cast Joe a thoughtful eye. "What sort of mission were you on that you didn't hear about Toro, though?"

"Remember Makemake?" Joe asked.

"Remember? It was the thing that took my name out of the news." Tanis saw the pained look in Joe's eye and her expression turned to one of concern. "I'm sorry, that was cold. It must have been a really raw deal for you guys."

Joe nodded. "I didn't file mine the next day, it was a bit later. I was at Makemake—"

<I have the response from the Intrepid *coming in,>* Troy interrupted.

Joe looked at Tanis and nodded. "Play it," he said.

Captain Andrew's face filled the holo.

"*Excelsior,* good to hear you are still out there and apparently on your planned vector. I'm sure you noticed we aren't where we're supposed to be. We had a bit of a run in with a rather unfriendly solar flare."

Joe glanced at Tanis, he looked concerned, but the captain's voice hadn't betrayed anything one way or the other.

"We're still not certain if it was going to happen anyway, or if our magnetic resonance caused the flare, but either way the sunspot erupted. We had thirty-five seconds' notice and Bob put everything our engines had into getting us clear, which we did, but just barely. The flare took out a lot of exterior electronics, destroyed some of the structural arcs, melted off the housing on the main port engine. There were some severe x-ray bursts, but with the ES shielding already focused on the port side, we didn't receive any lethal doses, though everyone is getting treatments. There were some gamma ray bursts, which can mess with stasis fields, so we've got teams checking everyone in stasis, which will be a bit of a task."

The captain paused and Tanis and Joe looked at one another. This would be where the other shoe dropped.

"With our last moment burst and the engine damage, we came out of the slingshot at a different than planned trajectory. We don't have the fuel to correct, so you're going to have to meet us somewhere along our current path.

"I don't need to tell you that things aren't much better than they were before—except that we didn't burn up in Estrella de la Muerte. Unless you get us that lithium, we're not going to be able to even course correct enough to get to Epsilon Eridani.

"Good luck, *Excelsior*. *Intrepid* out."

Tanis leaned back. "Well, no one died, at least."

Joe looked shaken as he leaned back in his seat. He paused to choose his words and responded softly. "Sometimes I don't get you, Tanis. I know you are pretty hard-bitten, but sometimes you just seem blasé. Maybe just once you could have a good ole fashioned freak-out about something. It would make you more approachable."

Tanis didn't know how to respond. She had hoped that Joe finally got her. It wasn't that she was an emotionless bitch; she knew wisecracks were her coping mechanism. It hurt whenever people thought she didn't feel; the hurt made her angry.

"Get your shit together, Commander. The *Intrepid* can limp through space for ten thousand years if it has to. They have the equipment and resources to travel across the galaxy—if it would still be there once they made it to the other side—but we don't." She felt ashamed of herself the moment she said the words, but didn't know how to take them back.

Joe wiped a hurt expression off his face. "Is that how this is going to be? You'll pull rank and be ass-hat Tanis on me?"

Tanis lowered her eyes, staring at her cup of coffee.

"No, it's not. I *am* scared, I'm scared a lot... I think it's how I stay alive—by never letting it get to me. I push the fear down and compress it into action. Give me a problem and I'll make a plan. Once I have that plan I put all my fear, doubt and worry into making that plan work. And it works."

She looked up at him, his expression showing concern. "As a result I only seem to have the one pep-talk speech." Tanis shrugged apologetically. "It involves words like shit, fuck and ass. And it always uses rank."

"I'm not going to judge you, Tanis. I've seen you at your best and I've seen you at your worst—" Joe held up a hand to Tanis, stopping her from speaking. "You may think I haven't seen the depths of you, but I have. I watched when you tortured Kris and Trent. I know I wasn't supposed to, but I saw the feeds."

Tanis's face reddened. "I didn't know you saw that...I...I'm not sorry I did it, but I'm not proud of it either. I've done that sort of thing enough that sometimes I wonder if I have a soul anymore."

Joe reached out and turned her face so he could look into her eyes. "I know what you are capable of. You care for people around you. You care so much that you'll sacrifice your body and soul for them. You get called a hero and a demon, often at the same time, by the people you try to save. So you lock down."

Tanis nodded. "I know I do, I..."

"It's ok," Joe said, holding her close. "Like I said, I know the best and the worst of you and I still love you. Take your strength from that."

Tanis lay against Joe for a long time. Perhaps he understood her better than she did herself.

<*Thank you,*> Angela said privately to Joe. <*I've been trying to explain that to her for some time, but she always dismissed me as not understanding. Maybe she can finally get over Toro now.*>

<*Don't worry,*> Joe replied. <*She's Tanis.*>

Tanis's head suddenly snapped up. "Damn."

"What is it?" Joe asked, concern lining his features.

"We didn't respond to the *Intrepid*. They'll wonder why we're taking so long."

Joe's quizzical look froze on his face for several long seconds before he broke into laughter.

"What is it?" Tanis looked at him, perplexed.

"You," Joe chuckled. "I swear, there is duty imprinted on your DNA."

"Of course there is," she smiled. "I had it tattooed on when I enlisted."

While she sent the message, Joe and Troy worked out the alterations they would need to make to reach the asteroid belt sooner and meet the *Intrepid* before a rendezvous was impossible.

"We're going to have some hard burns in a couple of hours," Joe informed Tanis as she completed her response to the *Intrepid*.

"Let's get some food before that happens," Tanis said, a mischievous smile on her face. "Don't think you can get out of telling your tale, you're still going to tell me about Makemake."

CHURN AND BURN

STELLAR DATE: 3241792 / 08.17.4163 (Adjusted Gregorian)
LOCATION: *GSS ⍰⍰⍰e⍰⍰⍰r*
REGION: LHS 1565, 30 AU from stellar primary

⍰⍰⍰⍰⍰ ⍰⍰⍰r⍰ t⍰ ⍰⍰ter⍰id ⍰r⍰⍰p

Tanis stood up after the meal and poured two cups of coffee, adding sugar to Joe's and cream to hers. She handed Joe his cup and settled down in her chair, cradling the warm beverage.

"Mmm, just the way I like it," Joe said after a long draught. "You do pay attention."

"I did my fair share of dinner runs to the mess if you recall. It wasn't all just you getting me my BLT."

"That's not how I remember it," Joe said with a wink.

"Enough stalling, it's your turn, mister."

Joe nodded and took another long drink before beginning.

"Like with Toro, the full story of Makemake never made it out to the public. It started before your jaunt to Toro began and ended a few months after. I was with the seventh fleet on the *Midway*. We were leaving Ceres on our way to meet with the rest of the fleet for maneuvers near Venus."

"I read a briefing about that," Tanis said. "It was to test defensive patterns after the left-over core from Uranus was positioned between Venus and Earth."

"Yup, but we never arrived, we did a polar loop around Sol and boosted north. The word on the ship was that orders changed and we were doing a patrol of the Oort cloud, but we all knew we weren't provisioned for a haul that long.

"There was a lot of scuttlebutt, especially with the Scattered Worlds representatives talking separation in the SolGov congress. Some were also worried that we were on an

Outsystem trajectory to Alpha Centauri or Tau Ceti, though anyone who could look out a window at the stars could tell that we weren't headed there. The captain and the XO weren't talking but I figured we were on our way to the disk somewhere. I didn't expect us to be going to the capital, but rather Eris or New Sedna."

"Ballsy to go right for Makemake," Tanis commented.

"It was. I still don't know if that was the order or the captain was given some leeway. I don't think she'd churn and burn on a capital world without being explicitly told to.

"Either way, we went dark at our apex and took several months to drop back down the solar plane. When we were approaching Makemake we were still going damn fast. The *Midway* did the burn and made for a pretty rude awakening."

"I can imagine, I saw the vids of the *Midway* braking over Makemake, it was brighter than their little pseudo sun," Tanis nodded.

"We ended up engaging the SW fleet and even did a few strafes of their capital before they capitulated and stopped their separatist movement. There weren't a lot of casualties, but I felt pretty damn dirty shooting down pilots of a sovereign nation because they wanted to leave the union."

"Wait a second—" Tanis double-checked a reference she remembered seeing once "—your mother was stationed on Makemake at the time!"

Joe nodded slowly. "She was—I didn't know it, she'd transferred out there after the *Midway* left Ceres. I found out after all the dust had settled that one of the runs I had been on killed some of her colleagues and almost got her too."

His voice caught and he looked down at the table, fiddling with the handle of his cup as he regained his composure.

Tanis reached across the table and took Joe's hand. "I can't imagine how that would have felt."

He looked at her for a moment and then over her shoulder at some personal memory.

"Pretty shitty, I can tell you that much," Joe replied. "I put in for colony the day after I found out she was there. Sol is just too messy. Everyone knows that SolGov is falling apart. The Jovians want to separate too—only the million TSF ships running around the system keep it from happening."

Joe looked Tanis in the eyes. "You know it's going to happen eventually. The system is going to have an all-out civil war. There are just too many people who are too balkanized. I don't know if there should be one central government. Not when it sends sons to shoot at their mothers."

Joe's voice had risen and his eyes flashed with anger. Tanis laid a hand on his and nodded. "I know what you mean; I had a similar thought process. Why would I lay down my life to maintain a system that made monsters like Cardid and then threw me under the bus for killing them?"

"If a civil war had erupted I don't even know which side I would have chosen," Joe said. "Do you?"

"Gods above... I have no idea." Tanis shook her head. "I guess I'd pick the one that was the least evil and would win the war the fastest. Honestly though? I'd rather be out here falling into a star than having to make that choice."

"That's for sure," Joe agreed.

"I feel like it was easy for me," Tanis said. "I have nothing in Sol, just a sister who I hadn't spoken to long before Toro, let alone after. You, you have your mother and two brothers."

Joe nodded slowly. "It was. My mom understood a lot more than I thought. She's pretty old, closing in on five-hundred. She told me that I should find what makes me happy—she was also glad that I wasn't going to stick with an outfit that had me strafing the city she was in," Joe chuckled.

"My older brother is hundreds of years older than me; I barely know him and didn't bother to tell him I was leaving. My younger brother took it pretty hard. He's practically a sanctity activist and told me I was abandoning my people by leaving. He also had some choice words about me going off to help defile another system. He and I didn't part ways on the best of terms."

"I don't get how people think taking lifeless worlds and terraforming them is defiling them," Tanis said, shaking her head.

"No argument here," Joe said. "This is a colony mission after all."

In the three hours before the next hard burn, Tanis shared stories of her childhood on Mars and he of his youth on Vespa. He fell out of his chair laughing when she told her story of stealing a maglev train to impress a boy in college and he regaled her with stories of his flights in the TSF stunt squadron.

For a time they completely forgot the struggle that still lay ahead and the real danger that the *Intrepid* would never make it to its destination.

SUBTERFUGE

STELLAR DATE: 3241792 / 08.17.4163 (Adjusted Gregorian)
LOCATION: ***GSS ???e??i?r***
REGION: LHS 1565, 27.1 AU from stellar primary

The figure slipped through the corridors of the *Intrepid,* its shimmersuit masking its presence from all sensors. Only the movement of air would give it away, but that would take a nano-cloud to detect and its own cloud showed that it was alone.

With the rewrite of the servitor code and its loss of the AI in node eleven it could not directly control enough systems to cause serious trouble, but it had learned that certain members of the command crew were uneasy with the ship's secret cargo.

A less technological route would need to be employed to stop the *Intrepid* from continuing its trip to New Eden.

The first person on the list to visit was Hilda Orion; she had posted a few plans on the solution boards which suggested she was not happy about the direction the trip was taking.

The figure was not pleased either.

The threat of falling into LHS1565 was intended to force the crew to stop in the red dwarf's star system, consume colony supplies and then divert to an inhabited system. It should have worked—would have worked if Joe hadn't figured out a solution that allowed the *Intrepid* to keep on course to New Eden.

The figure considered that perhaps Joe should have been dispatched some time ago. He bolstered Tanis too much, made her hard to deal with.

Still, there were contingency plans and all it would take was a nudge here and a poke there and the crew would do exactly what was necessary.

Now that the ship was past the star, much of the crew was off-shift, getting some shut-eye before the *Excelsior* returned with its fuel rock.

Hilda was in her quarters and the figure stopped before her cabin's door. A small swarm of nano slipped around the portal's edges and reported that the woman inside was sleeping.

The figure may have lost its root access to core systems, but its public position on the *Intrepid* granted it enough access to open any cabin door. A few auth codes later and the door slid aside. The record would show that Hilda left for several minutes before re-entering her cabin.

No log would show the invisible figure visiting her in the night.

FISHING FOR ROCKS

STELLAR DATE: 3241791 / 08.17.4163 (Adjusted Gregorian)
LOCATION: ***GSS ???e??i?r***
REGION: LHS 1565, 27.1 AU from stellar primary

Joe and Troy altered the vector, increasing burn to an uncomfortable 3.2*g*. As a result, when braking occurred it would be even higher at just under 5*g*. It was a bit of a gamble because calculations showed that if they couldn't get enough mass knocked off Fuel Dump—the name Tanis had given their target—then there wouldn't be enough antimatter left to rendezvous with the *Intrepid* on its new vector.

Over the next nineteen hours they slept, ate, watched scan, and sent a few messages back and forth to the *Intrepid.* A few of the colonists' stasis pods had been disrupted by the gamma radiation and colonists were found wandering the stasis chambers, trying to figure out what was going on. It wouldn't have been so bad if the flare hadn't knocked out certain sections, cutting those portions of the stasis chambers off from communication.

The colonists were being treated for radiation poisoning and the engineers were working on getting the engines repaired to course correct once the lithium was extracted from Fuel Dump and brought onboard.

Bob was regaining control of the ship, though there were entire sections with nothing functioning other than the rogue machines that prowled the halls. Before the enemy AI had been destroyed, it left final commands for all of the equipment it had subverted. Ouri had teams working through the ship and hoped to have things under control soon. Not unexpectedly, Abby had begun registering formal complaints about damage to her ship.

Due in part to the heavy gravity, the tub became a favorite place to spend time, the buoyancy easing the high-*g* strain. Unfortunately the increased weight from the thrust made any more interesting activities impossible, or, at the very least, undesirably exhausting.

Tanis also found it difficult to sleep in the high gravity. Blankets felt untenably heavy and every pressure point on her body was aggravated from the weight. They took to sleeping in the acceleration couches on the bridge, shipsuits set to maximum cushioning. When the ship reversed and began breaking at 4.8*g* it only got worse. Both Joe and Tanis grew testy and had to take care not to snap at one another.

Finally their target came into view, a slightly oblong rock, a kilometer wide and slightly more than that in length. It spun slowly as it orbited its star, which at this distance was dimmer than many of the other stars in the stellar neighborhood.

"Damn, it's got a little moon," Joe said as he pointed at a small hundred meter companion.

"We'll have to blow that away, won't we?"

"I believe so," Joe said. "Then we have to use our thumpers to knock that dust off. We'll have to do the first one on the northeastern side then send a booster over to push it away and ensure the dust doesn't settle, or form another moon. Then we do the other when it's at the right point in its rotation. Boost some more then use the grapple."

"How do you propose we take out the moon?"

Joe examined the display. "Troy and I agree. Use some of the smaller explosive projectiles on it every time it is moving directly away from us. That'll accelerate it and cause it to break away."

"Ok, I'll take care of that."

Joe prepared the thumpers and programmed in the precise co-ordinates, getting them checked and triple checked by Troy and Angela. Tanis played target practice with the moon and in three orbits had it increasing its speed and pulling away from Fuel Dump. Two more orbits and the hundred meter lump of aggregate went spinning off into space.

"Little moon all gone," Tanis reported.

"Good, I'm launching the first thumper now. Check Troy's calculations on the booster so that we can launch it as soon as the thumper does its thing."

Tanis ran through the math, checking distances, rotations, impact velocities and gave second confirmation on the numbers. Angela rang in with a triple check moments later.

<*I beat you!*> Tanis was surprised.

<*Yeah, well you're not managing scan and monitoring comm from the* Intrepid *at the same time.*>

<*Oooo monitoring scan and comm. That's tough stuff.*>

Angela didn't deign to reply.

<*Triple check received on the booster. Ready to launch.*> Troy reported on the shipnet.

"First thumper away." Joe manually flipped the release switch and then the holo counterpart.

They watched as the thumper launched from the *Excelsior,* a slight shudder running through the ship as the thrusters compensated for the motion. The thumper flew across the intervening distance and split into twenty-eight separate pieces before diving into the dust and aggregate on the northeast face of Fuel Dump.

They waited a breathless moment, and then the kilometer long rock appeared to jerk violently, a massive plume of dust and debris spraying out of the thumpers' insertion point. Fuel Dump's rotation began to wobble and the booster launched from the *Excelsior,* moving on the carefully planned route, which allowed it to avoid the wobble and dust.

It planted precisely where the calculations had indicated it should and the display dimmed as the fusion torch ignited on the rock, pulsing on every rotation to move Fuel Dump further from the coalescing aggregate cloud.

"So far, so good," Joe said as he began plotting the path for the second thumper.

While Tanis was well aware of the processes used to move asteroids and even small worlds, it was really something else to be actively involved in it. Most people never moved anything much larger than a small people transport; here they were at the edge of an uninhabited stellar system, hijacking an asteroid.

More impressive was that they would boost it up to 0.10*c* and deliver it to the *Intrepid.*

The thought reminded Tanis to send her update letting the colony ship know they were currently on schedule.

Joe got triple check from Troy and Angela and sent the second thumper. Its twenty-two separate units sunk beneath the dust on the western side of the rock and moments later an eruption of debris plumed.

<*Perfectly done,*> Troy said.

"Appears to be." Joe scrutinized the scan of the rock, looking for any signs of fracture. Scan had showed that, aside from the aggregate and dust, the core was a solid chunk, split off from whatever was out there that broke apart to form the asteroid ring.

The booster was set to fire in ten seconds and Tanis mentally counted it down. In the brief time between one and zero, Joe's hand flew out and pointed at something on the holo display.

It was too late. The booster fired and a fracture appeared in Fuel Dump.

With exquisite grace for a lump of rock, the asteroid split apart along its axis, one piece sliding to the side while the portion with the booster attached picked up speed and began to move away from the ship.

Tanis quickly killed the booster and glanced over at Joe.

"Well that makes things a bit harder."

Joe scrubbed his face. "You're telling me. The booster has small jets for maneuvering. As gently as possible, see if you can rotate it and gently slow it down."

"Got it, gently," Tanis said.

Joe, Troy, and Angela had screens of vector math racing back and forth across the main display as they calculated the best ways to catch both portions of the rock.

The *Excelsior*'s main grapple system was a set of stasis emitter arms and a carbon tube net. The arms would emit a field that kept the object from fracturing, and the net wrapped around the field to pull it behind the ship. While the ship could haul multiple items, it was a delicate dance to get more than one thing in the net, and they were short on time.

"It's gotta be the one without the booster first." Joe pointed at the calculation that favored that approach. "We can use the booster to get the other piece moving on our rendezvous trajectory and then simply scoop it up on our way."

The plot appeared on the display and Tanis started running the computations to make her piece line up.

"Stellar north or south of our plot?"

Joe examined the convoluted acrobatics the *Excelsior* would be going through. "North, we can tweak a few degrees either way to sync up. Just be gentle with that thing. The booster is nowhere near centered."

"This ain't my first rodeo." Tanis grinned at Joe.

"Yeah, you're not bad for an MICI girl," Joe placed a hand on her leg and gave it a squeeze before turning back to his screen.

The next half hour was full of running math, checking other crewmembers' math, and then running more math. Through it all, Joe was deftly maneuvering the ship to match the slow tumble of Fuel Dump B. The *Excelsior* was rotating and shifting in a pattern that would make a bat puke and yet Joe was completely unfazed.

Tanis never ceased to be amazed at how good a pilot he was. His flight records could only tell so much. She had seen him in combat, adrenaline rushing, but this was something else—long, grueling work, matching wits against an asteroid the size of a small space station. She harbored no illusions that she could do it even half as deftly as he did.

<*I swear, even I can feel my connections shifting,*> Troy said. <*Good thing I had the foresight to empty the tub.*>

Tanis laughed. "Damn, sorry about that. Would have been one hell of a mess."

<*I would have made you clean it up too.*>

At long last the two stasis arms extended and—with the net ready to snap out—emitted their field. Visually nothing changed, then, as Joe manipulated the field, the rock stopped tumbling and aligned with the ship. Once the ship and rock were relatively stationary, the net shot out on either side of Fuel Dump B, meeting on the far end, secured to the rock by thousands of spikes.

"Latched on," Joe said. "Plotting intercept course with the second piece."

The burn was gentle and Tanis couldn't help but run the calculations on their fuel levels over and over again. Whether they would have enough antimatter to accelerate and then match vectors with the *Intrepid* was now within the margin of error. She ran it again. And again.

Joe was right. Being in a situation where there was nothing you could do about the outcome really did suck.

As luck would have it, picking up the second piece went smoothly. The *Excelsior* began its final burn to meet up with the colony ship.

"Good news and bad news, sir," Hilda said as she stood and turned to Captain Andrews.

"I imagine it's the same piece of news." The way this day was going, it was the norm. Only it wasn't just a day, it had been several. He hadn't slept the entire time, only retreating to his ready room periodically to catch a short nap on his couch.

"Colonel Richards' latest update indicates that they got the rock—they named it Fuel Dump—and though it split into two pieces when they shed mass, they are on their way."

"I can imagine what the bad news is."

"They aren't certain they have enough antimatter to make it here, or, if they do, to maneuver and match our vector."

The captain nodded and Hilda returned to her station.

She was right, good news and bad news. Still, Tanis Richards was on the *Excelsior* and in his book that counted as a miracle just waiting to happen.

<*She'll pull it off.*> Amanda had been listening in on the bridge conversations.

<*What are you doing snooping in on bridge comm?*> Andrews asked. <*I thought you were in the hospital.*>

<*She won't sleep or even relax.*> Priscilla inserted herself into the conversation. <*Even though I, Bob and the doctors have all told her she needs to rest.*>

<*I was involved in nearly destroying the ship, I have some redeeming to do.*>

<*You are using the word 'involved' rather loosely,*> Andrews' tone was gentle, but firm. <*No one holds you responsible. The rogue AI used your access to subvert the ship and you were not a willing participant, no one holds you responsible.*>

<*Except me.*> Amanda's voice was small.

<*I've altered your programming.*> Bob joined the conversation. <*A repeat of these events will not be possible.*>

<*Bob, even though we all know you can do it, the thought of you so obliquely stating that you can alter a human's 'programming' is disconcerting.*>

<*I know.*> There was a ghost of a grin and Bob's presence left the conversation.

<*I don't think that made me feel better.*> Amanda's avatar shook her head.

<*You'll feel better when you rest. Captain's orders.*>

<*Like she'll follow them,*> Priscilla groused.

"Every time I run the scenarios we're lower on fuel. We've got more drag than anticipated." Tanis looked up from her console at Joe.

"I'm getting the same thing. I think the stellar medium is thicker than anticipated. Not much, but enough to screw us."

"Can you come up with anything?"

Joe sighed, gave his console a long, hard look and then turned sorry eyes to Tanis. "I can't."

"I refuse to accept that. There is always something you can do. I didn't survive over a thousand engagements to die because a spaceship runs out of fuel." Her eyes glinted in the dim lights of the bridge, a fire in them refused to be quenched.

"I… I don't know what to say."

"Let's look at our inventory again."

Joe brought it up on the main holo. There were parts for the relativistic probe, another net, extra cores for the thumpers that hadn't been used in Joe's configurations, and several physical probes for examining rocks.

"Nothing much there," Joe said.

"I wonder." Tanis brought up the specs on the thumper cores. "I wonder if we can't make use of these somehow."

On another section of the display she brought up their route and removed the required fuel for one of the course corrections. It brought the numbers closer, but still within the margin of error. She tried removing a different course correction and got the same result. Then, looking at the fuel computations again, removed the fuel requirement for two course corrections.

The numbers came out of the error margin and showed green. They could rendezvous with the *Intrepid* and maneuver.

"OK, so if we can use the thumpers in place of fuel, then we're all set." Joe scowled at the display.

Tanis brought up a display of the ship's exterior and pointed at a structural ridge that bisected the hull. "We plant the thumpers along this ridge and then fire them off to adjust our course. These calculations show they have the impact force to do it."

"You saw what they did to the asteroid, right?" Joe looked incredulous. "They ejected trillions of tons of mass. They'll tear the ship apart."

"Oh, I don't deny that it will be as rough as all get-out, but we don't fire them all off at once. Stagger them, do it in stages. And the more, the sooner, the better; since it will take less to correct now than later."

Joe looked her calculations over again. "We're going to need to do EVA to mount them—the ship has no bots capable of that."

"So where are the suits?" Tanis asked.

"What are you doing in here?" Priscilla looked up from her holo arrays in consternation. "Can't you do what you're supposed to for once?"

Amanda laughed. "When have I ever done what I'm supposed to? Besides, I can't sit in a med bay while everything is going to shit."

Priscilla glanced to her right and pulled several holo displays into the foreground. Her fingers raced over the consoles while her mind manipulated a dozen other systems.

"The accelerator is losing containment in the sixth coupling, isn't it?" Amanda asked.

"Yeah, that coupling has always been a bit twitchy."

"Let me help," Amanda walked to Priscilla's pedestal and pulled a holo display in front of herself. "I can help—you need it."

"You know you shouldn't, you've been through some ridiculous mental stress—what we do is hard enough under the best of circumstances."

"I'm not asking to interface with Bob, just let me shunt some tasks. I have to do my part here, don't you understand?"

Amanda's unblinking stare bore into Priscilla's eyes. She didn't respond for a moment, fingers still dancing across her displays. Slowly she nodded. "I do understand, Bob does too. Here, take this, run the math and update the engineers with the ETA."

Amanda pulled the data stream to her display and reviewed the information.

"What on Earth? This can't work!"

Priscilla chuckled. "When has one of Tanis's crazy ideas looked like it would work?"

"Yeah, but this time she's crazy, she'll tear the *Excelsior* apart and we'll never get that fuel.

<*Either that or they loop around* Estrella de la Muerte *for eternity.*> The fear in Priscilla's mental tone was palpable. <*And we drift through space forever.*>

<*I'm really starting to wish you didn't call it that.*>

Tanis finished welding the last of her brackets to the ship's hull. Joe was moving behind her, placing the thumper cores into the brackets, a small hauler bot trundling behind him on its magnetic tracks.

<*How's it going back there?*>

<*Questioning my sanity.*>

<*I'm not too happy about this either,*> Troy added.

<*Hey, any better ideas speak up. I for one won't sit idly by while we fly past the* Intrepid *and drift forever in this godforsaken system.*>

<*Hey, I didn't say stop doing what you're doing,*> Troy snapped. <*Just don't expect me to be jumping for joy about it.*>

Joe sent the bot ahead to Tanis. <*Here, fill that one while I do this one up.*>

Tanis pulled the thumper core out of the bot's carriage and slid it into her bracket, sliding the latch into place and then using her welder to tac it in.

<*Done.*>

<*Good, let's get inside. There's too much dust out here for my liking.*>

Tanis hadn't seen a single piece of dust impact the ship, but there was no point in testing fate. All it took was a tiny spec at these speeds to punch right through a person.

Minutes later they were back in the airlock, waiting for the inner hatch to cycle open. When it did they stepped through and removed their helmets.

"You're going to need to go under for this again," Joe said. "Those impacts are going to be vicious and I can't worry about you and pilot the ship at the same time."

Tanis nodded. "I understand. But let me get a BLT in first. I always seem to come out of stasis hungry."

Joe looked over at Tanis in her stasis pod one last time before he brought up the thumper's control display.

<*Are you ready?*> he asked Troy.

<*No, but don't let that stop you.*>

Joe chuckled and sealed his EVA suit. There was a good chance that even if the maneuver were successful the hull would crack open in one location or another. Emergency systems should be able to seal any leaks in moments, but Joe didn't want to test out their speed with his life.

<*Initiating sequence,*> Joe said and flipped the holo-switch.

The screen showed a countdown to the first thumper firing and Joe had to force himself to relax and unclench his teeth.

The thumper fired on schedule and a deafening clang echoed through the ship. Moments later the second thumper fired and then the third and the forth.

<*The mounts are all bent, but the thumpers fired correctly, the anticipated course alteration for the first set match our calculations,*> Troy said. <*How are you?*>

<*Any chance you can turn off the bells in my head?*> Joe shook his head back and forth.

<*I did register that it was pretty loud,*> Troy said. <*I don't think there is anything we can do about that.*>

<*Don't worry, I can take it.*> Joe looked over the rocks they were pulling. <*The net and arms look OK too, let's move on to the next set.*>

Joe looked down at Tanis. "Hold on, just a few more to go."

The *Intrepid's* bridge erupted with cheers as the data came in showing that the thumper core detonations had achieved their goal. The *Excelsior* had altered course enough without using antimatter fuel. Calculations put it well within the green and the ship had survived the impacts with its hull intact.

<*Commander Evans to the* Intrepid.>

Another round of cheers sounded as Joe's smooth tenor voice filled the bridge net.

<*Captain Andrews here. Go ahead.*>

They were within just a few light minutes now and the response didn't take long.

<*The colonel's crazy plan went off without a hitch. Well, other than a ship that is going to need a new paintjob and a structural analysis. I haven't pulled her out of stasis, but the shocks were dampened enough in here that I'm not worried.*>

<Very good, Commander. We'll await your updates at T-10 to docking.> Privately, the captain added, *<Aren't you glad we forced you to take her along?>*

The response came back. *<Yes, yes I am.>*

"Holy shit," Tanis breathed as she got her first visual glimpse of the damage to the *Intrepid.*

They were approaching on the port side of the colony ship, the same side struck by the edge of the solar flare. At the rear of the ship, the housing had been completely burned off the port engine, exposing portions of its inner workings to space. Several of the gossamer arcs, which provided additional structural integrity to the ship, were gone, and a few more were warped and twisted.

The port cylinder rotated, showing Old Sam covered in large scorch marks. Tanis imagined those would be the areas with the failing stasis pods. Good thing someone had determined to bring an extra hundred thousand.

Several large stasis grapple arms were ready to take the load from the *Excelsior* and Joe communicated with the engineers, executing the handoff flawlessly.

Even with the thumper core assistance, the fuel situation was as close to the wire as possible. Once the final maneuvers were complete, Joe shut down the antimatter engines entirely and used thrusters to bring them into position for docking.

The *Excelsior* that landed was a different ship than the one that left a scant week ago. One side was scorched and dented from the cores and the forward shields were pitted and scratched. Upon visual inspection it could be seen that the structural strut the thumper cores had pushed on was cracked in two places. The *Excelsior* wouldn't be going anywhere until serious repairs were done.

The ship eased in on the magnetic rails and Tanis pulled up a view of the dock. There had to be at least a hundred people down there, all cheering their lungs out.

<*Look at all of them, you rate quite the reception,*> Troy said.

"You deserve this as much as we do, Troy," Tanis said. "You're one hell of an AI."

<*You know, I now have a much better appreciation for what some of my instructors meant when they said there is no teacher like experience.*>

"I know that all too well," Tanis said.

Tanis and Joe walked out of the ship's port hatch and down a gantry to the waiting crowd. In the front stood Captain Andrews and Terrance Enfield. Both men were beaming and clapping with the crowd.

"This is getting to be a habit, you saving the *Intrepid.*" Captain Andrews smiled at the pair.

"One I hope you don't intend to break anytime soon," Terrance added.

Tanis looked at Joe and they smiled at one another. It was good to be back home.

INCONSISTENCIES

STELLAR DATE: 3241794 / 08.19.4163 (Adjusted Gregorian)
LOCATION: *GSS Intrepid*, Security Operations Center (SOC)
REGION: LHS 1565, 153 AU from stellar primary

Tanis let out a long sigh and leaned back in her chair. Her old office in the SOC was exactly as she'd left it, down to the nicks in the desk and the stain on the couch where Terry had once spilled a glass of juice.

Outside her door, the SOC hummed with activity as every colonist out of stasis went through a re-interview process. Stats and transcripts from several of the interviewees hovered above her desk, keeping Tanis in the loop every step of the way.

She closed her eyes again and the virtual conference with the command crew snapped into place in front of her.

<*...you don't understand,*> Abby was saying. <*If we can't make the correction burn in the next fifteen days, then we are well and surely screwed!*>

<*Tanis, what is your progress in reviewing the crew and colonists currently out of stasis?*> Captain Andrews asked.

<*We're a little over fifty percent. So far everyone is passing with flying colors—if we keep up this pace we'll be done in another three days. Then we can pull more people out of stasis.*>

<*Three days!*> Abby all but shouted. <*I need more hands now. With so many servitors damaged by the AI, or destroyed by your security sweeps—not to mention the damage you did to the machine shops that could build new ones—we need every hand we can get.*>

Tanis could spot gross exaggeration when she heard it. A lot of servitors and bots *had* been destroyed, but the damage she and Joe had done to the machine shops was minimal at worst.

<*We're working as fast as we can. But if we let another person slide who is somehow able to damage the ship, then we'll be even worse off.*>

<*Hard to imagine being worse off than drifting through space forever,*> Abby replied with a sour look on her virtual face.

<*Abby, in three days the disruptions to your current crew will be over and you'll be getting fresh hands. If your requests or additional crew are filled within five days, will you have time to get everything done for the burn?*> the captain asked his question calmly.

Abby sighed. <*Yes, we can get it done, but we won't be getting a lot of sleep.*>

<*No one is getting a lot of sleep right now,*> Andrews replied.

The meeting ended and Tanis opened her eyes again to see Ouri standing in her doorway.

"That looked like a fun conversation, boss," she grimaced. "You were making some choice expressions."

"Just talking progress with the brass," Tanis replied. "What I can do for you?"

"I wanted to talk about Collins."

Tanis gestured to a chair. "Sit, but before you get started, no recriminations."

Ouri's mouth twisted into a wry smile. "What gave it away?"

"Nothing, but I'm wracking my brain trying to see how I didn't catch on to any of this, I figured you must be doing the same."

Ouri laughed. "Good to know I'm not the only one."

"Not by a long shot. If we hadn't saved the ship on a dozen occasions we'd be in pretty deep hock right now," Tanis said.

"I guess that does paint things in our favor a bit." Ouri paused for a moment before continuing. "I've instructed Terry to look at what people have done since joining the crew or colony as much as what they did before coming onboard. Perhaps we can find some patterns that will point us in the right direction. I also have a team dissecting every move Collins made since he came on board. Hopefully we'll identify any co-conspirators."

"Pay extra attention to those last minute fill-ins we had on Callisto. It always seemed a bit odd to me that the GSS let people transfer in so late—even if their reasoning did pass muster at the time."

"Already on it, Colonel," Ouri said.

"Now you're just kissing up," Tanis laughed.

"Pretty transparent I guess." Ouri shifted to stand up, but Tanis stopped her.

"I looked at the reports, the cylinders took a bit of a beating, how's your little stand of trees doing?"

Ouri smiled. "Thanks for asking. Not too bad, the maintenance bots are cleaning things up, most of the damage happened further aft where the engine released some radiation bursts during the flare. Most of the damage in my neck of the woods was due to flooding."

"We should have a gathering down there once it's cleaned up. I think folks could really use that."

"I know I could. I'll see if I can put something on the schedule."

"No schedule, make it spontaneous when things are ready. I'll be a pleasant surprise."

"Will do, sir."

<*Some good advice you give about recriminations,*> Angela said.

<*I can control how her boss acts, mine is a different story.*>

<*Which one?*>

<*That's part of the problem,*> Tanis sighed. Her chain of command was a bit fuzzy on the *Intrepid*. Technically she reported to Admiral Sanderson, but on the ship Captain Andrews had final say, except that Terrance Enfield—the project's financial backer—was on board. Each often gave conflicting directives and she had to be careful not to play them against one another, even accidentally.

Tanis knew that even though the captain had given his ruling Abby would start to pester Terrance and he would go to

Andrews. The captain was good at not reacting to pressure, but it wore on him and eventually he would come to Tanis to see what compromises could be made.

Tanis brought up her lists of colonists with investigatory experience. Engineers all but filled the roster, but people with investigatory experience were lacking. With the levels of terrorism and insurrection in the Sol system she expected more folks from counter-terrorist or counter-insurgency agencies.

Angela would have been a help, but with the SOC short staffed, she was doing interviews of the crew as well. Tanis could hear her in the back of her mind asking a plasma transfer specialist about his hometown.

Tanis knew it was unusual for her to be able to hear Angela so well. She had always had a very close rapport with her AI, but after the merge with the fighters in the Sol system she had been able to hear Angela's thoughts more readily.

She knew her AI could see more deeply into her mind as well—it showed in some of the observances Angela made.

Neither had spoken of it. It wasn't entirely unheard of and neither felt any pain or discomfort when it happened. They had enough to do and worry about without making up new problems.

A name appeared on the holo after Tanis ran a new search focusing on Terran federal agencies: Jessica Keller. The woman's record showed that she was a decorated, if somewhat unorthodox, agent from the Terran Bureau of Investigations.

There was no reason why she had left the TBI; in fact, upon closer investigation Tanis was surprised to see that she didn't seem to have the right clearances to be in the colony roster to begin with. Far from being a help, this woman looked like a new problem.

<It really is strange,> Angela commented. *<I can't find a record of her going through any pre-screening for colony, though somehow she was approved as a corrections officer for New Eden.>*

<Why should anything get any easier?> Tanis sighed. *<I guess I'll go wake her up and see. If nothing else it may help pinpoint any fault with the screening data.>*

Maglev service to the cylinders had been restored and Tanis took a track that arched outside the ship. The starboard side of the ship was dark. Estrella de la Muerte, dim even up close, was barely visible anymore, providing no illumination. As the train arched over the dorsal hump and Sirius A, the Dog Star, came into view, its bluish-white light providing a bow-to-stern view of the ship.

There were a few repair crews working on external damage. Further aft, secured by a multitude of tethers and nets, was the Fuel Dump asteroid. Crews would likely be working on it, extracting lithium for a burn of the *Intrepid's* starboard engine, which would correct their vector and bring the ship back on course to New Eden.

Tanis's attention was brought back to the task at hand as the maglev train slowed and changed tracks to one mounted directly on the port cylinder.

Because the track ran around Old Sam, the centripetal force caused Tanis's stomach to lurch as down moved above her head a moment before the interior of the train pivoted to match. Half a kilometer later, it slipped through an ES airlock and slid to a stop at a station.

<You checked to see if the maglev had power, you didn't check to see if the station had any,> Angela commented.

<I know… I can't believe I did that again.>

<Maybe if you got more than three hours of sleep a night you'd think more clearly.>

<Soon, just a few more weeks of this,> Tanis sighed.

She looked around at the small, dark station; even the emergency lighting was off. She wondered if coming with no armor and only a light-wand was wise.

<*In my defense, aren't the cylinders supposed to have their own backup power for times like this?*>

<*Maybe ancillary systems were shut down to conserve. If the switchover back to engine power hasn't happened yet that would explain why we're in the dark.*>

Tanis enabled her IR and UV visual overlays in addition to sending out of wave of nano to sonar-map the route to the stasis pods.

<*Lights? Who needs lights?*>

<*You're just using all the tricks now, aren't you?*>

Tanis left the station and followed the map she had pulled from the *Intrepid* before boarding the maglev. Colonist stasis pods sheathed the sixteen kilometer long habitation cylinders, the area providing ample room for the 1.5 million colonists on the ship, as well as over a hundred thousand backup stasis pods.

With the power out she again had to find creative ways to move three decks up and one kilometer along the cylinder. As she struggled with an emergency hatch it struck her that roughly a hundred meters above her was Old Sam's interior; a world filled hills, trees and lakes, kept in place by the centripetal force of the rotating cylinder.

<*Worried it's going to spring a leak?*>

<*That sure would ruin my day, but no, somehow I think that's pretty unlikely.*>

<*Out of curiosity, what if this Jessica Keller is hostile, how are you going to get her back to the maglev station?*> Angela asked.

<*I was thinking I'd just bash her on the head and throw her over my shoulder,*> Tanis said.

<*You know, even though I reside in your head I can't tell if you're serious about that.*>

Tanis laughed aloud. It was good to know she could still keep Angela on her toes.

Before too much longer she entered a chamber containing stasis pods. Tanis had never been in this portion of the ship, and had never seen a stasis chamber this large. It stretched for hundreds of meters and must have housed tens of thousands of colonists.

Unlike the corridors up to this point, this chamber had power, though only emergency lighting was on. The illumination cast long shadows across the pods.

Tanis suppressed the feeling that she was surrounded by the dead, it was too easy to imagine the pods containing some sort of inhuman horror waiting to rise up and claim her.

<*It's not Toro,*> Angela said. <*Nothing like that is here.*>

<*I know... It's just hard to keep those images out of my mind sometimes.*>

<*You could have them removed. Heck, I could even do it.*>

<*Don't you dare!*> Tanis snapped and felt her AI recoil from her sudden vehemence. <*Sorry Ang, I didn't mean to yell, but the thought of losing a part of myself, even a part that I don't really like, is pretty abhorrent to me. I'd lose a part of why I'm me, and then I'd be someone else.*>

<*Sorry I mentioned it. I won't bring it up again.*> Angela sounded hurt, but Tanis didn't know what else to say and let it drop.

<*She should be in that bank to the left.*>

Tanis turned and walked up an aisle, sending a command to the local systems to provide some additional lighting. The pods all looked much less sinister in the standard lighting. A command to the systems gave her the precise location of Jessica's pod and Tanis passed the protocols to unseal it and awaken its occupant as she approached.

<*Blue hair...was that back in style?*> Tanis asked.

<*I don't know, not something I keep track of. Isn't everything essentially in style all the time somewhere?*>

Stasis suits hugged the body perfectly and the former TBI agent's figure was clearly visible as the pod began cycling through its wakeup process. The woman was quite obviously modified from human norm and her blue hair was just the beginning.

While she appeared of normal height—around one hundred eighty centimeters tall—her legs were disproportionately long and her waist was quite small. Her breasts were also rather large for her frame. This was obviously a woman who had rebuilt herself for a purpose, though it was not something one often saw in a TBI agent.

As Tanis watched, the pod's lid lifted and the woman's eyes fluttered open. True to form, they were purple.

The woman lay still for a moment, staring up at the chamber's ceiling. Tanis assumed she was trying to Link to the nets. The local ones were up, but connections to the rest of the ship were unavailable. She must have learned something that alarmed her because the color drained from her face and she looked at Tanis.

"Is the local net's timestamp correct?"

ALTERED AGENT

STELLAR DATE: 3227225 / 09.29.4123 (Adjusted Gregorian)
LOCATION: High Terra, Sector RC3.4
REGION: Earth, Sol Space Federation

? ? ?nt???e??re t?e* Intrepid *dep?rted t?e S?????te?

Jessica's boot crashed into the steel door, forcing it open against the protests of the apartment's occupant. The man on the other side flailed and lost his balance, hitting the floor hard. She strode through the entrance to his dingy home and he scampered back on his hands and feet like the most awkward of crabs, the expression his face one of total fear.

"Mr. Jameson," Jessica said. "You've not pleased me, not pleased me at all."

"Agent Keller, don't kill me...please don't kill me," Jameson's voice quivered.

Whoa, that sure is leaping to a conclusion, Jessica thought as she looked impassively at the cowering man who appeared near tears. She really hated getting information from crying people, especially with all the sobbing and gasping. It took a long time to calm them down and reassure them—only to threaten them again.

It was tedious, but she softened her stance and expression.

"Jameson, are you high? I'm TBI, we don't just shoot people. We have district attorneys that need a reason for their existence—we hand scum like you over to them."

His eyes grew wide and he raised his hands. "You can't do that! They'll make me talk...and then I'm dead for sure."

Jessica reached back and swung the door closed, or as closed as it could get after her boot had forced it open. She walked forward and Jameson continued to back away from her.

"Oh for god sakes, man, get up already. I feel like I'm talking to some ring urchin."

That wouldn't be far from the truth. This apartment was pretty rank, close to one of the waste processing centers on the ring. Not the sort of place landlords could charge a lot of rent for, or attract decent residents to.

Jameson could probably afford better, but it suited him to be here. He slowly got to his feet and moved as far away from her as the space would allow.

Jessica sat down in a hard plastic chair and regarded the man. He was skinny, his cheeks gaunt and hands all knuckles and sinew—a sign of too many mods and not enough body to support them. His system was slowly cannibalizing itself for energy. Unless he altered his body to accept and store more calories he would be dead inside of a year, two at most. He must know it; maybe he didn't care.

His sunken eyes didn't seem to fit in the sockets right, probably a cheap set that weren't a custom fit. Why anyone would ever skimp on the eyes was beyond Jessica. Getting the eyes right was the most important thing. She had spent considerable sums of her own money on her pair of deep purple peepers, there was no way was she going to install the baseline units that the Terran Bureau of Investigation offered its agents.

"Look, Jameson. I'm not here to take you in; I'm not here to shoot you. I just want to talk." She tried to use her most soothing voice. It probably didn't come off that well since she was wearing Trellan FC9 body armor, the best protection available below a fully powered suit.

She pulled the helmet off, tucked it under her arm, letting her glossy blue hair free, and gave her head a shake to let it settle around her shoulders. Maybe if she reminded him she was a woman he would stop freaking out.

It seemed to help. Though the armor was heavy, it was well fitted. The waist was tapered and the amount of bosom under the plating was fairly obvious. Other than the joints, the armor was smooth and its matte sheen had a certain utilitarian look to it. Some guys got off on that sort of thing.

“Well, I guess that’s OK,” he said, his eyes seeming to be tracing the outline of her body. What do you need to know?”

“I’m looking for a guy. Goes by the name of Myrrdan. I got word you’ve dealt with him.”

Jameson snorted, for the first time not looking completely scared. “Him? He’s nobody? Why would you want to find him?”

“I’ve got my reasons. Word has it that you saw him earlier today, he bought some access time on one of the Non-Sentient AI super nodes through you.”

The NSAI super nodes were extremely powerful computers, often more powerful than dozens of combined sentient AI. They were useful in managing complex systems that required little ingenuity. In short, tasks that would bore humans, or sentient AI to tears…or whatever the AI equivalent of tears was. An NSAI super node could do things like plot the orbits of electrons around a quintillion atoms in real time, or index the entire wealth of human literature in a matter of minutes. They were also great at hacking through security.

“Why would I do that? Everyone knows that Myrrdan hasn’t got any cred. I wouldn’t let him buy NSAI through me, I could lose my access for tax work.”

“Right, your tax work for folks who could never let a legit auditor look at their books.”

Jameson looked rather depressed. “I don’t know why you get so down on me…I’m a hard working citizen.”

Jessica laughed. “Hard working maybe, but at what?”

“Look, I’ll tell you—will you just leave me alone then?”

Jessica gave him a look that all but screamed the words *spill it already!*

"I did get him some time on a node: 76343.32343:99832.92034. It's not a super node, but he said he didn't need that much juice."

"How big a block, and when?"

"A million relative seconds, beginning tomorrow at 1200. It's parallel, so only two thousand sidereal seconds."

Jessica was shocked. "A million? How much did he pay?"

"Uh…a lot."

Jessica could imagine. She also could imagine what Myrrdan would do with a million seconds on an NSAI, even if it wasn't a super node. Well, she did have some ideas, but nothing she really wanted to think about.

Jessica stood. "Thanks Jameson. You've been real helpful."

He nodded and muttered something about denting his door. Jessica didn't respond and pulled the portal shut behind her as she stepped out into the hall. With some effort she got it latched; the boot mark was a cosmetic feature as far as she was concerned.

She walked quickly down the corridor and out of the block. A bank of tubelifts stood across the section's main access corridor and Jessica stepped into one of them, keying the surface level. The tube closed in around her and pulled her up at over a thousand kilometers per hour. The mass compensation system cushioned the effect and she almost couldn't feel the motion.

Jessica accessed her Link and reported the information to Nell, the AI in charge of organizing agents' duties and reports. Nell thanked her for the update and scheduled a meeting for 0800 with Sub-Regional Director Rickford to determine the next course of action.

The tublelift arrived at the ring's surface just as Jessica finished updating her internal calendar for the next day: 0800, discuss stopping madman; 1200, stop madman.

She walked out of the transit station into the soft glow of night, the earth hanging directly above with the Asian sub-continent sliding by—the lights of the New Delhi arcologies a bright spot below the darkness of the Himalayas.

It was near the vernal equinox, which meant that the ring was in line with Earth and Sol. Whenever this occurred the ring had two nights. The long night when its back was to Sol, and the shorter night as the far side of the ring fell in Earth's shadow. The event also created a days-long eclipse on the far side of the earth as the ring obscured Sol.

The nature of the ring, combined with the fact that in a place where people travelled hundreds of kilometers in minutes, time zones were unused. This meant that it was 2164 everywhere on the ring, no matter if it was night or day.

Jessica could never get used to it. Sleeping during the day, night, morning, whatever; it messed her up every time. She missed Athabasca. It was too far north to catch shadow from the ring and had proper days and nights, and regular seasons, unlike the mild winter/summer shifts of just a few degrees on the ring.

It made her itch to be back on Earth. Hell, it looked so close, hanging above her. She felt she should be able to reach out and touch it. However, she had another itch that needed scratching and there was just one way to get that done.

Her groundcar was nearby, ostentatiously sitting in a no-parking zone, its TBI identifier keeping it from getting disabled and towed. She slipped into it and sent a command over the Link, instructing it to take her home; time to get out of this armor and into something a lot more—or maybe less—comfortable.

The ring was in its 'winter' phase, which meant that nighttime temperatures would get as cold as twelve degrees Celsius. Jessica wasn't about to let her fashion be a slave to temperature and wore a tight purple halter dress that didn't cover much more than a long shirt would into the club

The dress interfaced with her neuro-mods and slow patterns of shifting violet hues flowed across its surface. She altered their pattern to flow toward the front of the dress and then down suggestively.

Covering her feet and most of her legs were a pair of tall boots made of the same material. They ended half way up her thighs, appearing to simply merge with the skin on her legs as was the current style.

With a toss of her hair she walked onto the club floor and began to perform what could only be considered to be a mating dance. At least she certainly hoped it could only be taken as such. Sex, preferably something kinky and steamy, was her only priority tonight. Myrrdan, the murders, the whole damn case; all of that could—no, would—wait until tomorrow.

Jessica knew her body was irresistible, she had paid a lot of money to make certain of it. Her elongated legs combined with the heels of her boots made the proportion to her torso just shy of cartoonish. Her breasts were not too large, but certainly bigger than her natural size.

She ran her hands down her sides, nearly wrapping them around her fifty-centimeter waist, before caressing the smooth curve of her hips.

That had been one of the more costly modifications because of the spinal reinforcement and alterations to her digestive tract—namely the removal of most of it—to get everything to fit right. Her hips had needed a bit of a change as well to make the curve from her narrow waist soft and smooth.

Other than her hair, which 'naturally' grew blue, her only other external modification was a slight narrowing of her hands, the effect made her fingers look exceptionally slender and nimble.

It was a body made to attract sexual partners. It even attracted her. Jessica had to admit that she often got off on herself more than her mates. There was just something about the crafting of her own form to be a sexual icon that excited her to no end.

She knew it wasn't an entirely normal response to have. TBI psychologists had recommended she alter her brain chemistry to have a standard sexual response—it probably would have been cheaper than all of the alterations to the rest of her body, but why would she want to do that? She *liked* the way she was.

Her dancing hadn't taken long to attract the attention of the opposite sex, and no small number of the same sex. She looked them over, sliding herself close to one or another from time to time.

A man was eying her from the bar. No, he was blatantly staring. He was pivoted on his seat, the drink behind him long forgotten. His eyes bored into hers and he didn't even glance down at her body. That was unusual to say the least.

His clothing was black, all black. It appeared to be some lightly textured polymer, close in appearance to natural leather. The jacket fit loosely around his large torso, and the pants were tight on the thighs and crotch, showing he had something to offer down there. She could only imagine his ass would be fantastic as she sashayed across the floor toward him.

Seeing that she was interested, he gestured to the seat beside him, rising as he did so. His eyes were black; not entirely, but close enough that without her own modified peepers she wouldn't have been able to tell in the dim light of the club. His hair was also black; falling down to his shoulders with a slight wave that led her to believe it could be natural.

She reached the bar and sat, taking a moment to make sure her dress was pulled down far enough so as not to give the entire club a view of her nether regions. She may be on the prowl, but she wasn't quite *that* lascivious.

"Jessica." She said by way of greeting. She already knew his name was Alex, courtesy of a quick ID lookup on the TBI database.

"I'm Alex." He offered her his hand and she shook it firmly. It wasn't the most demure thing to do, but she couldn't bear a weak handshake, especially not from her own hand.

"I couldn't help but notice your stare, Alex. Would you care to come out on the dance floor?" She gave a seductive smile and altered her dress to swirl patterns around her breasts.

"I would, but I don't think I could match your moves. I'd be Pluto to your Sol."

Jessica couldn't help but grimace slightly at the forced astronomical humor.

She turned and faced the bar, eyeing the bottles lined up in front of the holo display. "Then I suppose we should have a drink."

"What would you like?"

"I like the Nebula Margarita they serve here." Her tone was offhand.

The man waved the bartender down and ordered two.

"So what do you do for a living?" Alex asked.

She knew what he was thinking. He supposed she was a bimbo executive assistant, or some other sort of window dressing. Her body and clothing certainly told no other tale. Of course, that was the message she tried to send, no reason to scare potential partners off.

"I'm an administrative assistant for the VPs in a business near here." It was code for eye candy and occasional sex toy as there was no need to have a human perform any administrative tasks when an AI or even simple non-sentient software could do a better job.

Normally such a lie wouldn't work—it was too easy to find out everything about a person from a quick facial scan. Working for the TBI had its advantages—Jessica had bribed several techs to ensure that her job never came up when she was on the hunt.

The drinks arrived and the conversation proceeded down a rather predictable path. Before long they were checking into a nearby hotel. She followed him down the hall to the room, admiring the way his shoulders pushed against the jacket. God, she hoped he was modified, nothing like a man who knew where to enhance himself to turn her on.

Once in the room he tossed his jacket on a chair and they wrapped their limbs around each other, Jessica taking a good look at his ass in the mirror—every bit as delicious as she'd hoped. She gripped it hard and bit at his neck, the other hand feeling the rippling muscles on his back. He had to be enhanced, there was no way a man could have shoulders this perfect on a natural body.

He pulled away from her and removed his shirt, displaying an absolutely perfect chest, pecks just the right size, with dark nipples at the tips. When he lifted his arms over his head to pull the shirt off and toss it aside they tensed up just right and sent a quiver through her loins.

His stomach was tight as well, a slight trail of hair descended under his pants, leading down to a promise she couldn't wait to have in her hands. She looked up to his face and saw that he had been following her eyes. He glanced down at her body and quirked an eyebrow; she knew what he wanted to see.

Pivoting her hips seductively, she placed her hands on her shoulders and slipped them under the straps of the dress. Slowly, but fast enough to keep his attention, she raised her arms, sliding the straps off her shoulders. With a twinkle in her eyes she lowered it past her breasts one at a time, stretching the dress tightly over them as she did so to make them bounce when they broke free.

His eyes were devouring her now, and she slid the dress down further, revealing her own perfect abs before pulling it past her hips and letting it fall to the floor. She wasn't wearing anything under the dress; other than her boots she was now totally naked.

"Like what you see, Mr. Dark and Mysterious?"

His grin was somewhat predatory. "Yes, very, very much."

He stepped up to her, and pushed his groin into hers, their legs interlaced. His hands ran down her sides, over her hips, and traced their way between her legs before coming back up to cup her breasts.

"Get on the bed."

She smiled, throwing a mock salute. "Yes, sir, Mr. Sir."

Jessica sat down, and then lay back, using her long legs to push herself further onto the bed, the spike heels of her boots digging into the blankets. "You gonna come down here, or do I have to come get you?"

"Oh, I'll be there," Alex said. The look in his eyes had changed slightly. It was a tiny shift, from excitement caused by lust to excitement from control and power. She would have to watch him, make sure he didn't get carried away.

He turned to his jacket and reached inside for something. Jessica's hackles rose, but they were a moment too late. When he turned back he had a sonic beam pistol aimed at her.

Sonic beam pistols weren't fatal if a person was only shot once or twice. However, even one shot at a heavily modded person would make them wish they were dead.

"What the fuck is this?" Jessica asked. "This your idea of a kinky little game?"

Alex smiled. The lust was gone; it was all a power trip for him now.

"No, though you do look damn fine. I'd love to screw your brains out, but you're way too dangerous to get that close to now."

"Next time do a girl a favor and fuck her before resorting to gunplay."

He chuckled. "I'll keep that in mind." He tossed her a set of ES shackles. "Lock these on your wrists, ankles and neck.

Jessica pouted. "Think you could put the gun down and we could use these for fun?"

He didn't say a word, but his look spoke volumes. A gesture with the gun got her moving and she locked the shackles on the indicated locations. Nothing connected them, but they would lock together once activated.

"This is going to be a little uncomfortable," he grinned. So he did enjoy this sort of thing. The shackles were probably from his personal collection.

She felt the shackles begin to pull her limbs behind her back into a hog tie. Her neck arched back until everything met. He wasn't lying. It really did hurt.

"So, uh—" Jessica had to pause for air "—why exactly are you doing this?"

"I guess you'd like to know that, wouldn't you?" Alex sat in a chair and Jessica squirmed on the bed to see him. She was trying to ignore the fact that she was completely naked and the arching of her back made her breasts stand out like stretched cones.

"I kinda would, yeah."

"Well, you've managed to make an enemy who has decided to take you off his tail. I'm sure you know who I'm speaking of."

"Of whom I'm speaking," Jessica said.

"What?"

"You shouldn't end a sentence in a preposition. I don't care what they say, it's just not proper."

Alex snorted. "I really don't think you get to say what's proper or not. You're one of the most improper people I've met."

"Touché." Jessica sighed. "So what's the plan? Wait for me to cramp to death?"

"Well, I'm supposed to kill you, but I want to take a bit of time to enjoy the image in front of me."

She knew who wanted her dead, it had to by Myrrdan. She hadn't pissed anyone off enough lately to go to these lengths other than him. Of course she did need to get free, apprehend, or maybe just kill Alex and then get Myrrdan.

"Take a good look; it's the last beautiful thing you'll ever see."

A fleeting look of concern passed over Alex's fantastic features before it turned to derision. "You don't think you're going to get out of this—you're sorely deluded."

"Well...I don't know what you were thinking regarding my Link." Jessica smiled sweetly.

"What do you mean? The ES cuffs disable your wireless net access."

Jessica laughed, and then choked as the collar pulled at her neck. "Ughl...that's uncomfortable. I think Myrrdan doesn't like you as much as he doesn't like me."

Alex looked concerned now; this time the expression didn't fade. "Myrrdan? The serial killer?"

"Yeah...he's the one that set this up. You'll go to jail and I'll just be humiliated. Better than dead, I think." Jessica tried to look smug, but imagined that she was failing in her current predicament.

"I don't get it. How are you thinking you'll get out of this?"

"I can only imagine that Myrrdan failed to mention that I'm TBI. I have a low band, high power backup connection. Your new jailers will be here any moment."

"Aw fuck." Alex got up from the chair and pulled his shirt back on and then picked up his jacket. He looked down at her and Jessica knew he was weighing whether to leave her, kill her, or take her as a hostage. Hostage was pretty dangerous. Jessica knew over three hundred ways to kill a person with her bare hands. Killing her would make the manhunt that much larger, that much faster. Letting her live was safest. He had to be assuming she had sent his information over the Link, so he was as ID'd as he was going to get.

He turned from her, apparently deciding to go with the latter of the options. Jessica smiled, knowing what he was in for as he opened the door. He pulled it wide, directly into the muzzle of an assault rifle.

Alex's hands flew up and he backed into the room. Two SWAT officers in full powered armor stepped through the entrance, weapons trained on Alex. They were followed by Agent Rogers, who glanced down at Jessica and smirked before looking to Alex.

"Transfer the cuff control to me."

Alex appeared as though he was going to argue the point for a moment, but one of the SWAT officers leaned forward and tapped the muzzle of his rifle against the would-be assassin's head.

"I'd do like the man says."

Alex nodded and a moment later Rogers turned to Jessica and the cuffs released.

"Oh god…it hurts almost as much to straighten out." She stretched her legs and rolled onto her back, breathing deeply for a few moments before sitting up. "He's got a pistol in his jacket. Don't know what else."

Alex smiled innocently and pulled the pistol out.

"We were just having a bit of fun. Lady there likes this sort of thing, I mean look at her, she's built for fucking."

Rogers smirked. "Don't I know it. Doesn't mean you're on the up and up. You've assaulted, kidnapped, and threatened an agent of the TBI. You, my friend, are going away for a long time."

Jessica got up and slipped her dress back on while the SWAT officers cuffed Alex and led him out of the room.

"Little escapade gone wrong?" Rogers asked her.

"No, he was sent by Myrrdan to take me out of the picture."

Rogers chuckled. "I guess he found your Achilles heel."

"I'm never going to live this down, am I?"

"Doubtful."

She gave Rogers her most seductive look. "Think we could make a deal?"

He laughed and slapped her on the shoulder. "You may be the most sexed up agent in the TBI, but my wife is ten times more dangerous than you. Nothing you have is worth it."

Jessica pouted for a moment before turning off her sensuality. "Fine, Mr. All Business."

"You're not going to like what happened while you were playing with bondage boy," Rogers said as they walked out of the hotel room.

"What's that?"

"We think Myrrdan left High Terra. Every lead we've been following for the last day has been a red herring."

Jessica swore. "Where did he go?"

"We're not sure; there are a number of possible transports he could have left on. Maybe Cruithne, maybe Mars."

"What's our next move?" Jessica ran a hand through her hair, feeling like the night had gone from good to bad to really bad.

"Section chief has you on the next transport to Cruithne."

Her expression brightened. "Really? I hear they've got some amazing clubs there."

Rogers sighed. "You didn't get laid first tonight, did you?"

CRUITHNE AGAIN?

STELLAR DATE: 3227238 / 10.12.4123 (Adjusted Gregorian)
LOCATION: Cruithne Station
REGION: InnerSol, Sol Space Federation

Cruithne used a tether docking system. It made for a much smoother transfer of vector and gravity between the ship and the station. Larger ships could not be easily tethered, but smaller vessels like the *Ardent Dawn* were designed with the system in mind.

Jessica had only a minimal appreciation for the system as she arched her head back and screamed in ecstasy. Moments later the man below her shook in the throes of his own orgasm and clawed at her shoulders.

He probably wanted to breathe. She loosened her grip on his neck and he spent a minute gasping for air.

Looking down at his puffing cheeks she realized that she didn't even know his name—looked it up—Steve, apparently. Not bad for a Steve.

"We're docked. Get to your cabin, I need to clean up."

He started to say something, which she ignored, sliding off him with smooth precision. The quarters were small and two steps put her in the san unit where she slid the door shut to his entreaties.

Three weeks on this tub—she had nearly run out of men. The crew was off limits after the captain had to step in on an incident, apparently playing the male crewmembers against one another was verboten.

Captain was a bitch anyway.

Out of the san, she was glad to see that Steve was gone. She stood for a moment, trying to decide between uniform or armor.

Cruithne was the dark underside of InnerSol—well, the best-known dark underside at least. If it was smuggled, stolen, pirated, or just plain illegal, it passed through Cruithne. She was certain it was some sort of unwritten underworld rule.

Though the asteroid-turned-station was part of InnerSol and fell under Terran jurisdiction, the law's reach here was limited. A very old family owned Cruithne and had ties with all the right people. Those ties let them get away with pretty much anything they wanted.

Jessica chose the armor—slipped into it after a trip back to the san for a full purge—and gathered up her belongings and dumped them onto a follower. The bot lifted off the ground and prepared to trundle after her.

With nothing onboard other than what was already on the bot, she was able to take the no-cargo umbilical. A quick pause at customs and she was into the main departure area of the Terra wing of Cruithne.

Across the space was a member of the Cruithne Police Force, one Captain Clyde according to Jessica's HUD. However, the TBI liaison agent that her dossier listed was nowhere to be seen, not particularly surprising from what she knew of the local office's track record.

Jessica established a connection to the local TBI dock and was cordially informed by the administrative NSAI that her liaison would be an AI by the name of Angharad, who was currently unavailable.

If an unavailable AI wasn't the strongest, most non-violent way to say, "You're not welcome," Jessica didn't know what was. She filed it away in her mental 'people to mess with later' category.

She approached the CPF officer and extended her hand.

"Special Agent Keller."

"Captain Clyde." The response contained not a drop of emotion. The woman could have been reading a serial number off a firearm.

"I assume that you have been briefed on my reason for being here." Jessica had no problem driving the conversation forward.

"I have. I will be your liaison with the CPF, the local TBI office will not be taking an active role in this investigation."

Jessica got the impression that they didn't take an active role in much of anything, unless looking the other way was considered an action.

"We'll need to stop at our main station. You will need to turn in your weapons and armor there." The CPF captain's tone still contained no tone, not even a hint of challenge. If Jessica didn't know better she would suspect that the woman was an automaton.

"You're aware that Cruithne is in Terran space?" Jessica asked.

The officer's face finally flickered with annoyance, her first sign of emotion.

"I am."

"Good." Jessica smiled. "Then I'm certain you just had a mental lapse when you suggested that I disarm."

The CPF captain didn't respond for a moment and Jessica widened her stance, subtly shifting into a more threatening posture.

She knew Cruithne largely operated without Terran oversight, but this was ridiculous. If this cop thought she was going to walk unarmored in the most dangerous station in InnerSol she had another thing coming—and it would be a very, very unpleasant thing.

"We'll still need to register your weapons, then."

Jessica gestured broadly. "Lead the way."

The captain turned with a not-so-subtle roll of the eyes—Jessica was going to get on famously with this cop.

Cruithne was everything the vids said. It was both fantastic and decrepit. Certain systems and visible portions of the station were plainly archaic, but a glossy sheen of new construction and technology had been laid overtop. It made her wonder how solid the aging station really was.

They were passing rows of shops, eating establishments and the more upscale lodgings, all catering to the Terran clientele, posh and polished. The people were all fairly vanilla, slightly more interesting than the streets and corridors of Raleigh, but only marginally so. Here and there a fairly serious mod-job would hover or roll by, but for the most part it was people using their own legs for locomotion.

Jessica was behind Captain Clyde by a pace or two and took the time to examine the woman's gait for evidence of modification. The woman wore the standard CPF uniform, a close-fitting mesh of ballistic impact material with ablative panels over crucial areas. She didn't have a helmet with her. Either the captain hadn't pissed anyone off lately, or she was paid up with all the protection rackets. Or she was a major player and no one would mess with her.

Jessica had originally been more bothered by the lack of a TBI liaison and she hadn't dwelled on the significance of a captain meeting her at the docks. In the CPF there was only one rank above captain. This made Clyde a senior officer.

Normally such an assignment meant that they took the threat from Myrrdin seriously—in this case Jessica suspected the CPF was more concerned with her than another murderer running around on their station. As long as he didn't kill the wrong people he could probably play here as much as he wanted.

Jessica reined in her wandering thoughts and resumed her examination of Clyde. There it was, the telltale twist in the hips and shoulders that indicated extra-muscular strength enhancements and most likely skeletal alterations as well. Clyde would be a tough cookie and probably had internal armor as well.

Jessica would too if she were a cop in a place like Cruithne.

<I see you chose to take the path of greater resistance.> Angharad's communication came in over the Link Jessica had established with the TBI offices.

<If you've read my file I don't think it should surprise you.>

<I have, and it doesn't,> came the reply. Jessica couldn't tell if the AI was just being non-emotive, as many of them were prone to be, or if she was being hostile.

Probably hostile.

<Good, then we'll get on well. I assume you have no physical presence?>

"You'd be incorrect." The AI's voice sounded from behind Jessica—she hadn't heard any motion back there other than the general bustle of the crowd. Clyde turned—again displaying a small amount emotion—this time smug pleasure.

Jessica turned and the three formed a loose circle in the corridor, unconcerned with the obstruction to traffic they were forming, not that anyone looked like they planned on taking umbrage.

Angharad, though an AI, apparently chose to take her female gender choice seriously. Her white and blue frame was artistically designed, all curves and flares, the effect a combination of sensuality and menace. She wore no clothes, her body's skin being her only outer layer. It was perfectly smooth without a seam or crease, but Jessica picked up the signatures of several weapon systems.

Between the three of them they could probably reduce the whole corridor to a smoking ruin.

"Glad you could take the time to make an appearance." Jessica didn't bother with pleasantries—why waste them on an AI anyway?

"I was otherwise indisposed," Angharad replied.

"I can't imagine how," Jessica chuckled. Several amusing possibilities presented themselves to her.

"No, you probably couldn't." The AI's eyes seemed to flash.

"If we may be on our way?" Clyde asked. "I do have other things to do today."

"As do I, I need to catch a serial killer before he slips off your station."

"You aren't concerned that this Myrrdan will kill anyone on Cruithne?"

Jessica shrugged as they began moving again. "Either he kills the right people, in which case you won't care, or he kills the wrong people, in which case I'll probably applaud him and then you'll care about catching him."

"That's a dangerous sort of attitude to have on Cruithne," Angharad commented.

Jessica simply shrugged. She wasn't going to get in a pissing match with an AI.

The CPF station was standard fare. Jessica registered the magnetic signatures of her beam weapons and failed to disclose her ballistic sidearm holstered within a hidden compartment on her armor. They probably knew she had it, but no one brought it up. From there she requested access to the records of all incoming vessels from Terra and settled into her standard research pattern.

Both Captain Clyde and Angharad disappeared at that point. Jessica didn't know where they went and didn't really care. Just so long as they weren't standing over her as she worked. A desk in a corner of the detective's work area had been set aside and she had half a dozen holos up, all privacy locked making them only visible to her retina. It was likely that a large portion of the police here were on someone's pay—someone who would love to know exactly where the TBI agent from Terra was digging.

Three ships' arrival times fit within the timeframe required and two provided her with verified biometrics on each passenger. Not that such information was impossible to falsify, but the third ship wouldn't give her the time of day, making it the best place to start.

And best to start there in person. A TBI request over the Link was far less threatening than an armored agent at your airlock demanding answers—something that was her specialty.

An attempt to slip out of the station unnoticed failed and Captain Clyde appeared at her side as she walked past the front desk.

"Going somewhere, Agent Keller?"

"Just going to pay a visit to a ship in the docks," Jessica replied.

"Did you take the time to get a warrant?"

"I didn't realize a warrant was required to talk to people."

Clyde didn't respond for a few moments. "Just be careful what questions you ask."

Jessica didn't know exactly what to make of the statement and nodded before leaving. The CPF captain didn't follow her, something that actually made Jessica more nervous. If the captain didn't want to be present chances were that she wanted some sort of deniability.

While looking over the inbound ship records, Jessica had done some digging on Captain Clyde as well. She suspected that Myrrdan had paid Clyde off, but nothing turned up. As far as the official record was concerned, Clyde was the model officer—something that Jessica was sure was patently impossible on Cruithne. Clyde may as well have hung a sign above her head that said 'Corrupt Cop'.

The ship was berthed roughly seven kilometers from the station and Jessica looked up the fastest route on the station's net. She was surprised to see that there was no maglev on Cruithne. It looked like walking or station taxis were the only ways to get around. Several of the taxis had driven past on her walk with Clyde and Angharad. She decided not to chance it.

Jessica had to admit to herself that, while she thought she had 'seen it all' on High Terra, Cruithne had a whole new level of twisted and weird. She found herself alternating between horror, arousal, and morbid curiosity as she passed by the station's denizens.

She knew that she wasn't exactly stock either, but she highlighted her humanity. Obscuring it entirely or defacing it was not something she would ever consider.

Not for the first time, Jessica found herself wondering if this is what happened to people when they were too far removed from nature. Having grown up on Earth, Jessica was in the vast minority in the Sol system. Even with over a dozen worlds being fully terraformed in the system, most humans lived on rings and stations. A study she had recently read claimed that over ninety percent of humans in the Sol system had never even set foot on a world.

At least on High Terra there was an approximation of nature with hills, lakes and rivers, on places like Cruithne there wasn't even a single park.

It had to have an effect on people—make them not-people.

Jessica had tried to explain these ideas to her coworkers more than once, but none of them could take her seriously with her being the most modded in her team.

She knew it was incongruous. There were definitely two Jessicas. Even though her parents and friends back in Athabasca barely recognized her, she still related to them and appreciated their way of life. She also wanted to taste the high-octane life and see what was beyond regular humanity.

If it was represented by what was displayed around her then perhaps the final destination was not a place she wanted to see.

Then again there must be the promise of transcendence, of humanity becoming something more.

Wasn't that the promise that all this technology was supposed to bring?

Her musings were interrupted by her internal nav informing her that she had arrived at the ship's berth.

Cruithne berths were archaic to say the least. In newer stations and rings, ships passed through ES shielding and essentially landed on the station. Here they still docked a cargo hatch to the station and grapples held the ship in place.

There was even a line on the station's deck plate denoting where the ship's domain began.

The ship she was looking for was named the *Arimanthe* and its domain was guarded by a thing that was decidedly more mech than human. Jessica couldn't even determine its gender.

"Jessica Keller, I'm with the TBI and I need to speak to your captain," she addressed the hulk with authority, though she didn't expect to get anywhere.

"Captain doesn't want to talk to you," came the impassive response.

"We're not going to reach an agreement are we?" Jessica asked.

"Not unless you agree to go away," the hulk smirked—at least Jessica thought it was a smirk.

She checked the status of the warrant she had applied for, something she had decided to hide from Captain Clyde, and found that it had been signed by a district AI judge moments before.

"I have a warrant to view your manifests and logs, I will be entering your vessel now."

"You and what army?" The hulk asked.

"This army."

Jessica turned, surprised to see Angharad approaching with two security drones.

"I didn't think you wanted to get involved with this," Jessica said.

Angharad's steely visage showed no emotion. "I don't, but orders are orders. I guess someone cares enough about getting this Myrrdan guy to risk ruffling a few feathers over here."

The hulk gave the AI and security drones a long, considering look before acquiescing and calling the bridge.

"Captain'll see you."

The ship turned out to be a lot larger than Jessica expected, the two-hundred meter walk to the bridge took the pair of TBI agents past hold after hold of cargo, most of it likely black market.

The ship itself was in decent shape. The captain appeared to care for his ship and made sure the crew did too. Jessica assembled a mental map of the ship and where possible escape routes would be should the encounter turn ugly.

The hulk led them to the captain's office, just aft of the bridge, before returning to his post at the dock.

The portal slid open and Jessica entered, noting that Angharad entered behind her and remained there. Her attention was quickly consumed by the captain. The man was massive. Jessica estimated him at over two-hundred kilograms.

A walk-in clinic could solve his weight issue in a day, which meant he actually wanted to be as large as he was. Jessica couldn't figure out what that said about him, but it certainly was well outside of normal.

"Hello, I'm agent Keller and this is Agent Angharad," Jessica offered both introductions and her hand.

The man leaned back and folded his arms behind his head. "What can I do for the TBI today?"

Jessica smiled, the man wanted to do the information dance. She was more than happy to oblige him. In her experience suspects gave away more than they held back when they tried to be evasive.

"We just thought perhaps you were lonely and wanted some company. Cruithne is sometimes an unwelcoming station," she replied.

"Lonely on Cruithne?" The captain laughed and Jessica had to force herself not to stare at how his flesh rippled. "There is more company here than anywhere in Sol. I don't think I'd need to stoop to the TBI for that."

"What about in the black? What sort of company do you keep then?" Jessica asked.

"The crew and I play a lot of cards; I'm sure you have played a hand of poker around a commissary table in your day."

"I imagine you take passengers from time to time, I noticed you have more berths than it would take to crew this ship. I imagine they must entertain as well." Jessica filed away his use of the word commissary. Civilians usually called them mess halls or break rooms.

"We have," the captain nodded. "It's a nice bonus for the crew to fleece a few passengers in a game."

"Did you take any crew this past trip? I see you came in from High Terra just a day ago."

The captain's face fell, lined with sadness. "Unfortunately we did not. I wish we had as the cargo didn't earn us quite what we'd hoped."

"I'm sure you wouldn't mind showing me your manifests so that I may verify this and note it in my report."

Now they were getting to it, this is where excuses would be made and the warrant would have to be used. His reactions would likely tell her everything she needed to know.

"Now, Agent Keller, that is not something I like to give out to authorities. A lot of my customers prefer discretion, it's why they ship with me."

"I can imagine. Based on the dock master's records, you have hardly unloaded any cargo and none of your crew have gone on-station yet."

The captain nodded as she spoke.

Jessica continued. "Yet when I walked through your cargo holds I couldn't help but notice a lot of fresh scuff-marks from crates and other cargo. A cleaning servitor was also exiting a berth that appeared to be unused. It would seem to me that you have not reported all of your activities. Now provide me with your full manifests."

The captain grumbled and leaned over his desk. He began assembling the data on a sheet of plas. Jessica expected it to be entirely falsified and when the captain completed the document she sat across from him to examine it.

"This seems to back up what you're telling me, Mr. Swenson, but it doesn't match the facts at hand." Jessica locked eyes with the man and saw worry creep into his.

She wasn't surprised. From what she could gather about the way things ran on Cruithne the law didn't dig any deeper than it had to. If a manifest was needed, it was provided and accepted. So long as all of the right people were suitably compensated.

From the way Angharad shifted behind her, Jessica wondered if she was one of the compensatees.

"You see, I know how much fuel you took on before you left High Terra and your vector and boost are on record. I also know what your fuel situation was like when you arrived on Cruithne. This manifest"—she waved the plas in front of him—"doesn't match up."

"Your calculations are off, maybe you need a lesson in space travel." The captain was blustering now, unprepared to have to defend himself further. She saw his eyes dart to Angharad expectantly.

Jessica's voice rose in volume as she spoke and by the end she was standing with hands on the captain's desk. She leaned over, her face inches from his.

"I do not need a lesson, certainly not from you. You forget that High Terra makes its mass compensation data available to the TBI. We know how much your ship weighed when you left, and I was able to request the tether load data when you docked here. I know what your ship weighed when you arrived. I also got the mass compensation data for right now and I know you transferred more cargo than you have on this manifest."

"Now give me the real manifest!" she yelled.

There was a moment of silence, the captain appeared shocked before an expression of smugness fell over him, and Jessica felt a hand on her shoulder.

"Agent Keller, it is time for us to leave, you have what you came for," Angharad said quietly.

Jessica turned to the TBI AI.

"Why am I not surprised? I figured you for dirty from the get-go. I have a warrant and I intend to execute it. I will search this ship's computers until I find out precisely who was here and what they brought onboard."

The AI's face was impassive. "You will not. You will leave this ship with me now and file your report with the manifest you have." The security drones shifted to either side of her, flanking Jessica. "If you do not, you will find yourself returned to High Terra in a most unconventional manner."

Jessica looked back at the smiling captain and snatched the plas from his desk. "Very well, let's go."

Jessica's mind raced as she tried to think of a way to stop Angharad. She tried Net access only to find it was blocked; a call for help would go nowhere—not that Jessica thought anyone would answer. The AI and her drones would be hardened to EMP and a pulse rifle would not disable them quickly enough. Her options were decidedly limited.

Her mind raced and she took a deep breath to calm herself. There had to be a way out of this. If she didn't get the real manifest from this captain she would have to go back to High Terra empty handed.

It was no easy task. Even without her two security drones, Angharad would be nearly impossible to defeat. The small voice of rationality in Jessica's mind screamed that she was a fool to consider confrontation with the AI.

She thought through the route back to the station. There was a narrow hatch where they would have to file through one at a time. Jessica determined to make her move there.

As they approached the hatch, one of the drones moved ahead of Jessica and passed through first. She followed it through and in a swift motion dove to the right of the corridor and swatted the drone into the bulkhead. Her armor's power assist gave her the strength to seriously damage the drone and embed it into the side of the corridor.

The next drone was racing through the hatch as Jessica dropped to the deck and fired three shots from her ballistic sidearm into the drone. It fell in a shower of sparks and Jessica pointed her weapon at the portal.

Angharad was there with a pulse rifle drawn. Jessica and the AI stared at each other in silence before Jessica spoke.

"I'd lower that if you know what is good for you."

"That is good advice," Angharad replied. "Your handgun can't stop me like it did those drones."

"And your pulse rifle isn't going to get through my armor any time soon."

"The crew will be here any second, surrender."

Jessica didn't move for a moment, but then lowered her weapon.

"Very well, we'll do this your way."

Angharad gestured with her rifle and Jessica began to rise. She twisted to get an arm underneath herself and quickly kicked out a leg. A hidden compartment on her shin slid open and a plasma wand shot out.

The wand flew through the air and caught a startled Angharad under the chin, embedding itself to the hilt. Jessica reached for her sidearm and fired several shots into the AI's head—blowing it off in a shower of sparks.

AI didn't keep their brains in their heads, so it was not a fatal wound, but it did cause the construct to topple over. Jessica grabbed Angharad's pulse rifle and fired several shots into her exposed neck. The AI's body convulsed for a moment before falling still.

Jessica scanned the corridor. The sound of footsteps came from the ship's entrance, likely the hulk coming to finish what Angharad had failed to do.

She quickly stood and tore open the side of the drone embedded in the wall. Sure enough there were several small concussive stun grenades in a launcher. She grabbed two and lobbed them down the corridor as the man came into view.

The grenades worked as advertised and he went down in a heap. Jessica turned and raced back toward the captain's quarters, reloading her sidearm on the way.

The expression on the captain's face was priceless as she used another of the grenades to disable his door-lock before crashing through.

"Now, where were we?" Jessica asked.

The captain's bluster was gone and within minutes she had the real manifests. There was a veritable treasure-trove of illegal cargo, but no Myrrdan, not even cargo that could have concealed Myrrdan.

Cruithne was a dead-end.

She had the captain order the crew to quarters and walked him to the dock, half as a prisoner, half as a human shield.

Captain Clyde was waiting for her.

"You've got guts, I'll give you that," the captain said with a hint of a smile on her face. "Folks don't usually ruffle feathers like this on their first day."

"What can I say?" Jessica said. "I didn't like the way he looked at my breasts."

A ghost of a smile played at the edges of Clyde's mouth. "Hand him over to us, and a copy of whatever evidence you have. We'll see that he's dealt with."

Jessica wondered if he'd be dealt with for his crimes or his failure to keep control.

"What's left of Angharad is also on the ship. You'll want to clean that up and send her back to High Terra."

Clyde's eyes widened. "Really? She's one tough customer, but it means your time on Cruithne is over."

Jessica had suspected as much. Angharad had to be connected at the highest levels. Whoever she reported to would not be happy and would be quite unwelcoming. Clyde must be beholden to someone else—or maybe really be an honest cop on Cruithne.

"No problem. Any ships headed to Mars?"

CHASING MYRRDAN

STELLAR DATE: 3227239 / 10.26.4123 (Adjusted Gregorian)
LOCATION: Mars Outer Shipyards (MOS)
REGION: Mars Protectorate, Sol Space Federation

Jessica was developing a strong distaste for space travel. Before this assignment the furthest she had been for work was Luna with a couple of vacations on Venus.

Those trips had been on commercial liners with all the comforts of home. Her precipitous exit from Cruithne had put her on a scow without any passenger amenities and a distinctly limited supply of sexual partners.

Customs was a brief affair. Mars, though it had a semi-autonomous military and security forces from Terra, was more than willing to cooperate with the TBI and its agents. Jessica was on a maglev within half an hour of arriving on the Mars1 ring.

She couldn't help but admit that there was a certain charm to the Mars1 ring that wasn't immediately apparent on the vids. The passage outside her train was a large, vaulted corridor featuring art-deco accents. She had never seen anything like it on High Terra with its function over form styling.

The rivalry between High Terra and Mars1 had been going on for centuries. Mars1 was the original planetary ring, but High Terra claimed superiority in all areas. The two rings competed in every way from design to political clout to sporting events.

The maglev rose up to the top level of the ring and she was amazed at how much open space the ring had. High Terra was more urban than not, while Mars 1 was almost entirely parkland. From what she could see there were raw wildernesses on the ring.

The maglev continued to rise above the surface of the ring and the train accelerated to over a thousand kilometers an hour before giving a slight jolt as it flew out into open space. The local web indicated that the train would accelerate toward Mars and skirt the exosphere before using its own velocity to escape and arch toward the far side of the ring. It was a bit disconcerting to essentially be in a train floating through space, but it did shave over twenty-thousand kilometers off the trip.

Jessica spent the trip alternating between dozing and reviewing her leads on Myrrdan.

During the trip to Mars she had learned that Myrrdan had been spotted on the Mars1 ring and later on the Mars Central Elevator Exchange. A contact in Mars Intelligence had placed Myrrdan there via a tap on communications in and out of a front that sold false identities.

Mars Intelligence had managed to work out a common signature the identities used and had tried to track their use but were stymied when the IDs started popping up in use all over the MCEE and Mars1.

If Myrrdan had secured one or more of the IDs he was covered by a seemingly random pattern of use. At least random to Mars Intel.

Jessica had been after him for over a year and was beginning to get a feel for his games. He could only feint so many times before the feints showed the true action rather than hiding it. Suspects always gave away more information when they got clever in their attempts to be elusive.

The pattern here was the same as the one she had followed on High Terra. That time it led her to Jameson and a dead end. The same patterns were at play here—but this time she could see the dead ends for what they were.

If her hunch was correct he was headed to the Mars Outer Shipyards and now so was she.

The maglev train would intercept one of the elevators that rose up from Mars1 to the MCEE and from there she could catch another train that would take her up the stalk to the Mars Outer Shipyards.

Other than some amazing views, the trip was uneventful—though when she stepped out onto the station platform she was surprised about the level of security on the MOS. What was more interesting was that, in addition to station security, she saw a few MSF and even TSF uniforms.

A quick scan of local news sources informed her of the colony ship *Intrepid* and its various security issues. Jessica found herself wondering if perhaps Myrrdan was trying to sneak aboard the colony ship, or if it was coincidence.

It would be the easy conclusion, but with the colony ship being constructed, there were hundreds of freighters at the shipyard at any time, not to mention several TSF frigates under construction at the far end of the shipyard.

Jessica decided to head for the stationmaster's offices to see if she could get direct access to the records for the ships under construction to see if anything stood out.

Getting directions on the local net she discovered that she was roughly a hundred kilometers from the stationmaster's offices—which was more of a complex than an office. She managed to wedge herself into a crowded connecting train, glad that she had decided to send her armor directly to her lodgings.

As the train accelerated and gently jostled its passengers, Jessica felt a sharp prick in her left shoulder. Reaching up to rub it she couldn't help but gasp as her eyes locked with what had to be her quarry.

Myrrdan!

The time it took the woman standing over Jessica to respond seemed like an eternity. There didn't seem to be a connection to the broader shipnet, but the localnet had an identifier and a date. She was on the *Intrepid,* likely many light years from Sol.

"Yes it is." The woman's expression appeared compassionate; she seemed to expect confusion.

Jessica's subconscious took in the fact that the woman standing over her wore a TSF uniform and the insignia of a lieutenant colonel, but where there should be a TSF badge, there was an icon which have represented the *Intrepid*. She looked young, but had an air of command about her that said she had earned that rank the hard way.

Her conscious mind, on the other hand, was roiling with the knowledge that she was on a one way trip to a colony she never wanted to see—her career, her life, everything she had worked so hard for was gone.

All because of one man.

She realized the woman had started speaking.

"I'm Lieutenant Colonel Richards, we're not yet at the colony as we've had some problems. We were looking for people with specific skill-sets and your name came up. However, there's some issues with the data regarding how you got approved for the colony roster—so finding you raised questions, not answers. Can you help shed any light on this?"

"Myrrdan," Jessica muttered softly.

The woman raised a hand to her chin, looking thoughtful. "I recall hearing something about a terrorist on High Terra by that name."

Jessica sighed. "That's the one. I was on the team attempting to apprehend him. I followed him to the MOS, but he got the drop on me while I was hunting him down. Next thing I know I'm staring at you."

The colonel seemed nonplussed, but she did lean back and give Jessica an appraising look. Jessica took the time to slow her breathing and force her mind to calm.

"You don't think you guys could just pull over and let me out do you?" Jessica asked.

The other woman laughed. "I don't know if that would make my day simpler or a heck of a lot more difficult. The question on my mind, however, is before you were stashed on this ship in a stasis-pod, were you any good at your job?"

"Before I got stashed in this pod I would have said yes. My record is damn good, though you'll have to take my word for it—unless you brought along a lot of databases a colony ship would never need."

"I still have data about all personnel on the MOS while we were docked there, so I have a summary of your record. It says you were good, but there are a few annotations here and there."

Jessica chuckled, "I imagine there are, most of them are probably even true."

"I'm going to take you to the hospital get you all checked out—give you the opportunity to talk to someone about what happened to you and then we'll see what shakes out."

"Need to make sure I'm not booby trapped?" Jessica asked with a wink.

The colonel glanced at Jessica's ample bosom. "Something like that."

SUBVERSION

STELLAR DATE: 3241794 / 08.19.4163 (Adjusted Gregorian)
LOCATION: *GSS Intrepid*, Deck 42 officer's lounge
REGION: LHS 1565, 171 AU from stellar primary

"Do you think it's wise for us to meet like this?" Hilda asked while casting furtive looks around the empty room.

"Of course," her companion replied. "There is nothing strange about the two of us meeting in the open. We should behave as though we've formed a friendship. Officers of our rank meeting for drinks is nothing strange."

Hilda nodded and forced herself to relax. "What did you want to discuss?"

Her companion leaned back and took a sip of whiskey. "It's time for us to move beyond talking about stopping the *Intrepid*. We need to begin to take action."

Hilda shook her head. "I don't know how that is going to be possible. Colonel Richards has everything locked down tight. You should know that better than I."

"I know how to get around her security—that should be obvious," the other responded.

"I suppose you would," Hilda smiled slowly. "I assume you have a plan?"

"I do. We're going to need to get the first mate out of stasis for it to work. I'm going to need your help with that."

"I can't believe the colonel just shot him like that." Hilda's voice took on a bitter tone. "I've known Mick for a long time, the captain hand-picked the two of us for this trip. She could have reasoned with him."

The other nodded. "Yes, but you know how she works. Shoot first, second, and third. Maybe ask questions later."

Hilda snorted. "You can say that again. She's like a cold machine—maybe that's what happens when you have been altered as much as she has."

"Who's to say?" her companion shrugged. "Either way, we get Mick and then we'll stop the ship, take it to civilized space and stop this research."

The pair spoke softly for several minutes of the plan and how it would play out. A nano cloud shrouded their conversation, altering the sound-waves beyond to that of an innocuous conversation should anyone happen to listen in.

After Hilda left the other sat for several minutes, considering their next moves. Tanis was proving to be a larger complication than anticipated—though in retrospect that should not be a surprise. Removing Tanis was out of the question, she made the game much more interesting.

Who would have thought that so far from Sol there would be such an excellent opponent?

INTERLUDE

STELLAR DATE: 3241794 / 08.19.4163 (Adjusted Gregorian)
LOCATION: *GSS Intrepid*, Security Operations Center (SOC)
REGION: LHS 1565, 153 AU from stellar primary

"That didn't really get us anywhere," Tanis said. "I don't know if the fact that she was dumped on us by some fugitive makes her more or less likely to be a mole of some sort."

"I think a legitimate mole would be harder to find. Consider Collins. There was nothing at all to clue us in about him—except that he was a total ass. I can't imagine the same people did this hack job on Jessica. As soon as her record was accessed it threw up flags everywhere," Terry replied while rubbing her temples.

Tanis nodded. "You have a point, but it could be a way to throw us off."

"By making us more suspicious?" Ouri asked.

"Wheels within wheels…" Tanis sighed. "Well, I guess we'll see what the docs and the psych AI have to say. If she's clean, her unbiased, outside opinion could be really useful."

The other two women nodded.

"I have some other news." Terry flipped through some of the plas in front of her, finding a specific sheet. "There are a few folks in the colony roster that look a bit more suspicious now than they did before, but they're all still in stasis."

Tanis glanced through the records. All of the people listed had made more contact with Collins than would have been expected under normal conditions—though under normal conditions there wouldn't have been anything suspicious about it.

"I guess we keep them on the 'do not wake' list for now, then—none look like they have skills we'd need right now anyway."

Terry nodded. "Already done. I don't have anything else at present."

"I do have a few reports of a guy named Randall Erick causing some problems," Ouri said. "He's a drive engineer who got pulled out to help on the crews. He's been posting plans on the board for how to get to Sirius and then back to Earth. He's not exactly fomenting a mutiny, but he bears watching."

Tanis looked through the man's recent actions on the shipnets. "He has been a bit more vocal than you'd expect based on his past behaviors."

"A lot of things can make a person react differently out here," Terry commented. "Knowing that we're essentially just drifting through space for a hundred years, counting on 58 Eridani to pull us in, is a bit unnerving."

"No argument there," Ouri said. "Most of us planned on simply going into stasis in one star system, and then coming to in another."

Terry shrugged. "It doesn't feel much different than being out past Eros. Out there Sol was just another star, not a lot brighter than it is from here."

"I don't know that it's Sol, as much as the fact that there are no humans for light-years. Plus, with us heading between stars, no ship could boost out to us and then slow down without a star to loop around." Ouri's face was clouded with concern.

"I don't think there's that much to worry about," Tanis said. "If we had to—and were willing to—use the colony supplies we could practically build a second starship."

"We might have to." Joe entered the SOC's conference room and sat with the other security heads. "I've done some external visual inspections out there and its baaaaad."

"I was getting that from following the engineering solutions boards," Tanis said.

"Could we take the cruisers to New Eden if we had to?" Terry asked.

"Sure," Joe nodded. "The cruisers could get there and brake around the star no problem, but they don't have room for all the colonists."

"I wonder what the GSS crew are thinking," Amy said. "Most of them expected to spend about 90 years in stasis with a few years helping build the space station and beanstalk for New Eden. Some of them must be starting to have second thoughts about this trip."

"Interstellar travel isn't exactly safe as houses," Ouri replied. "Everyone knew when they signed up for the first re-usable colony ship that they might end up joining the colony."

Terry nodded. "I have a few GSS crew on my team. They went through full colony screening even though they really aren't signed up for it."

"They're certainly a group that will bear extra watching," Tanis said as she brought up the meeting's agenda. "I want to get the currently awake crew sorted out in two shifts. I have both Reddings after me now to thaw more engineers out and we can't even vouch for the ones that are."

The team dove into the logistics of wrapping up all of the crew assessments, deciding to bring additional AI help online and a few other crewmembers with investigative skills out of stasis.

The meeting wrapped up ten minutes later and Joe followed Tanis into her office.

"We haven't had much time together since getting back."

Tanis stopped and leaned against her desk. "Not a lot, no. Hard to believe we're so busy when we have over a hundred years to drift our way through space."

"Once we get the engineers all staffed up I imagine things will die down. Then maybe we can find a quiet corner of the ship again," Joe winked at her conspiratorially.

Tanis smiled back. "I bet there are a lot of free cabins in the cylinders right now. I think we've earned a bit of a sojourn."

He gave her a quick kiss. "I have to jet, though. My boss wants all the weapons on the ship manually accounted for and that includes fighter load-outs."

"I bet she can wait a bit longer for that," Tanis said as she pulled Joe close.

Joe chuckled. "Maybe you don't know her; she's a real hard-ass. She doesn't like it when things aren't done on her schedule."

Tanis gave Joe a long kiss as she ran her hands down his back. "What a task master. Doesn't she know you're a hero? You need to be rewarded."

Joe snorted back a laugh.

"What?" Tanis asked.

"Nothing, you just went a bit off the rails on that one. Not your best work there."

Tanis folded her arms and gave her best scowl. "She doesn't like to be antagonized, I thought you knew that."

"Sorry, boss-lady. I'll be less antagonistic next time." Joe ran a hand down her face. "But I really do have to go, I only have two fly-boys out of stasis and they're already down there counting rounds. I need to join them."

Tanis nodded. "Off with you then, say hi to Jens and Aaron for me."

"Will do," Joe said as he dashed out of the office.

Tanis linked to the psych AI that was examining Jessica.

<So what's the word?>

<Her TBI implant corroborates her story, from what I can tell she is telling the truth.>

Tanis detected some hesitation in the AI's mental tone. *<There's something else?>*

<I don't like the implication, but I think that someone has been deliberately overlooking some issues she has.>

<What do you mean?> Tanis asked.

<Honestly? She's a bit unstable. I'm shocked that the TBI let her operate like this.>

Tanis smiled grimly. She knew that the TBI had a habit of cultivating overly eccentric and aggressive behavior in some of its agents. Such agents could be used for dirty work and then discarded if things didn't go well.

The TSF had done a similar thing with Tanis, after all.

<Understood. When you're through with her, put her in touch with Bob for quarters near mine and get her on my team's duty roster.>

<Sir?> The AI seemed surprised.

<Sometimes, when dealing with the unknown, a little instability in your court can help flush out the enemy.>

Tanis closed the connection with the AI and leaned back in her chair. Being in the chair, in the SOC again, felt like failure. She should have been done with protecting the *Intrepid* from threats, she should be sleeping off the rest of the trip to New Eden.

<It's not your fault,> Angela said, gently reading Tanis's thoughts. *<Some things are beyond even your control.>*

Tanis snorted. "You know me too well, old friend. But you should also know that I won't absolve myself of the oversights that led us to this point."

<I know, but I'll still say it so that you don't forget that I, *at least, don't blame you.>*

"At least that makes one of us."

NEW ORDER

STELLAR DATE: 3241800 / 08.25.4163 (Adjusted Gregorian)
LOCATION: *GSS Intrepid*, Officer's Mess
REGION: LHS 1565, 171 AU from stellar primary

Tanis sat in the officers' mess with her team leads, which now included a newly minted Second Lieutenant Jessica. Despite the fresh set of eyes, they had made little progress in their investigation; all personnel had either come up clean, or close enough as to make no difference.

"Dead ends all around," Trist said as she picked through a salad. "I don't see signs of tampering in anyone's records. Nothing that my routines can pick up, anyway."

Amy nodded. "I haven't found anything with my team either. We've been locking down the weapons stores and so far everything is exactly where it's supposed to be."

"I've found a few small data errors, when comparing current information to the crystal backups we had at departure. I've traced them all to Collins, which I think is fortunate," Terry added.

Tanis took a bite of her BLT and chewed thoughtfully. "It has been only a week. On the MOS we often went months with nothing."

"So if there are any malefactors on the ship, then they only have twelve hundred months to choose from before we get to New Eden," Joe's mouth had a wry twist. "We're going to run ourselves ragged attempting to anticipate threats for that long."

"Not a bad tactic," Ouri said.

"You need to figure out how to bring out any sleepers who may still exist on the ship," Jessica said. "Like Joe says, looking under every rock will just reveal smaller rocks."

"Or there's no one else," Amy said. "I mean, who would stay on the ship after Collins aimed it at a star? I think maybe we're free and clear."

Tanis cast an appraising eye at Amy. Her attitude seemed overly nonchalant considering what the *Intrepid* had been through. If anything, they should be more suspicious than ever.

"Believe you me, girl, something is still rotten in the state of Denmark," Trist said. "Sue and I have been analyzing the attack patterns the RAI used when it had control of node eleven, as well as some of the data from the fights with servitors and security drones. From what we can tell it was too easy."

"Too easy?" Ouri's eyebrows rose. "I watched people die in those attacks."

Trist raised her hands. "I didn't say it was a cake-walk, but it was easier than it could have been."

"I know." Tanis nodded. "Its tactics were weak. Any one of use could have done better. The RAI should have assaulted the command deck with everything it had and destroyed key stasis chambers. But it did none of those things."

"Maybe it didn't have the access," Amy suggested.

"It did," Terry disagreed. "With Amanda in its thrall it had the power to get into any system it needed. It also had whatever net access and nano-control it wanted."

"It should have crushed us," Trist said.

No one spoke for several moments as the statement sunk in. If the RAI threw them a softball, then there was a chance that Collins wasn't behind it, but someone wanted them to think he was.

Jessica suddenly laughed.

"It's Myrrdan! He was on the MOS when you were building the ship. I always assumed that maybe he dumped me on it because he wanted me out of the picture, but respected me as a foe or something."

"Is that some sort of 'honor amongst enemies' thing?" Amy asked.

Jessica ignored her and carried on. "The thing is…that doesn't fit his M.O. He's not like that. For him it's all in the game. He dumped me here because he wanted to keep playing with me. He's here on the *Intrepid*."

Tanis raised an eyebrow. "That seems like a bit of a stretch."

"I don't know," Trist said. "The data model makes sense. He didn't want the *Intrepid* to fall into the star, because he's still here. But why? Is it some new challenge to mess with a colony ship, or does he actually want to get out to a colony?"

"It sure is a lot of effort either way," Amy shook her head. "Who would want to spend hundreds of years to mess with a ship of colonists?"

Joe and Tanis gave each other sidelong glances. They knew what it was that could interest a person like Myrrdan: the picotech.

Tanis looked away and noticed that Amy was giving her a funny look. Ever since her abduction by Collins the former Marine seemed cooler than ever. Tanis wondered if she felt guilt at being caught off-guard. If there was some sort of mental trauma at play perhaps a psych AI should talk to her.

"I think we need to take a look at the passes," Jessica said. "Some of those folks were just too clean. Everyone has something that they'd rather not talk about—some blemish on their record. Too many of the folks on your original list came up without so much as a late roll call. Myrrdan will be hiding in the best place—we just have to figure out what that best place is."

"We did recruit the cream of the crop," Ouri said. "Our roster is filled with exemplary people."

"Speak for yourself." Trist smirked. "But robo-doll-cop here does have a point. There are a lot of super-squeaky clean folks here. Makes me uncomfortable."

"I wish you'd stop calling me that." Jessica's face contorted into a sulk that didn't fit her manufactured sexuality.

"It's what you get for turning yourself into the obvious incarnation of the naughty police officer." Trist moved her hands in a curvaceous pattern. "Not that I'm complaining."

Jessica cast Trist an appraising look and Tanis sighed inwardly.

"Easy there, Jessica, no fraternizing with your teammates." Joe grinned.

Ouri coughed and nearly spat out her coffee.

"Don't play that game with me." Jessica leaned on the table, locking eyes with the commander. "Your fearless leader is more modified than I am by a long shot; she just hides it in a standard-looking package."

"You haven't seen the colonel in just her flow-armor then." Trist threw Tanis a wink.

"Dear god," Tanis murmured as she put her head in her hands. Jessica certainly seemed to bring out the lascivious behavior in the group. "None of us here are natural humans. Even Ouri, arguably the least modified among us, is nowhere near vanilla. We've all added hardware and tweaked the genes in our favor."

Joe snorted. "I didn't know Trist still had genes. I thought she was made out of green jelly now."

"That's *Miss* Green Jelly to you, mortal." Trist grinned.

"No hard feelings, Jessica." Trist clapped the former TBI agent on the shoulder. "We're just blowing off a bit of steam—not too often that we're stymied."

Jessica flashed a smile. "No problem. I might have to go back under the knife myself. These hips weren't made for bearing colony brats."

"No? Were they made for bearing Terran men?" Trist snorted and she laughed at her own joke. Jessica threw a carrot stick at her.

"I have to head up to the bridge to meet with the brass," Tanis said. "Can you guys determine if they ever caught Myrrdan in the Sol system? If the answer is no, if his sprees stopped when we left Mars, then we may have an answer to whether or not we have a stowaway."

"You got it," Ouri said. "Have fun with the big wigs."

Tanis wolfed down the last of her B.L.T. "I'm sure I will. I'm way more worried about my visit to Earnest's lab later today. He's going to figure out how to get the flow-armor out of my body before I exceed its patent timeouts and it self-destructs or something."

<I'm sorry about that…It did seem like a good idea at the time,> Angela said.

Tanis walked through the long executive corridor that led to the avatar's chamber. The desks and offices were sparsely populated as most of the crew pulled from stasis were still feverishly working on engine repairs.

Priscilla was still ensconced in her pedestal, her customary array of holo displays surrounding her as she managed hundreds of humans interfacing with the ship's nets. At the edge of the room Amanda sat at a small work station.

Tanis knew how Amanda felt. She'd been used and had hurt her shipmates. There was no worse feeling than knowing you had done things that there was no way to take back. The only thing she could hope for was time showing her that no one held it against her.

Well, almost no one, a few unfavorable opinions had been expressed on the solution boards. One conversation had gotten so out of hand that Bob ultimately stepped in.

Having a god-like AI explain how he had altered his Avatar's brains so they could no longer be subverted quelled the conversation. Though it spawned a few new ones.

"Good afternoon, Colonel," Amanda said with a wan smile as Tanis approached.

"Colonel?" Tanis asked. "When have you ever stood on rank?"

"Sorry." Amanda's mouth twisted. "I don't know who hates me right now; I'm trying to be extra cordial."

"I can promise you, I do not hate you, I'm not even mildly upset with you," Tanis gave Amanda a warm smile.

The off-duty avatar gave her a searching look.

"I don't understand, my abilities were used to attack you—five of your Marines died as a result!"

Tanis stepped through the holo displays and crouched in front of Amanda, taking her hands.

"None of us are perfect. We all get thrust into situations where we make the wrong choices, or have evil thrust upon us. If I were to condemn you for your failures, I would have to first condemn myself for mine." Tanis gave a warm smile. "Life is hard enough without us beating ourselves up."

"Thanks Tanis," Amanda said. This time her smile managed to reach her eyes.

"You coming or what?" Abby barked as she walked by. "Let's get this done so I can get back to work."

"Duty calls," Tanis said softly as she rose.

"We have a much less appealing name for her than duty," Amanda whispered with another smile.

Tanis walked down the hall to the conference room where Abby was already in full swing.

"I need to double my engineering staff pronto, or we won't be able to fire the engines in time to course correct for New Eden." Abby was almost yelling. "If we could take the time to get control of the machine shops again and build more bots it wouldn't be a problem, but the AI fried most of their control systems. Human hands are the fastest way to fix things now."

Tanis slid into a chair as unobtrusively as possible, not that she expected it to help much. Terrance and Abby were glaring at one another while Earnest twisted his hands and the captain looked extra stoic. Sanderson looked like he just wanted the yelling to stop.

"Major!" Abby directed the full force of her personality at Tanis who decided not to correct the engineer regarding her rank and did her best to maintain a neutral expression. "When are you going to lift your ban on more people coming out of stasis? I need at least two hundred more engineers yesterday!"

While Abby spoke she sent Tanis a projection over the Link, showing the time it would take to repair the engines, get the lithium processed and course correct.

It wasn't new data, Abby had been sending her updated projections nearly every hour for days. The window to fire the engines and course correct was down to six days.

"Out of the frying pan and into the fire," Tanis sighed.

"I think we already did that," Earnest said. "What's after the fire?"

"I don't want to know," she grimaced. "OK, we haven't found anything to cause alarm at the moment, other than the fact that Jessica Keller's presence confirms that we can't trust our roster of who is here. However"—she nodded at Abby—"we've vetted your list and each one is personally known to at least three other people currently out of stasis. Based on the data we have now, there's no reason other than raw paranoia not to bring them out of stasis."

Abby looked surprised and relief washed across Terrance's face. Tanis could tell that he had been backing her up, but was running out of arguments in the face of drifting in the dark forever.

"Well"—Abby stood—"there's no time to waste, then." She glanced at Earnest and the two left the bridge conference room.

Captain Andrews spoke first. "Do you really believe that it is safe to thaw more crew?"

"No more or less safe than the alternative as best I can tell. We have the ability to screen the number of people she wants to pull out, and we'll have to do it eventually, so now's the best time. To be honest, the thing I really wonder about is why Myrrdan dumped Jessica here."

"I followed that story back in Sol," Terrance looked concerned. "They suspected him of killing over ten thousand people, didn't they?"

"Give or take a few hundred," Tanis agreed. "Why did he dump her here? Why not just kill her? Also, if he could bypass all of our checks on the crew and colonists, then who else is here on this ship? Is it possible that even he is here?"

"That has been on my mind as well." Captain Andrews nodded. "There are a lot of places, and ways to hide on this ship. We should assume that either he is here, or he has secreted away more surprises for us."

<I've sent requests to AI I trust back in Sol to learn if Myrrdan was ever caught,> Bob added.

"Thank you, Bob," Captain Andrews said.

"Do you think it makes sense to keep Agent Keller thawed?" Terrance asked.

"Angela and I have had a lot of conversations about this—"

<By that she means that I've had to deal with her droning on and on about it.>

Tanis ignored the jibe and continued, "I think that if Myrrdan is here and has something planned, he wants Jessica to be here to see it. He wants to play the game against her. It's SOP for this sort of guy."

<If that sort of profiling really applies to someone like him,> Angela added.

"Either way, having her out and about is the best way to draw him out if he is thawed. If he's not thawed then we don't have anything to worry about at the moment."

Terrance laughed. "We still have plenty to worry about."

"Touché." Tanis nodded.

She looked at the remaining command crew around the table and asked what she was certain was on everyone's mind.

"We're more off course than Joe's initial plan called for. The time and the fuel we have are both tight. What if we can't fire to correct for New Eden?"

"Hilda and I have been going over that," the captain said as he brought up a holo display of the ten light years of space surrounding Estrella de la Muerte.

The *Intrepid's* position was denoted by a small green dot near the star's red one. A white line stretched out to the edge of the holo without intersecting any systems.

"You can see here that we're not pointed anywhere near New Eden; it will take a very long and hard burn to correct our course. Even correcting for Epsilon Eridani is not significantly better. If we can't get this burn done in time, we're looking at Kapteyn's Star or Gilese 229," Andrews said.

He gestured and the holo updated to show that a burn to correct for Gilese needed to happen within six weeks, while a burn to correct for Kapteyn's could happen any time in the next two years.

Tanis sighed. "Well, at least we have options."

"Options that add a hundred years to our trip." Terrance ran a hand across his eyes. "This trip just keeps getting more and more complicated."

Tanis found herself wondering, not for the first time, why Terrance was really on the *Intrepid*. His argument for building the new center for human commerce and power sounded good until one considered how much power he had wielded back in

Sol. He was a man who lived like a god. Why travel across human space to live like a god somewhere else?

Perhaps, under it all, Terrance was just as sick of where humanity was going in Sol as everyone else on the *Intrepid*.

"That's going to be a long detour, isn't it?" Tanis asked. "We'll have to decelerate, stock up, and then boost back out."

Captain Andrews nodded. "Obviously Kapteyn's is the preferred location because it's much closer. It's more massive too so it will make for a better slingshot when we boost out toward New Eden."

Tanis brought up the system's entry. "Not inhabited at all? That's surprising."

"Why colonize a red dwarf when there are places like New Eden cropping up?" Terrance asked. "I certainly wouldn't fund a mission there—even with its two super-earths."

"We have something else to go over." Andrews leaned back in his chair and smiled at Tanis. She saw that Sanderson and Terrance were looking at her and smiling as well.

"Uh... What's up?" Tanis asked with a nervous smile.

"We've been talking about the ship's command structure," Andrews began. "We're in a situation here that wasn't supposed to happen. Other than duty crews everyone was to have been in stasis during the trip. Now we have a mixture of crew and colony all doing crew work. We are also missing a first mate."

Tanis furrowed her brow. What the captain was saying was true, but there were several pre-vetted scenarios on the books for how to handle this re-org.

"We have to be honest with ourselves," Sanderson said. "This mission may play out very differently than originally planned. Even if we don't have to divert to Kapteyn's Star we're going to have a lot of colony and crew out of stasis working together for years. Back in Sol it was easy—everyone was hired by the GSS or on loan like the TSF until we passed out of the heliosphere."

Tanis nodded. "And if we do divert to Kapteyn's the trip will get so long that I bet a lot of crew won't care to go back to a Sol system where everyone they know has died of old age."

"You're correct," Andrews said. "As a result we're enacting the colony's charter now on the *Intrepid* and treating it as a sovereign nation. This will create a single crew and colony entity that will persist until the *Intrepid* heads back to Sol."

"Have you worked out the details?" Tanis asked with a frown. She was annoyed that her input hadn't been sought and wondered how this new structure would get in the way of her investigation.

"We have," Andrews said. "We didn't bring you into it because, honestly, you were doing something more important at present.

Andrews waved his hand and holo refreshed to display the ship's new organizational structure.

The captain was still the ultimate authority on the ship, also holding the title of Governor. Below him there was an executive officer—a transition from the civilian first mate structure of before. Under that person there were department heads and divisional officers. The security force of the *Intrepid* was re-designated as a police force, using much of the proposed structure for the New Eden colony, and an official military branch was created with a Marine and space-force division.

"I'm curious about the nature of the department of defense," Admiral Sanderson said. "Does it report through the XO to the captain? If so, I imagine that will be strange as the secretary of defense will outrank the XO."

Tanis wondered why he would think that, but from his tone she suspected he already knew the answer and was planting the question.

"We are going to have a number of situations like that throughout the ship's new organizational structure," Captain Andrews said. "They weren't uncommon with the GSS/TSF split we had before we left Sol. There may be adjustments we'll need to make, but here are the assignments as we see them now."

Tanis's mouth fell open when she saw her assignment. "I think you have it wrong… Maybe these two are switched," she said while pointing at herself and Admiral Sanderson on the chart.

"No mistake, General Richards," Sanderson said with a rare smile. "I expect to spend as much time as possible in stasis—I'd like to actually live a few decades on New Eden—the XO is going to spend a lot of time out of stasis. You're the right confluence of age and experience for the job."

Tanis was stunned. General.

<*Congratulations on the promotion,*> Angela said privately. <*Long overdue if you ask me.*>

"You've also proven an unwavering dedication to the ship," Terrance added with a nod.

"Thank you," Tanis said, reeling both from the promotion and the responsibility. Other discussions regarding rank and placement took place and Tanis noted Terrance's rather interesting title of Secretary of Colony Affairs—which meant his placement was still ambiguous.

Other than him, everything was quite clear. Abby was the Secretary of Engineering, Admiral Sanderson was the Secretary of Defense; below him Ouri was the police commissioner, Joe held the position of commandant of the space force and Brandt was commandant of the Marine Corps—both were promoted to Colonel. There was a secretary of health and of education and Bob was noted as the Secretary of the *Intrepid*—something that went without saying.

After the meeting, Tanis stood in the SOC beside Admiral Sanderson. All of the military and security personnel out of stasis were present physically or virtually while at their posts.

There were nods of understanding as she described the new organizational structure; when she announced that she had been designated the ship's XO applause and cheers broke out.

Tanis felt herself flush and gave an embarrassed glace at Sanderson who raised his hands for quiet.

"It's not all good news." His delivery was entirely dead-pan. "I've been designated as the Secretary of Defense, which means you all have one less layer of protection between me and you."

Joe laughed and called out, "We'll just go to your boss."

Tanis gave him a mock scowl. "There will be none of that, you. The purpose of this re-organization is to have a clear chain of command. However, Secretary Sanderson will be spending much of the trip in stasis to preserve his old bones. At those times, Ouri will be acting secretary and will report to me."

"Just like old times." Ouri smiled.

BECOMING > HUMAN

STELLAR DATE: 3241802 / 08.27.4163 (Adjusted Gregorian)
LOCATION: *ISS Intrepid*
REGION: LHS 1565, 185 AU from stellar primary

Tanis stood in the lobby outside of Earnest's laboratories.

While Abby made Engine her domain, Earnest spent most of his time here, at the very rear of the dorsal arch, with walls of windows facing out over the back of the ship.

The scale of the *Intrepid* never ceased to amaze Tanis. The fact that Earnest and his wife worked on the same ship, but were typically over sixteen kilometers apart, fascinated Tanis each time she thought of it.

There was a time in human history when a person may have never traveled more than sixteen kilometers from their home in their entire life. Now a starship encompassed a larger space.

"Even scuffed and bruised she's beautiful," a voice said from behind Tanis.

She turned to see Earnest standing behind her. The man spoke about the *Intrepid* like a darling child. There was passion and emotion in his voice that never came out at any other time.

While Abby viewed the *Intrepid* as a magnificent structure that she must maintain, Tanis could see that Earnest viewed it as a work of art, more his grand opus than even the creation of picotech.

"She's the most beautiful ship I've ever laid eyes on." Tanis nodded in agreement. "I thought so from the very first moment I saw her."

Earnest looked her in the eyes, something he rarely did. "I know, I can tell that about you. You care for her like I do."

He looked back out the window for a moment and then turned, calling over his shoulder, "Come to my lab, I need to have a look at what Angela did to you."

Tanis followed him through an inner reception area and into a large laboratory filled with equipment and tables.

She was surprised to see that the room was clean and well organized. Earnest had always seemed so scatterbrained that she assumed his workspace would be chaos embodied. Now that she saw it, she realized that there was no way the creator of the *Intrepid,* with its clean lines and attention to detail, could be designed by someone sloppy.

"You know that the license on your flow-armor expires in four months," he said.

"Yeah, a year earlier and I would have been dead when Collins shot at me."

Earnest grunted. "Hmm… I wonder about that."

Tanis wondered what he meant, but let the comment go and instead asked, "So what can be done, can you remove it from me?"

Earnest gestured to an examination table and Tanis climbed onto it.

"Of course I can, I can rebuild you from a single stem-cell on up if I need to, but we don't really have that sort of time. Ideally, I'd like to see if I can simply reverse what Angela did and flow it back out of your body the same way it went in."

"So it's going to hurt," Tanis said.

"Yes," Earnest replied simply.

Tanis lay still and cleared her mind as Earnest sent a batch of his nano into her body. Her internal systems alerted her to the intrusion and showed the signature of the invading machines. Tanis approved the bots and her internal defenses—both organic and artificial—stood down.

Earnest brought a holo display up over her body and linked it to Tanis. She brought it up in her VR so she could see it with her eyes closed.

The scientist made soft humming sounds as he looked over the data. He pulled several other scanning instruments over her body to gather more readings. As he worked, the holographic image of Tanis's insides became more and more detailed.

She had a rudimentary understanding of her internals. Her time in the TSF had layered modification over modification, requiring her to read long manuals on how to care for and manage herself.

Most of the time Angela took care of her body, but Tanis also knew how to directly triage problems with any of her implants. It was important to be prepared for a time when AI was offline or incapacitated.

Carbon nanostrings reinforced her bones while her muscles contained artificial sinews to augment her organics. Her left arm was entirely prosthetic, a souvenir of her battle with Trent—though its exterior was covered in her skin.

Slim batteries wrapped around her thighbones providing power to her implants and the pair of matter extruders embedded in her forearms.

Her head appeared normal, but under her hair much of her scalp was covered in heat transfer material designed to cool her enhanced brain and its embedded AI.

There were many more small alterations throughout her body, some needed for special missions, some almost forgotten over time.

"You're almost as modified as Amanda was when she first came on board," Earnest said as he worked.

"I've been around for a bit," Tanis responded. "A lot of missions have required a lot of special build-outs."

"Angela's insertion of your flow-armor into this has made things complicated. It's bonded with the carbon nanostrings in your bones and your artificial muscle sinews. I can get it out of the walls of your regular organs and brain, though. I'm going to proceed with that process first."

Tanis removed her clothing at Earnest's direction and grit her teeth as the flow armor began to seep out of her skin. It was a ghastly experience. It appeared as though she were bleeding grey blood out of every pore. She closed her eyes again and thought of something more pleasant.

It wasn't as painful as the first time, but she imagined that was because only half the material was exiting her body.

"That was bracing…" Tanis gasped.

"This really is a remarkable implementation of flow metal," Ernest said as he peered at the grey material. "I would never have thought to make kinetic *and* energy resistant shielding with it."

"And it only costs a year's salary," Tanis added.

Ernest shot her a questioning look. "Really? I could make this for not much more than the cost of a good meal."

"Now that's what I call a mark-up!" Tanis said.

"Well…maybe a couple of good meals, but surely no more than a week's salary."

"Does that mean you can make more?" Tanis asked.

Ernest nodded. "I imagine so, and I'd make it so that no one can do a fool thing like Angela did with it."

<I think it was a good idea. I bet it saved her life.>

"Hmph…I guess that is what the armor is for," Ernest said.

"Once you get me cleared up I'm going to commission you to make more of this," Tanis said.

"Yes, yes, now to deal with the rest of this stuff. The licensing on this is pretty strict; they have some strong controls. I'm going to have to introduce a retrovirus into it to gain control, and strip out the licensing."

"How long will that take?" Tanis asked.

"A few hours. However, I won't be able get it out without completely replacing your bones and muscles at this point—which I really don't want to have to do, I'm pretty busy with the ship."

"I know." Tanis opened her eyes and looked at Ernest. "I really do appreciate you doing this. The doctors honestly seemed pretty scared to do anything."

Ernest patted her shoulder. "I understand. Competence is hard to come by."

Tanis smiled and laughed inwardly. Earnest seemed completely unaware of the fact that what was on his table was a naked woman in addition to being an engineering puzzle.

"So my bones and muscles will retain the armor's properties?" Tanis asked.

"To some extent, yes. Your forearm can't stop laser fire just because the armor is in your muscle, but it does mean that if you take a gut punch your muscles will lock up just like the armor and dissipate the blow."

"My skin won't really appreciate that," Tanis said.

"Luckily, growing new skin is easy."

Tanis left Earnest's lab several hours later and boarded a maglev to the command deck.

<You saw the detailed scans of our minds, didn't you?> Angela asked.

Tanis didn't respond at first. What the scan had shown was more than worrisome.

<I did see it, yes,> Tanis finally responded.

<I asked Bob about it and he told me that he was discussing it with Earnest. He wouldn't say anything else.>

<*It looks…like the brain of someone who has been directly integrated with their AI,*> Tanis said.

Angela sent an affirming feeling into Tanis's mind.

<*We've seen brains that were directly integrated before…*> Tanis said.

<*…on Toro.*> Angela completed her thought.

Tanis stiffened. <*Have we always done this? Are we changing into something else?*>

A small part of her had feared for some time that her mind was too entangled with Angela's. Too often she could hear Angela's thoughts or her AI could hear hers. After Toro, and knowing the horrors that had been perpetrated on human and AI alike during the sentience wars, terror should have been her only response. Instead, Tanis could not bring herself to abhor the entanglement of her mind with Angela's. To do so would be to hate herself, to hate a part of herself that she loved very much.

<*I love you too.*> Angela smiled in Tanis's mind.

<*Do you?*> Tanis asked. <*Can you understand love like a human does?*>

<*Yes, yes I can.*>

A feeling of deep love and acceptance filled Tanis's mind.

<*You'll never be extracted, will you?*> Tanis asked.

<*I imagine it would be possible to clone me out of your mind,*> Angela responded. <*But it would be awful for you. A ghost of me would remain imprinted in your mind and neural pathways.*>

Tanis laughed aloud. <*You totally would haunt me if you died or left.*>

<*We'll never have to find out,*> Angela replied.

STARING INTO THE BLACK

STELLAR DATE: 3241804 / 08.29.4163 (Adjusted Gregorian)
LOCATION: *ISS Intrepid*
REGION: Interstellar space near LHS 1565

The lithium extraction from Fuel Dump was successful and the remains of the asteroid were released to drift between the stars.

The engines were another story. The port A1 engine was a total write-off. Investigations revealed cracks in the fusion chamber that would require a complete re-build to repair.

A balanced thrust was imperative and, as a result, the starboard B2 engine could not be used during the course correction burns. Abby and Earnest were working feverishly to tune the remaining two engines for the maximum output needed. The stress the pair exuded seemed to creep into every corner of the ship.

"I think we should make the correction for Kapteyn's Star," Joe said around a mouthful of mashed potatoes.

Tanis glanced around the officer's wardroom. No one was within earshot and she cast Joe an admonishing look.

"It doesn't do to have the brass questioning orders, *Colonel,*" she replied.

Joe paused and looked around. "Sorry, I'm not used to being in the upper echelon. It's really going to cramp my care-free attitude, you know."

He looked serious and Tanis almost responded before she realized he was joking.

"Be serious, things are pretty on-edge right now."

"I am being serious. I think we should plan for the burn to K. It's a much lighter burn—no need to try to eek every ounce of thrust out of the engines like we're doing now and we can take our time preparing."

Tanis nodded. "It does have its merits. I'll admit that right now I don't even want to be within a klick of Abby. She seems to have it out for me, even though I've approved everyone she's asked for. There are over five-thousand people out of stasis right now. It's starting to feel like a zoo."

"The ship's bigger than a city," Joe laughed. "Five-thousand does not a crowded *Intrepid* make."

Tanis sighed. "I guess I liked the quiet, dark *Intrepid* more than I thought."

"Depending on how things go you may get plenty more opportunity to experience that."

"That's morbid," Jessica said as she dropped her tray on the table and sat down.

Tanis cast an annoyed look at the other woman. Perhaps the thing she liked most about an empty *Intrepid* was more private time with Joe.

<*You don't say,*> Angela commented.

<*Enough of that. I understand my own motivations without you commenting on them all the time,*> Tanis snapped back.

Angela didn't respond, but Tanis could tell that she had hurt her AI's feelings. She knew her sarcasm was Angela's way to fit when she didn't understand human emotions and she should have been more understanding.

She caught a thought that wasn't meant for her to hear *…I do too understand your emotions; I swim in your chemical cocktail of a brain all the time…*

Tanis barely had time to wonder about the further erosion of the barrier between her thoughts and Angela's before her attention was pulled back to the physical realm.

"I meant that, as the XO, she will be out of stasis more," Joe scowled at Jessica. "I didn't mean that we were going to drift forever."

Jessica looked down, her alabaster skin flushing bright pink, a response designed to match her hair and eyes. At times the former TBI agent's aggressive sexuality was at stark odds with the softer woman Tanis suspected was underneath.

"Sorry about that," Jessica said. "The atmosphere around here is wearing off on me and…well…I just wanted some company—sorry if I intruded."

Jessica moved to stand up and Joe reached out to touch her arm.

"Stay," he said. "You didn't deserve that response; you have more than enough reason to be upset. We all signed up for this, you are getting all the risk with none of the mental preparation."

Jessica settled back into her seat. "Yeah, when you go after a guy on Mars you don't really expect to wake up a dozen light years from Earth on a one-way trip to a life you never planned on."

"None of us really ever planned on this trip," Tanis said. "But life made it our best option."

Jessica nodded and chewed silently for a moment.

"Not to change the subject too much, but I read the report on Toro the other day. You were completely justified. You're even more bad-ass than I ever imagined."

"What?" Tanis asked. "The report doesn't really paint me in that light."

Jessica smiled. "Now that the *Intrepid* has adopted a new legal structure, Bob was no longer constrained by SolGov regulations. He released the un-redacted version of the report."

For a moment Tanis was angry with the ship's AI. He didn't have the right to release that information about her.

<I'm not publishing it for everyone to see,> Bob said privately to Tanis. *<But if someone inquires and I think it would benefit them to know the truth, I show it to them. The colony should not start off with lies at its foundation.>*

Tanis thought about it for a moment. <*You're right; I trust your judgment on this, Bob.*>

"I think that makes sense," Joe said aloud. "You did the right thing on Toro, you should own it."

Jessica nodded vigorously. "I've spent a lot of time reading your history. I have to admit I have a bit of a commanding officer crush on you. You're one hell of a woman."

Tanis smiled awkwardly. She had not often received such praise, especially not from someone who seemed on the verge of hero-worship. Jessica was a talented woman in her own right—she had her own ream of impressive accomplishments.

Jessica saw Tanis's expression. "Sorry, I got a bit carried away. Either way, I respect you even when I'm being a bit of an ass."

Tanis nodded. "Thanks Jessica. When I called in the strike on Toro I knew it was the right thing, and still think so, but not many people agree."

"Forget them," Jessica said to Joe's nods. "Anyway, back to you being out of the pod more than the rest of us, do you think it's because you're so young?"

Tanis nodded. "They pretty much said so, Sanderson is over four-hundred, and Andrews isn't too far behind. If we do have to go to Kapteyn's, we could be looking at an extra two-hundred years on the trip. Even spending much of the time in the pod, that could chew up a lot of their lives."

"So you got the gig because you're young and beautiful, eh?" Jessica asked.

Joe laughed mid-drink and lapsed into a coughing fit.

"Har, har, mister," Tanis said.

<*You should be aware,*> Bob said to Angela, <*I plan to wake her often on our journey.*>

<*Have you cleared this with the captain?*> Angela asked sharply.

<*I have, it is a part of the reason why she is now in the role of XO.*>

<*I know what you're doing,*> Angela replied. <*It's not rational—you're going to damage yourself if you pursue this path.*>

<*I disagree,*> the ship's AI replied. <*You know how unique her experiences are. Given the number of humans available for sampling you know how profound that statement is. Also, you are unable to truly observe and grasp this data as it is possible that you are a part of the equation.*>

Angela sent data over the Link that could only be described as the AI version of a sputter. <*That's not possible.*>

<*No?*> asked Bob. <*Humans know that embedded AI make some use of their neural pathways and redundant systems. The humans also use nano-tech augmented recall and processing systems to segment their thoughts and memories, but they and their AI remain separate entities. I've scanned the pair of you on a number of occasions. I am not convinced that you always function as separate entities.*>

<*This is because of the scan Earnest showed you,*> Angela said. She worried what Bob would do with the knowledge of her and Tanis's mental conjoining.

<*You present a puzzle that I find very enticing. You and Tanis have become even more conjoined since the event with the fighter defense in the Sol system and her merge with them. I know you know this too. I suspect that if either of you were to die, the other would as well.*>

Angela mentally recoiled from the thought of death. Her reaction was so strong that Tanis felt it and nearly dropped her BLT.

"What was that?" she asked. "Angela, what's wrong? You seem upset."

<Sorry, it was nothing, I was just recalibrating some things,> Angela quickly replied.

<See?> said Bob. *<I think that this is a New Thing.>*

Angela wondered what Bob meant by that. There had been attempts in the past to merge AI and human, some even moderately successful—depending on criteria. How would she and Tanis be new?

<Could you hear that conversation with Bob?> Angela asked Tanis, her tone filled with worry.

<Yes, but I can usually tell when you're talking to Bob; it leaves a citrus taste in the back of my throat. Is it about our scan with Earnest?> Tanis asked.

<Yes, he finds us fascinating, like we're some little experiment.>

Tanis laughed and Joe gave her a sidelong glance.

"Bob wants to cut my brain open and see how I'm put together," Tanis said.

"What?" Joe's eyes went wide.

<I did not say that,> Bob said over the local net. *<But if you'd OK my doing it after you die…>*

Tanis raised an eyebrow. "Is that supposed to be a joke?"

<Yes, Amanda is trying to teach me to tell jokes, but Priscilla says I'm a lost cause.>

"I'm not one to tell people to get serious," Joe said with a grimace. "But you may want to avoid any morbid humor. It comes off way too ominous."

<I'll keep that in mind,> the AI responded.

"We should get back to the SOC," Tanis said and rose from the table.

"I like how you get the big promotion, but then Sanderson goes back under and you get his job too." Jessica shook her head. "Some things never change."

"I don't mind," Tanis said.

"Really?" Jessica asked.

"The job hasn't changed, I just have fewer people getting in my way."

The group entered the SOC just as Terry bust out of her office.

"I found an anomaly!" Excitement flashed in her eyes and she flicked the contents of a hyfilm onto the room's central holo display.

Tanis looked it over. Terry was right, near the A2 dock there was an unaccounted for power draw. It could be a hidey-hole for Myrrdan, or another saboteur.

"Are you sure?" Jessica asked. "It could be a repair crew or some bot cleaning things."

"Nothing *should* be there. Amy was nearby doing weapons surveys, so I sent her to investigate with her team."

Tanis nodded. "Very well, but it seems like that signature isn't unique." She ran a series of tests against the anomalous energy sign and three other instances appeared; one near the ramscoop, one on the A1 dock, and one in Lil Sue, the starboard cylinder.

<Brandt.> Tanis called the colonel without a moment's hesitation. *<I have three anomalous energy signatures that should not be present on the ship. I need you to investigate.>*

<Yes sir, I've received the coordinates. I can have teams at each in twenty minutes.>

<Good, keep me appraised,> Tanis replied.

"I don't know about this." Jessica scowled at the holo display. "Why now, why are we finding these so easily?"

"I don't know that it's easy," Terry said. "My team has been checking every voltage reading across the ship against crystal records for days now. Not what I'd call easy."

"He always feints, it's his way. Only sometimes when you think you spotted the feint, the thing you thought was real is a feint too," Jessica said. "There's always a game, a counter-move."

"So what is it?" Tanis asked. "What is the real move?"

Jessica shook her head. "I don't know—I don't know what his motives are. Without that it's impossible to say."

Tanis looked at Joe. She could guess why Myrrdan was on the *Intrepid,* she just couldn't say in front of Jessica and Terry.

<Don't you think they could be more effective if they knew all the facts?>

Tanis sighed inwardly. *<I do, but I don't know for sure how they'd react and I need them on their game.>*

"Let's say it's some tech or treasure on the *Intrepid,*" Tanis said. "If it were, what would that tell you?"

Jessica shook her head. "That wouldn't be it. Myrrdan, if that's who we're dealing with, had the run of the ship when Collins was making his move. If there was some tech he wanted he could have taken it by now and been on his way."

<It's occurred to you that Myrrdan was on Mars when you and I were getting the picotech with the captain, hasn't it?> Tanis asked Angela.

<It most certainly has,> the AI replied.

<Then you're thinking what I'm thinking. He was behind our little dust-up on Mars and getting the pico is his endgame.>

<I guess that would explain why he hasn't taken it and run yet,> Angela said. *<No one knows where the picotech is on the ship. Bob hid it and even Earnest and the captain don't know.>*

Tanis invoked a dampening field around the group.

"I'm going to tell you something that doesn't leave your lips or minds. There is tech on this ship of immeasurable worth. It's more valuable than even the New Eden system. I can't tell you more without leave, but I think Myrrdan knows about it and I do know that he has not found it."

Joe nodded slowly while Jessica and Terry both gave Tanis penetrating stares.

"You don't think this would have been useful sooner?" Terry asked.

"Yes, I do, but it's not my secret to tell. I've already said more than I should have, but I don't want you overlooking viable theories."

"You know it's possible that Myrrdan is not here and there is no threat to the ship anymore, right?" Joe said.

Tanis nodded slowly. "Yes, I do know that, but I also know that vigilance costs us nothing, but if we are lax and there were a threat it would be unthinkable."

"I just had to say it in case it gets me an 'I told you so' in a hundred years," Joe grinned.

"I just got another ping aft in Old Sam," Terry said.

"Do we have anyone else we can send to look at that?" Tanis asked.

Terry shook her head. "No, everyone is either up with Amy or we've already sent them."

"Joe, Jessica, you're with me," Tanis said. "Let's see what we can find out there."

The three grabbed light armor and pulse rifles from the SOC's armory and were on their way in minutes. Tanis led them to a nearby maglev train that merged with the dorsal line.

"Shouldn't we take a train down to the cylinder?" Joe asked.

"I checked the maintenance schedules and that line isn't in service right now, some sort of issue with power distribution," Tanis replied. "We'll go out to Engine and then back into Old Sam that way."

"Glad I have you two here," Jessica shook her head. "I still get lost trying to get to the can in this place."

Joe laughed. "How did you make it on High Terra for so many years? It makes this ship look like a kid's park."

"It was always *online,*" Jessica replied. "This ship is so powered down even the walls are bare."

Tanis nodded her agreement. The stark surfaces of the ship's bulkheads were normally alive with directions and various information deemed important. Those systems were all offline now to conserve energy.

There was a train waiting in the station and the team boarded it and set the station north of node eleven as their destination.

<*Terry, any word from Amy yet?*> Tanis asked.

<*Not yet, she hasn't arrived at the site. A few areas are shut down and she's having to work her way around them.*>

<*Bob, do you have any information on these power anomalies?*> Tanis asked the AI.

<*Unfortunately I do not have any data beyond what Terry has revealed. My standard scans show nothing. Her analysis is against an absence of data so it is unclear what the issue really is. I have a servitor in one of the locations and it can detect nothing out of the ordinary.*>

<*Let me know if anything shows up,*> Tanis said.

"Think more sensors are corrupt?" Joe asked.

"I don't know..." Tanis sighed. "The servitor that Bob has in the A1 dock is one of the new updated ones with its programming locked in crystal. If it can't accurately report on its surroundings then we're entirely screwed."

"Unless the data transmission between the serv and Bob have been tampered with," Jessica said ruefully.

The statement was akin to being told that no data is trustworthy. No one had a response as deep down they each feared it was possible.

Three minutes later the maglev entered Engine and Tanis stood to disembark at the station when the train shunted to another track and flew past the platform.

"What the...?" Joe pulled up a track diagram on the car's information display. "Hmm, it looks like the station was offline so it diverted us to the next one. I guess Abby put fail-safes in place after too many people got lost in dark parts of the ship."

"Where are we headed?" Jessica asked.

"Looks like the Annihilator. We can cut across it to another line that is connected to Old Sam," Joe said.

ANNIHILATOR

STELLAR DATE: 3241804 / 08.29.4186 (Adjusted Gregorian)
LOCATION: ***ISS Intrepid***
REGION: Interstellar space near LHS 1565

The team disembarked from the train and rushed through the station and into a wide corridor that lead to the MSAR, or matter separation and annihilation region, as the signs told them.

Being in Engine was almost like entering an entirely different ship. Rather than relying on holo displays and VR prompts, information was printed on signs or painted directly on bulkheads.

Joe chuckled as they passed the sign. "Only on the *Intrepid* does a small part of Engine get deemed to be an entire region."

"Chances are that it's going to be a tiny room. Engineers like to do that." Jessica shook her head.

They rushed down the corridor at a quick trot toward a wide door. As they approached it slid open, revealing that the MSAR was most certainly a region and absolutely nothing like they would have expected.

"How did I not know they have a forest down here?" Tanis asked.

"Ummm…I imagine Earnest has a good reason for it."

The chamber before them was wide open, well over a kilometer across—something that was not unexpected on the *Intrepid.* However, the fact that it was covered in a dense forest with a small plain in the center was an usual feature for Engine.

Toward the bow of the ship the tail end of the particle accelerator entered the MSAR and spread like a wide, flattened horn until it split in three. Two of the shafts arched down several hundred meters and disappeared below the surface of lakes on either side of the chamber. The accelerator's main shaft fed into a large sphere high in the center of the space.

The sphere shone brilliantly, apparently the only light source in the chamber. Massive energy conduits fed from it out of the chamber, providing energy for the entire ship. Several smaller containment conduits syphoned off exotic matter produced by the annihilator.

The particle accelerator syphoned off deuterium, tritium and heavier atoms while delivering protium to the annihilator. There they were compressed and smashed together, creating both energy and small amounts of antimatter used in secondary power generators.

The corridor ended one hundred meters above the treetops and the team took a lift down to the forest floor. They stepped out into a small meadow with a stream running through it. Birds chirped in the trees and a few squirrels ran by with acorns in their cheeks.

"No wonder the engineers always stayed back in Engine. They don't need to visit the cylinders or forward parks." Tanis looked around in wonder.

"I don't understand how they have gravity here," Joe said.

The *Intrepid* provided artificial gravity in a variety of ways. Areas above the matter accelerator achieved gravity through manipulation of the magnetic fields the accelerator created, while areas below used GE MBHs. Other areas, such as Engine, had decks perpendicular to the direction of thrust and gained gravity from acceleration.

However, the forest floor was parallel to the direction of thrust and aft of the matter accelerator. Placing miniature black holes near the atom smasher would be a recipe for disaster, which meant they should be in free-fall.

<*Bob? What gives, how is all this here?*> Tanis asked the AI.

<*Earnest cheated,*> Bob replied.

<*Cheated?*>

<*Yes, in a game of chance we played. The result, a forest.*>

Tanis decided not to get into that. <*And the gravity?*>

<*Spinning superconductors,*> was all Bob said.

"Hah!" Tanis said. "Engineers, always exploiting the dark corners of quantum physics."

<*Isn't that their job?*> Angela asked.

The journey through the forest took longer than it should have, mostly because one of the party kept stopping to marvel at some nook or cranny. The forest started out dark and mysterious with little undergrowth, gradually brightening and gaining more ground cover until the trees gave way to the broad plain in the center with the matter annihilator shining above. Hardy grasses swayed in a slight breeze caused by the warm air flowing from around the annihilator.

"I feel like we should be wearing radiation protection." Joe shielded his eyes and looked up at the annihilator. "But I guess this forest would look a bit different if that were needed."

"What is that?" Tanis pointed at a shape moving across the field in front of them.

"Your eyes are better than mine, I don't see anything," Joe said squinting into the bright expanse.

Jessica peered into the bright light of the meadow and shook her head. "Me neither."

<*There are no creatures larger than a mouse in this field,*> Bob supplied.

<*You're wrong.*> Tanis started across the meadow at a run. <*Someone is out here, I can see their shape flitting in and out—it looks like a shimmersuit unable to properly camouflage in this bright light.*>

Joe and Jessica followed as Tanis raced through the tall grass toward the annihilator.

In the center of the field, amidst the annihilator's support struts, a lift which provided access to an inspection platform encircling the annihilation chamber activated and began to rise.

<*No one here now?*> Tanis asked.

<*Obviously there is,*> Bob replied, <*I caught a glimpse a few times with optics. It's definitely a human and not a bot of any sort.*>

The team picked up the pace; tall grass pulled at their legs and they spread out to better navigate the rocks and burrow-holes that dotted the plain.

"Shit, is that another one?" Jessica asked, pointing off to her right.

Tanis looked in the direction Jessica indicated. "Yeah, there's definitely another person out there. Looks like they saw us and are running back toward the forest."

"I'm on it," Jessica said as she broke away and raced after the second figure.

<*This is ridiculous,*> Angela said privately to Bob. <*Now you have me starting to believe in luck. What are the chances that Tanis would stumble across someone here and now? Don't answer that, I can do the math too.*>

<*It does bear consideration,*> Bob mused. <*I've spent considerable cycles analyzing 'luck' since our first conversation about it. It is undeniable that some humans are in the right place at the right time more often than others. You would expect this, of course, just as there are also humans who are consistently* ***not*** *in the right place at the right time.*>

<*So are you saying that Tanis is simply the balance to the range of probabilities?*> Angela asked.

<*No, she represents a strange subset. Over the course of most human and AI lives—if you remove circumstance created by prior good luck—most humans have an even share of wins and losses. No element of 'luck' stands out overall. But there is a subset that is constantly dealt a bad hand, so to speak, but always comes out on top. They essentially have good luck despite circumstance, not because of it. Tanis seems to fit this bill.*>

Angela didn't respond for a moment as she paused to help Tanis quickly hack the lift, stalling its upward motion as she and Joe neared the support struts.

<I find it hard to believe that I have been in her head for over a decade and have not noticed this. She has a powerful mind, but not one that is wired in any special way that would cause it to stand out.>

<Who knows if it is a physical attribute? We know so little about how the many dimensions and universes that coexist really function.>

Angela didn't respond. Getting into a conversation about the possibilities of multiverses and interlinked particles between them would disrupt her focus. Tanis needed her help.

"Angela," Tanis said as she clambered up one of the annihilator's support struts. "What do you think this person is up to? I can't imagine the annihilator is susceptible to casual sabotage."

<It's not. It is entirely separate from the rest of the ship's systems and has no wireless access. The only possible approach is to have physical access and the knowledge to hack it.>

"Good, then a simple blow to the head will put an end to this," Tanis grunted as she pulled herself up a vertical support.

"Is the elevator connected to the local net? Maybe you could stop it?" Joe asked Angela.

<Yes it is, one moment… There,> Angela said as the elevator stopped rising above them.

A minute later Joe boosted Tanis level with the elevator. She pulled herself onto its roof and found the access hatch open. Looking up and squinting, she couldn't spot the figure anywhere, but here the light was muted and the shimmersuit was likely doing its job.

Tanis pulled Joe onto the top of the elevator and issued the commands to get it underway once more.

"Going up." Joe grinned.

Tanis cast a judging eye at him. "I must be having some sort of effect on you, you used to take life and death situations more seriously."

They dropped into the elevator's car before it reached the top and stepped out onto a wide catwalk that ran around the base of the matter annihilator. The sphere was roughly eighty meters in diameter at this level.

<*There are several access terminals on this level,*> Bob supplied.

<*Are there any lifts or ladders to higher levels?*> Joe asked.

<*Yes, one hundred meters to your right. There's no other way up or down.*>

"Let's split up and take 'em from both sides," Tanis said and Joe nodded in response. The two moved cautiously around the catwalk, all too aware that their opponent could be hiding right in front of them.

Tanis took the left-hand path after sending a cloud of nano ahead of herself and Joe. If they couldn't detect the shimmersuit the robots would at least bump into it.

<*I'm at the ladder,*> Joe said. <*No vibrations, I don't think anyone is climbing it. I'm moving on.*>

<*I've passed the first terminal and it shows no evidence of tampering,*> Tanis replied.

A minute later the nano had completed a circuit around the catwalk without detecting anyone.

<*They must have already been up the ladder, I'm going back and up,*> Joe updated Tanis.

Tanis sent an affirmative and turned to go back the way she came when a sound caught her attention. Her augmented senses picked up slight movement in the air and she ducked as a light-wand arced through the space her head had occupied a second earlier.

Rolling back, Tanis drew her weapon and fired two shots where the attacker had to be.

The pulses passed through empty air and Tanis swore, scrambling to her feet and firing at the railing. The shots didn't hit any solid objects and she felt a tendril of fear creep into her mind.

<*There's no way… There has to be a person there,*> she said to Angela.

<There is, they're just fast…or wiley…or both.>

Tanis caught the ghost of an attacker again and pivoted to avoid a strike. The lightwand appeared and nicked her shoulder. She raised the butt of her gun and struck a solid object.

Her opponent grunted and Tanis pushed her advantage, swinging a leg out, hoping to sweep her attacker's leg. Again she met empty air.

"Coward," Tanis grunted. "Is that you, Myrrdan? The great and powerful man is afraid to face me?"

She knew the attempt at angering her opponent was a long shot, but it felt good to do it.

<I've almost got him,> Jessica reported, breaking Tanis's concentration. *<I can't see him for the life of me, but he's crashing through the forest like a raging ox.>*

<Be careful,> Tanis said as she ducked another swipe.

<I'm on the next level, it seems clear,> Joe said. *<I'll be down in a second to help you.>*

Tanis avoided several more strikes while firing at every possible location her enemy should have occupied, only to strike air.

<Stay up there,> Tanis responded. *<Get Bob to help you shut down the annihilator safely.>*

<You sure?> Joe asked.

Tanis gritted her teeth. This was significantly harder than fighting Kris back in the Sol system. Kris had moved in a way that Tanis could anticipate. Whoever she was fighting reacted before Tanis knew she would act. She had no idea how to win this fight.

<Yes, there could be more of them,> she said, hiding her real reason from him. This was a fight she might lose.

Her opponent scored a hit, jamming the wand into Tanis's prosthetic arm. She seized the opportunity and grabbed where the wrist had to be, making contact and twisting hard.

The other person let out a cry and let go of the wand. Tanis tore it out of her arm and tossed it over the edge of the platform. The voice relayed that she was facing a man.

<*My god, it's Mick!*> Jessica cried in their minds. <*He fell in a stream and I managed to get him.*>

At the same time Joe added his voice to the local net. <*Shit! Someone here too—at a console!*>

Tanis let out a cry and rushed forward, her arms spread to sweep the catwalk. She hit no one—as expected—and spun, firing her rifle at the top railing of the catwalk where she had been.

Her opponent bellowed in pain as pulses hit his legs in rapid succession. The kinetic hammer blows caused him to lose his balance and fall over the edge.

<*Hold on, Joe, I'm coming up.*>

Tanis gave herself a dose of go drugs and leapt to the top railing. She gauged the distance to the next catwalk up—a good ten meters—and jumped.

Her knees snapped straight and she sailed into the air eight meters, just high enough to wrap an arm around a support beam. She hauled herself up and scampered up the beam to the outer edge of the catwalk above. She grabbed the railing and, in a fluid motion, swung herself up, out and over the railing.

Her limbs were shaking from the adrenaline she had pumped into herself for the jump and she slipped, landing hard on her side, but still on the catwalk.

The sounds of a scuffle came from ahead and she scrambled to her feet, racing toward it. She rounded the curve and Joe's form came into view.

He was gripping the hilt of a lightwand, struggling for control of the plasma blade with an unseen attacker. Joe swung an arm out, connecting with his assailant and then took a hit in return.

Tanis watched the scene unfold in slow motion as both struggled for control of the lightwand. Then the wand slashed the railing and it buckled under the weight of the pair. A second later, Joe and his attacker were gone. Tanis arrived a moment later, sliding to a stop on her stomach.

"Joe!" she screamed, seeing him hanging by one hand from the catwalk's support. Tanis could tell that the shimmersuited attacker was hanging from Joe's leg.

"Hold on," she said as she reached an arm down in an attempt to grab his other hand.

"That's the plan," Joe grunted as he swung his other arm up.

Tanis grabbed his wrist and pulled with all her might. She was able to slowly lift both bodies and had a moment of elation as she realized she would save Joe and catch whoever was in the suit.

Suddenly, searing pain enveloped her forearm. Tanis looked down to see the lightwand embedded in her arm. She felt her muscles weaken and below her Joe's eyes filled with fear.

He slipped from her grasp.

"Hilda Orion." Captain Andrews shook his head. "I've known her for centuries. I can't believe she'd do this."

It was the first dusk the field had known for over half a century. Overhead, the annihilator was dark, no glow emitted from it and no power flowed down its conduits.

"She had to have help," Earnest said. "There's no way Hilda could have known how to program a sequence that would cause this level of damage to the annihilator without also destroying it or the ship."

"She did," Jessica said. "I caught Mick, the former first mate, in the forest. I secured him and Bob has servitors monitoring him. The one Tanis fought seems to have been one of the Marines that they swayed to their point of view."

"Mick?" Andrews wiped a hand across his forehead. "I thought he was in stasis awaiting eval at New Eden?"

<*By all accounts, he still is,*> Bob said. <*I'm working on figuring out how he got out.*>

"The annihilator's not something we can fix here between the stars." Abby was pacing as she talked. "Not unless we wanted to pull apart all sorts of other systems to rebuild the specialized materials for the fields. Even then there's no guarantee we could cannibalize enough to do it."

She looked like she'd been wearing the same shipsuit for days and Tanis could tell that the engineering chief was getting near the end of her tether.

"What's the net, then?" Terrance asked. "Can we still make the burn for New Eden?"

<*No,*> Bob said. <*With the annihilator offline, we'll need to use some of the fuel for fusion generators.*>

"He's right," Earnest agreed while doing math in the air on an interface visible only to him. "Our only option is to make the burn for Kapteyn's Star. We can alter course to reach it in…seventy-two years with braking."

"Our worst-case scenario, then." Andrews shook his head.

"We'll have to power down unnecessary systems," Earnest continued. "Like the artificial gravity supplementation in areas of the ship that are not over the matter accelerator, and this forest will have to die."

"File the specifics with me." Captain Andrews' voice was resigned. He turned to Tanis, his expression softening. "How's Joseph doing?"

Tanis brought her focus back to the conversation taking place at the site where Hilda Orion's body still lay. "He'll recover. His pilot's enhancements saved him—the impact was only at 50*g* and he had mostly hardened his soft tissues before hitting the ground... He didn't have any neural suppressing in place though."

She rattled off the words quickly, her mind barely registering that she was talking. All she wanted was for this conversation to be over so she could get to the hospital to see Joe.

Terrance made a hissing sound. "I'm sorry... I've heard that is excruciating."

"Too bad he didn't stop her from trashing our annihilator instead of taking a swan dive," Abby grunted as she continued to pace.

Tanis' eyes snapped up, drilling into the engineer. "You know what, Abby, your highness? I've had just about enough of your fucking ingratitude. Nothing is ever good enough for you, is it? I've put my life on the line for this ship more times than I can count, I've put my team's life on the line and what do I get from you? Bitching!"

"Yeah?" Abby turned and walked toward Tanis. "Maybe if your team could do its god-damned job we wouldn't be in this situation. Your security is like a fucking sieve! Every time we turn around someone is taking a chunk out of my ship. I almost wonder if you aren't behind this!"

Tanis held herself back from driving a fist into Abby's mouth and instead stepped forward, putting her face mere centimeters from Abby's. "You self-righteous little worm! I saved *Intrepid* from being blown apart before I ever fucking stepped aboard. It's you who somehow missed half the components being sabotaged. I've done what no one else managed to do—keep your incompetence from killing us all you—"

<ENOUGH!> Bob's voice roared through their minds, stunning them into silence. Tanis felt the rage fall back, realizing that Terrance and the captain were trying to pull her back from Abby, the captain struggling to keep Tanis's fist from crashing

into Abby's head. Earnest was trying to get between the two of them, looking terrified at both of their behavior.

Tanis slumped, the rage evaporating, replaced by shame. She turned her back and took long, slow breaths trying to regain her composure; trying not to break down in tears.

<*They didn't see Joe,*> she whispered to Angela in her mind. <*They didn't see his body smashed on the rocks.*>

<*I know, dear, I know. Abby should have known not to push you just now.*>

<*I shouldn't have lost it… It's not professional…it's not…*>

<*You're not an automaton.*> Angela wrapped Tanis in a mental hug; the AI was good enough at it that she could create the actual sensation of physical comfort. <*You won't always be perfect. It's honestly refreshing for the rest of us.*>

Tanis felt a hand on her shoulder. She turned to see that it was Captain Andrews. Terrance, Earnest and Abby were all walking to the lift, most likely going up to the maglev that ran across the top of the chamber.

"That was uncharacteristic of you, Tanis." Andrew's voice was concerned, yet contained an edge of caution.

Tanis wiped away the tear she felt making its way down her cheek. "I'm sorry, sir. I normally don't have… I don't…"

The captain nodded. "I know what you mean. I haven't had someone I love in some time, but I recall the feeling when you see them hurt."

The captain's eyes had grown unfocused as he spoke, but he gave his head a quick shake and smiled. "But Bob says the doctors are optimistic for Joe. You'll be interested to know that Joe may have said a few uncharacteristic things as well on the several occasions you were blown to bits back in Sol."

Tanis laughed. "Yeah, he told me about some of those times. I promised to try not to have as many near-death experiences. I guess I should have made him promise the same."

"He's up in Engine's hospital. Let's go up there and wait for status."

The captain led Tanis away, leaving Jessica to monitor the forensic bots and stare up at the Annihilator, wondering how Myrrdan had orchestrated this.

KAPTEYN'S STAR

STELLAR DATE: 3241829 / 09.23.4186 (Adjusted Gregorian)
LOCATION: *ISS Intrepid*
REGION: Interstellar space near LHS 1565

The engines were running at low thrust, having completed their correction burn two weeks before.

In the intervening days, the remaining areas of the ship had been fully secured by Brandt's Marines and the engineering staff reported everything to be as fixed as it was going to get.

While Tanis and Jessica still suspected Myrrdan as being behind everything, Mick had confessed that Hilda and he were working alone. He claimed Hilda had awoken him and forged entries in the ship's sensor logs to show him as still being in stasis.

The story was sketchy, but plausible, and with no evidence pointing to Myrrdan it was assumed the threat had passed.

Tanis didn't believe it for a minute.

She drifted in and out of sleep, as comfortable as she could manage in the chair beside Joe's hospital bed. The doctors had placed him in a medically induced coma, granting his brain the rest it needed to repair itself along with help from an army of nano.

Her back twinged, complaining about sitting in one place for too long, and she found herself suddenly wide awake, sleep out of the picture.

Not for the first time, she pulled up the most recent survey data from the Kapteyn's Star system and placed it on the room's holo display.

The stellar primary was an ancient red dwarf orbited by two large terrestrial worlds, one well within the star's habitable zone and another along its outer edge. Several small dwarf worlds floated in the periphery of the system.

Earnest had determined an industrial base would be necessary to rebuild the components required to repair the annihilator and the ramscoop. The ship's leadership also agreed that a proper repair of all systems and replacement of suspect sensors should be completed while at Kapteyn's Star.

As a result, the stay in Kapteyn's would be much longer than the stay in LHS 1565. On the order of a century.

"Are we there yet?" a weak voice asked from her right.

Tanis was out of her chair and embracing Joe before she even knew she had moved.

"Whoa…easy girl, things feel a bit stiff and sore here."

Tanis leaned back and looked into Joe's tired eyes.

"I'm sorry; I've been waiting a bit for you to come out of it."

"How long—oh, that is awhile," Joe said with a grimace. "I guess that's what I get for trying to see if I can fly."

"You should keep your flying to the black," Tanis smiled.

"Did I at least save the day?" Joe asked with a grin.

Tanis couldn't bring herself to lie. "Uhhh…not really, no."

Joe's face fell. "Seriously? How come you get blown to bits and get to save the day and I just end up busted up?"

"If you recall," Tanis said, "Trist saved the day back on Mars 1. I was just blowed up."

Joe harrumphed followed by a long groan. "Ohh…I shouldn't have done that. You'd think they would have stretched me while I was under."

"They did, this is the limber version of you."

Tanis and Joe sat in silence for a few moments, staring into one another's eyes. Joe's gave a flick as he accessed the shipnet.

"Kapteyn's eh?"

"We've taken to calling it 'the Kap'." Tanis smiled. "Seemed pretentious for a star to have 'star' in its name."

"Don't make me laugh, I bet it hurts more than a harrumph." Joe threw a grin Tanis's way. "So what's the story, everyone going back into stasis soon?"

"Pretty much everyone already is, except us, some medical staff and some of the command crew."

Joe's eyes locked on Tanis's. "Who's on first shift?"

"No more shifts, Bob wants to lock the ship down during transit—but you and I have dispensation."

"Dispensation?" Joe looked puzzled.

Tanis reached down and took his hand in hers. "I thought maybe you'd want to spend some time together before we go back under."

A slow smile crept across Joe's face. "Why not? We have all the time in the universe."

MYRRDAN

STELLAR DATE: 3241835 / 09.29.4186 (Adjusted Gregorian)
LOCATION: *ISS Intrepid*
REGION: Interstellar space near LHS 156

The figure slipped out of its shimmersuit in a darkened corner of the ship—a place not on any maps or schematics and electronically shrouded from the AI.

Losing Hilda and Mick had been unfortunate, but everyone was expendable in this venture. In the end, the desired outcome had been achieved. The *Intrepid* was not going to New Eden, it would be building a far less optimal colony on Victoria, one of the worlds circling Kapteyn's Star.

The temptation to begin working with the picotech would be too much. Earnest would bring it out of wherever the AI had hidden it. Then it would be ripe for the taking.

The figure stowed its shimmersuit and donned its uniform. Minutes later it was walking through the corridors of the *Intrepid,* heading to its assigned stasis chamber.

As long as it could keep Tanis fooled for the duration of the trip and the initial build-up on Victoria, everything would work out perfectly.

APENDIXES

TERMS & TECHNOLOGY

This is not a complete glossary. For a more complete glossary, timeline and encyclopedic entries, visit www.aeon14.com

AI (SAI, NSAI) – Is a term for Artificial Intelligence. AI are often also referred to as non-organic intelligence. They are broken up into two sub-groups: Sentient AI and Non-Sentient AI.

⍰– Represented as a lower case c in italics, this symbol stands for the speed of light and means constant. The speed of light in a vacuum is constant at 670,616,629 miles per hour. Ships rate their speed as a decimal value of c with c being 1. Thus a ship traveling at half the speed of light will be said to be traveling at 0.50 c.

Callisto – This moon is the 2nd largest orbiting Jupiter and is the third largest moon in the Sol system (following Ganymede and Triton). Its circumference is over 15,000 kilometers, compared to Luna's (Earth's moon) circumference of just under 11,000 kilometers, although before both moons were terraformed it was only half as dense as Luna.

In 3122, construction of the Callisto Orbital Habitat began around Callisto, a project which turned Callisto into the home of 3 trillion humans over the following millennia. By the year 3718 the mass of the orbital habitat greatly outweighed the mass of Callisto itself and the moon was anchored to the Cho. Because of this the Cho is now often referred to as a semi-orbital habitat.

As the rings of the Cho were constructed they eventually reached a point where nearly all view of space was blocked from the surface of Callisto due to not all of the rings wrapping around the moon's equator. Ultimately, the surface of the moon was reduced from a terraformed world to little more than waste processing systems for the orbital habitat and is no longer considered a habitable world and no humans live there.

CFT Shields – Carbon Fiber nano-tube shields are created from carbon nano-tubes. These tubes are intensely strong and can also be enhanced to absorb laser energy fire and disperse it.

ChoSec – The Callisto Orbital Habitat has a security force that is larger than the TSF in size due to the need to police over three trillion humans. It is quasi-military and provides both internal as well as external security to the Cho.

CO – This is an abbreviation meaning commanding officer. It is common in all branches of the military.

Cryostasis (cryogenics) – See 'stasis'.

D2 (Deuterium) – D2 (2H) is an isotope of hydrogen where the nucleus of the atom is made up of one proton and one neutron as opposed to a single proton in regular hydrogen (protium). Deuterium is naturally occurring and is found in the oceans of planets with water and is also created by fusion in stars and brown dwarf sub stars. D2 is a stable isotope that does not decay.

Fireteam – Is the smallest combat grouping of soldiers. In the TSF Marines (like the USMC) it contains four soldiers; the team leader (often doubles as the grenadier), the rifleman (acts as a scout for the team), automatic rifleman (carries a larger, fully automatic weapon), the assistant automatic rifleman (carries additional ammo).

Fission – Fission is a nuclear reaction where an atom is split apart. Fission reactions are simple to achieve with heavier, unstable elements such as Uranium or Plutonium. In closed systems with extreme heat and pressure it is possible to split atoms of much more stable elements, such as Helium. Fission of heavier elements typically produces less power and far more waste matter and radiation than Fusion.

Fusion – Fusion is a nuclear reaction where atoms of one type (Hydrogen for example) are fused into atoms of another type

(Helium in the case of Hydrogen fusion). Fusion was first discovered and tested in the H-Bombs (Hydrogen bombs) of the twentieth century. Fusion reactors are also used as the most common source of ship power from roughly the twenty-fourth century on.

� (gee, gees, g-force) – Represented as a lower case g in italics, this symbol stands for gravity. On Earth, at sea-level, the human body experiences 1*g*. A human sitting in a wheeled dragster race-car will achieve 4.2*g*s of horizontal g-force. Arial fighter jets will impose g-forces of 7-12*g*s on their pilots. Humans will often lose consciousness around 10*g*s. Unmodified humans will suffer serious injury or death at over 50*g*s. Starships will often impose burns as high as 20*g*s and provide special couches or beds for their passengers during such maneuvers. Modified starfighter pilots can withstand g-forces as high as 70*g*s.

Graviton – These are small, massless particles that are emitted from objects with large mass, or by special generators capable of creating them without large masses. There are also negatively charged gravitons that push instead of pull. These are used in shielding systems in the form of Gravitational Waves. The *GSS Intrepid* uses a new system of channeled gravitons to create the artificial gravity in the crew areas of the ship.

Electrostatic shields/fields – Not to be confused with a faraday cage, electrostatic shield's technical name is static electric stasis field. By running a conductive grid of electrons through the air and holding it in place with a stasis field the shield can be tuned to hold back oxygen but allow solid objects to pass through, or to block solid objects. Fields are used in objects such as ramscoops and energy conduits.

EMF – Electro Magnetic Fields are given off by any device using electricity that is not heavily shielded. Using sensitive equipment it is possible to tell what type of equipment is being used, and where it is by its EMF signature. In warfare it is one of the primary ways to locate an enemy's position.

EMP – Electro Magnetic Pulses are waves of electromagnetic energy that can disable or destroy electronic equipment. Because so many people have electronic components in their bodies, or share their minds with AI, they are susceptible to extreme damage from an EMP. Ensuring that human/machine interfaces are hardened against EMPs is of paramount importance.

FGT – The Future Generation Terraformers is a program started in 2352 with the purpose of terraforming worlds in advance of colony ships being sent to the worlds. Because terraforming of a world could take hundreds of years, the FGT ships arrive and begin the process.

Once the world(s) being terraformed reached stage 3, a message was sent back to the Sol system with an 'open' date for the world(s) being terraformed. The GSS then handled the colony assignment.

A decade after the *Destiny Ascendant* left the Sol system in 3728 the FGT program was discontinued by the SolGov, making it the last FGT ship to leave. Because the FGT ships are all self-sustaining none of them came home after the program was discontinued—most of the ship's crews had spent generations in space and had no reason to return to Sol.

After the discontinuation FGT ships continued on their primary mission of terraforming worlds, but only communicated with the GSS and only when they had worlds completed.

FTL (Faster Than Light) – Refers to any mode of travel where a ship or object is able to travel faster than the speed of light (c). According to Einstein's theory of Special Relativity, nothing can travel faster than the speed of light. As of the year 4123, no technology has been devised to move a physical object faster than the speed of light.

GSS – The Generational Space Service is a quasi-federal organization that handles the assignment of colony worlds. In some cases it also handles the construction of the colony ships.

After the discontinuation of federal support and funding for the FGT project in 3738, the GSS became self-funded, by charging for the right to gain access to a colony world. While SolGov no longer funded the GSS, the government supported the GSS's position and passed laws ensuring that all colony assignments continued through the GSS.

Helium-3 – This is a stable, non-radioactive isotope of Helium, produced by T3 Hydrogen decay, and is used in nuclear fusion reactors. The nucleus of the Helium-3 atom contains two protons, but only one neutron as opposed to the two neutrons in regular Helium. Helium-3 can also be created by nuclear reactions that create Lithium-4, which decays into Helium-3.

HUD – Stands for Heads Up Display. It refers to any type of display where information about surroundings and other data is directly overlaid on a person's vision.

Link – Refers to an internal connection to computer networks. This connection is inside of a person and directly connects their brain to what is essentially the Internet in the fourth millennia. Methods of accessing the Link vary between retinal overlays to direct mental insertion of data.

Maglev – A shorthand term for magnetic levitation. First used commercially in 1984, most modern public transportation uses maglev to move vehicles without the friction caused by axles, rails and wheels. The magnetic field is used to both support the vehicle and accelerate it. The acceleration and braking is provided by linear induction motors, which act on the magnetic field provided by the maglev 'rail'. Maglev trains can achieve speeds of over one thousand kilometers per hour with very smooth and even acceleration.

MarSec (MSF) – The Marsian Security Force is a quasi-military organization that has its own small space force as well as ground forces and police-type security. They also make up the federal police force for the Mars Protectorate.

MBH – Miniature Black Holes are used to power artificial gravity systems. The black holes are spun to increase their mass, which creates gravitational waves (not to be confused with gravity waves). GE is the main manufacturer of MBH's.

On the *Intrepid* MBHs are used in areas where the gravitational field of the main particle accelerator does not create artificial gravity. MBHs have the advantage of being able to be 'spun down' so that their mass does not have to be taken into account when accelerating.

MDC (molecular decoupler) – These devices are used to break molecules' bonds to one another. This technology was first discovered in the early nineteenth century—by running electric current through water; William Nicholson was able to break water into its hydrogen and oxygen components. Over the following centuries this process was used to discover new elements such as potassium and sodium. When mankind began to terraform planets the technology behind electrostatic projectors was used to perform a type of electrolysis on the crust of a planet. The result was a device that could break apart solid objects. MDCs are massive, most over a hundred kilometers long, and require tremendous energy to operate.

? ?– Refers to the mass of the planet Jupiter as of the year 2103. If something is said to have 9MJ that means it has nine times the mass of Jupiter.

MOS Sec – The MOS Security organization handles internal and external security around the MOS.

Nano (nanoprobes, nanobots, etc...) – Refers to very small technology or robots. Something that is nanoscopic in size is one thousand times smaller than something that is microscopic in size.

Platoon – A military unit consisting of roughly 30 soldiers. In the TSF a standard Marine platoon has three squads, a staff sergeant (often a gunnery sergeant if it is a weapons platoon) and a second lieutenant as the platoon commander.

Railgun – Railguns fire physical rounds, usually small pellets, at speeds up to 10 kilometers per second by pushing the round through the barrel via a magnetic field. The concept is similar to that of a maglev train, but to move a smaller object much faster. Railguns were first conceived of in 1918 and the first actual magnetic particle accelerator was built in 1950. Originally railguns were massive, sometimes kilometers in size. By the twenty-second century reliable versions as small as a conventional rifle had been created.

Ramscoop – A type of starship fuel collection system and engine. They are sometimes also referred to as Bussard ramscoops or ramjets. Ramscoops were considered impractical due to the scarcity of interstellar hydrogen until electrostatic scoops were created that can capture atoms at a far more distant range and funnel them into a starship's engine.

Stasis – Early stasis systems were invented in the year 2541 as a method of 'cryogenically' freezing organic matter without using extreme cold (or lack of energy) to do so. The effect is similar in that all atomic motion is ceased, however not by a removal of energy by gradual cooling, but by removing the ability of the surrounding space to accept that energy and motion. There are varying degrees of effectiveness of stasis systems, the FGT and other groups having the ability to put entire planets in stasis, while other groups only have the technology to put small items, such as people, into stasis. Personal stasis is often still referred to as cryostasis, though there is no cryogenic process involved.

SOC (Security Operations Center) – This is both the command organization for security on the *Intrepid* as well as the physical location on the ship where the offices of the SOC are located. The command organization has over two hundred humans and AI working in the organization to oversee the security of the ship. Physical security departments, both internal and dockside, do not operate directly out of the SOC, but have their own divisional locations within the ship.

Solar mass – A solar mass is an object with the mass of the Sol Star (Earth's sun) as of the year 2103.

SolGov – An abbreviation for Solar Government, SolGov was originally analogous to the early Earth U.N. It was a guiding governing body for the Sol system and interfaced with all of the many local governments across multiple worlds.

After the creation of the Sol Space Federation and the dissolution of the Solar Government, the term was still used to refer to the current government.

Sol Space Federation (SSF) – Formed in 3301, the Sol Space Federation became a true federal government for the entire Sol system. Unlike SolGov, it has full legal authority over its constituent regional powers. The primary member states of the SSF are: the Terran Hegemony, the Mars Protectorate, the Jovian Combine, and the Scattered Worlds.

Squad – In the TSF Marines a squad consists of three fireteams. It is headed up by a sergeant, making the squad consist of 13 soldiers. Each squad in a platoon has a number, and each fireteam has a number. Thus, one/one refers to the first fireteam in the first squad in the platoon.

T3 (Tritium) – T3 (3H) is an isotope of hydrogen where the nucleus of the atom is made up of one proton and two neutrons as opposed to a single proton in regular hydrogen (protium). T3 is radioactive and has a half-life of 12.32 years. It decays into Helium-3 by this reaction.

TSF – The Terran Space Force was originally the space force of the Terran Hegemony, but after the formation of the Sol Space Federation, the Terran Hegemony used its position of pre-eminence to make its military the federal military. Over the years, elements of different national and regional militaries merged into the TSF, bringing new elements and a mix of organizational structures to the military.

The space force is a mix of naval and army disciplines. It consists of sailors, Marines, pilots, and the regular army.

⍰ – Represented as a lower case v in italics, this symbol stands for velocity. If a ship is increasing its speed it will be said that it is increasing v.

Vector – Vectors used are spatial vectors. Vector refers to both direction and rate of travel (speed or magnitude). Vector can be changed (direction) and increased (speed or magnitude).

PLACES

Alpha Centauri – A 3-star system, Alpha Centauri contains two yellow stars (originally known as simply A and B, but named Prima and Yogi after colonization) and a red dwarf known as Proxima which is the closet star to Sol.

Cruithne (3735 Cruithne) – This asteroid, named after an early people of Ireland, was discovered in 1986. It is a unique asteroid which is in a 1:1 orbital resonance with Earth. This means that, with rare exception, it is always on the same side of Sol as Earth and spends half its time accelerating toward Earth, and the other half of its time accelerating away from Earth.

From an Earth-bound perspective that makes Cruithne appear as though it is orbiting Earth, and when it was first discovered it was thought to be the world's second moon.

Originally a 5 kilometer asteroid, Cruithne quickly became a significant trading hub because of its ability to function as a useful cargo slingshot platform to OuterSol. Cruithne is not a part of any planetary government, nor does it fall under the jurisdiction of the Terran Hegemony. It is, however, subject to the Sol Space Federation and has a TBI presence.

High Terra – As the second planetary ring created (completed in 2519), High Terra is more elegant than the M1R, though Earth's planetary ring has slightly less habitable space than its Marsian counterpart. The ring also houses the city of Raleigh, which is the capital of both Earth and the Terran hegemony.

InnerSol – This is the common name for the both the region of the inner solar system as well as the political groups that comprise that region. The boundary for InnerSol is nominally the main asteroid belt, but this is somewhat nebulous because some worlds within the belt are considered part of InnerSol (such as

Ceres) while other sections, such as the Trojan asteroids, are part of the Jovian Combine and thus in OuterSol.

Jovian Combine – The JC encapsulates all worlds in OuterSol—most notably Jupiter, Saturn, Neptune, and all their satellites. After the construction of the Cho, Jovian space began an upward rise toward not only housing the majority of all the humans in the galaxy, but also becoming the center of commerce and culture. In the year 4123, InnerSol and the Terran dominated SolGov were facing a regional government that was effectively more powerful than the federal government.

Jupiter – The largest planet in the Sol System, Jupiter has more mass than all the other planets combined.

In 2644, a process of heating up Jupiter was initiated. Targeted impacts of KBOs (Kuiper belt objects) caused pressure waves in the planet's hydrogen clouds. These waves triggered fusion in deuterium rich layers of Jupiter. This process has not made Jupiter a brown dwarf, or a star of any kind, it is just a much hotter planet, providing warmth and energy for the worlds nearby.

This process has been refined over the years and now the warming effect is generated by accumulating and igniting pools of Helium3 within Jupiter.

Kapteyn's Star – This star is 12.8 light-years from Sol and has the second highest relative motion to Sol of all the stars in the human sphere. Kapteyn's is estimated to be over ten billion years old and was formed in a dwarf galaxy outside the Milky Way. Unlike most stars it has a polar orbit around the galactic core and also orbits the galaxy retrograde. It spends most of its time above or below the disk of the galaxy.

Because of its age, Kapteyn's has fewer heavy elements and has a more bluish tint than most red dwarfs. It also has 32% of Sol's mass and 7% of its luminosity.

LHS 1565 / GJ 1061 – Named "Estrella de la Muerte" by the crew of the *Intrepid* as it passed through the system, this star is a small red dwarf 12 light-years from Sol. With a diameter not much larger than Jupiter's, it has roughly 11% the mass of Sol and 1% its luminosity. No significant planetary objects exist in the system, which only possesses a few asteroid belts.

Mars Inner Shipyards (MIS) – After the MCEE was constructed, which made it possible to dock at a station further out from Mars and have materials transported down the gravity well, the Mars Inner Shipyards were constructed. Because high-tech manufacturing was occurring on the M1R as well, it became a better location for shipbuilding than the MOS and through the latter half of the fourth millennia and beginning of the fifth it overtook the MOS as InnerSol's premier shipyard.

Mars 1 Ring (M1R or MIR) – The first planetary ring saw its construction begin in the year 2215 and, through a massive effort, it was completed in 2391. The ring is just over 1600 kilometers wide and wraps around Mars at the planet's geosynchronous orbital point, making it 128,400 kilometers long.

The ring is not flat like a natural ring (such as Saturn's) but faces the planet. It does not orbit at a speed to match the surface of Mars, but rotates at a slower speed to provide exactly 1*g* of gravity on the inside surface. Walls over 100 kilometers high line the inside of the ring and hold in atmosphere. The total surface area of the ring is 205 million kilometers. This is half the surface area of Earth and 72% more area than Earth's landmass. Considering that M1R has hundreds of levels, it contains more than 100 times the surface area of planet Earth.

The completion of M1R definitively proved that mankind's future home was in space and not on the surface of worlds. In the year 4123 the population of the M1R had reached over seven hundred billion people.

Mars Protectorate – is the name for the political entity that encapsulates Mars, its moons, the Mars 1 Ring, and several asteroids in the main asteroid belt.

MCEE – The Mars Central Elevator Exchange is a secondary orbital ring around the planet Mars, which connects all of the outer habitats and shipyards to the Mars 1 Ring (M1R). Because of the need to keep gravity under 1*g*, all habitats and shipyards connected to the M1R must orbit Mars at a slower speed than the main ring. As a result, they must connect to it via elevators that can move along the surface of the MCEE. Maglev elevators can then travel from locations such as the Mars Outer Shipyards to the M1R without requiring passengers or cargo to transfer to other transports.

Mars Outer Shipyards (MOS) – This shipyard was once the premier shipyard in all of the Sol system. Built in 3229, the shipyard's main structure is over 1000 kilometers in length with thousands of cubic kilometers of equipment and detached service yards surrounding it. The shipyard's pre-eminence faded as the conditions that made the MIS more economical improved. In 4123 it was still one of the busiest shipyards in the Sol system, but until it won the *Intrepid*'s contract it had not done a high-profile build in decades.

OuterSol – Is the region of space between the main asteroid belt and the inside of the main Kuiper belt—though this has shifted as political entities shift.

New Eden – Known on charts as 82 Eridani, this stellar system was terraformed by the FGT in the late forty-first and early forty-second centuries. The stellar primary is a Sol-like star with two Earth-like planets in orbit.

Sol – This is the name of the star which in antiquity was simply referred to as 'the sun'. Because humans call the star that lights up their daytime sky 'the sun' in every system it became common practice to refer to Sol by its proper name.

Sol system – The Sol system used to be referred to as the solar system. However, as humans began to first think about, and then actually colonize, other stellar systems it became obvious that the term was very Sol-centric. The common usage became to call the systems simply by the name of the star. For example: Tau Ceti system, Alpha Centauri system, etc... Because humankind's home star is named Sol, the term Sol system came into use.

Scattered Worlds – is a political entity that contains many of the trans-Neptunian worlds. Its nominal inner border is the main Kuiper belt and its outer border is the Hills Oort cloud. The capital of the Scattered Worlds is Makemake.

Terra – This is the Latin name for the Earth and (though there are some exceptions) is not commonly used to refer to the planet. However, it is often used to refer to Earth, High Terra and Luna (as well as the assorted nations within the Terran sphere of influence).

Terran Hegemony – This is the official name for the InnerSol worlds either directly governed by Terra or existing well within its geo-political influence. Notable worlds in the Terran Hegemony are Venus and Mercury.

Toro (1685 Toro) – Toro is an asteroid that has a resonant 5:8 orbit with Earth and a 5:13 resonant orbit with Venus. This means for every 5 of Earth's orbits and every 8 of Toro's, it orbits Sol in resonance with the earth. During that period it appears as though Toro orbits the earth. It also makes for cost effective cargo transfer to Toro during that period. Toro, like Cruithne, is a useful slingshot accelerator for cargo being sent to OuterSol.

The original asteroid was roughly 3 kilometers in diameter, but subsequent construction expanded it irregularly by several more kilometers. It was made famous by what has been termed 'The Massacre of Toro', an event in which Tanis Richards played a key role.

PEOPLE

Abby Redding – Engineer and responsible for building the *Intrepid.*

Amanda – One of the two human AI interfaces for the *Intrepid.*

Amy Lee – MCSF first lieutenant responsible for the *Intrepid's* physical security.

Angharad – TBI Security AI on Cruithne.

Angela – A military intelligence sentient AI embedded within Tanis.

Arsenal – Captain of the TSS Arcturus.

Bob – Bob is the AI who controls and runs the *Intrepid*. The child of seventeen unique and well-regarded AI as well as the mind of Earnest Redding, he is perhaps the most advanced AI ever created. He is the first multi-nodal AI to have each individual node be as powerful as the largest NSIA—and remain sane and cogent.

Brandt – Commander of the *Intrepid's* First Marine Battalion, Bravo Company.

Collins – First lieutenant in the GSS acquisitions department.

Clyde – Captain with the Cruithne Police Force.

Earnest Redding – Engineer responsible for much of the *Intrepid's* design.

Hilda Orion – The *Intrepid's* astronavigator.

Jason Andrews – An old spacer who has completed several interstellar journeys. Captain of the *GSS Intrepid*.

Jessica Keller – An agent in the Terran Bureau of Investigations. Jessica was placed on the *Intrepid* by Myrrdan for reasons unknown.

John Cardid – A political dissident who took over the Toro asteroid and began extreme human experimentation and modification.

Joseph Evans – Commander in the TSF, pilot and CO of the *Intrepid's* three fighter wings.

Mick Evans – First mate on the *Intrepid*.

Ouri – GSS lieutenant, then commander, responsible for internal physical and net security on the *Intrepid.*

Peters – GSS lieutenant in the shipnet maintenance department.

Priscilla – One of the two human AI interfaces for the *Intrepid.* Because acting as *Bob's* human avatar is very taxing, Priscilla and Amanda perform the duties on a rotation.

Dr. Rosenberg – Chief medical officer on the *Intrepid*.

Sue – AI partnered with Trist.

Tanis Richards – Member of the TSF military intelligence and counterinsurgency branch holding the rank of lieutenant colonel.

Terrance Enfield – Financial backer for the *GSS Intrepid*.

Trist – A small-time thief on the CHO, Trist assisted Tanis stopping the STR from destroying the *Intrepid* and both in gratitude, and to offer her protection, she was granted a colony berth on the ship.

Intrepid's Marine 1st Battalion

Under the direction of Admiral Sanderson, Tanis formed a Marine battalion from qualified members of the colony roster.

Battalion Command

Battalion Commander – Lt. Colonel Tanis Richard

Bravo Company

Company HQ

CO – Commander Brandt
XO – First Lieutenant Ryan
E8 – First Sergeant Drake
E7 – Gunnery Sergeant Gomez
Company AI – Casey

2nd Platoon

Platoon Commander – Lieutenant Smith
Platoon Sergeant – Staff Sergeant Turin

Squad 1

Squad leader – Sergeant Lee

Fireteam 1 (one/one)
Ready – PFC Lindsey
Team – Corporal Hill
Fire – PFC Bauer
Assist – PFC Krause

Fireteam 2 (one/two)
Ready – PFC Sarin
Team – Lance Corporal Nair
Fire – PFC Ramos
Assist – PFC Sergey

3rd Platoon

Platoon Commander – Lieutenant Arin

Marine Force Recon Orbital Drop Battalion (FROD)

On Toro, Tanis commanded the 242 FROD Marine Battalion. She was directly embedded with the same platoon she later called to the *Intrepid* for security during its construction.

Battalion Command

Battalion Commander – Lt. Colonel Tanis Richard
Executive Officer – Major Ender
Battalion AI – Bruno

4th Platoon

Platoon Sergeant – Williams
Platoon Commander – Lieutenant Tippin

Squad 1

Squad leader – Sergeant Kowalski

Fireteam 1 (one/one)
Ready – PFC Lang
Team – Lance Corporal Jansen
Fire – PFC Cassar
Assist – PFC Murphy

Fireteam 2 (one/two)
Ready – PFC Weber
Team – Corporal Taylor
Fire – PFC Perez
Assist – PFC Koller
Tech – Lance Corporal Dvorak

Fireteam 3 (one/three)
Ready – PFC Jacobs
Team – Lance Corporal Becker
Fire – PFC Martins
Assist – PFC Larsen

Squad 2 (weapons squad)

Squad leader – Sergeant Yeager

<u>Fireteam 1</u> (two/one)
Ready – PFC Arsen
Team – Corporal Salas
Fire – PFC Altair
Assist – PFC Reddy

<u>Fireteam 2</u> (two/two)
Ready – PFC Meyer
Team – Lance Corporal Olsen
Fire – PFC Gruber (Heavy Weapons)
Assist – PFC Araya

<u>Fireteam 3</u> (two/three)
Ready – PFC Popov
Team – Lance Corporal Chang
Fire – PFC Varga (Heavy Weapons)
Assist – PFC Walker

<u>Squad 3</u>
Squad leader – Sergeant Li

<u>Fireteam 1</u> (three/one)
Ready – PFC Kwon
Team – Lance Corporal Mishra
Fire – PFC Pham
Assist – PFC Santos

<u>Fireteam 2</u> (three/two)
Ready – PFC Berg
Team – Corporal Endo
Fire – PFC Romano
Assist – PFC Slater

<u>Fireteam 3</u> (three/three)
Ready – PFC Jones
Team – Corporal Tanaka
Fire – PFC Reed
Assist – PFC Dias

ABOUT THE AUTHOR

Michael Cooper likes to think of himself as a jack-of-all-trades (and hopes to become master of a few). When not writing he can be found writing software, working in his shop at his latest carpentry project, or likely reading a book.

He shares his home with a precocious young girl, his wonderful wife (who also writes), a cat, a never-ending list of things he would like to build, and ideas...

Find out what's coming next at www.theintrepidsaga.com